LAST CHANCE

"Now, Grimes, I'm going to be frank," said the admiral. "There are many people in the Service who don't like you, and who did not at all approve of your last two promotions. I didn't altogether approve of them myself, come to that, although I do admit that you possess one attribute that might, in the fullness of time, carry you to flag rank. You're lucky, Grimes. You could fall into a cesspit and come out not only smelling of roses but with the Shaara Crown Jewels clutched in your hot little hands. You've done it, figuratively, more than once. But I only hope that I'm not around when your luck runs out!"

"You mean, sir," asked Grimes, "that this is some sort of last chance?"

"*You* said it, commander. *You* said it. . . ."

The Big Black Mark

by

A. Bertram Chandler

DAW BOOKS, INC.

DONALD A. WOLLHEIM, PUBLISHER

1633 Broadway, New York, NY 10019

DEDICATION:

To William Bligh

FIRST PRINTING, FEBRUARY 1975

5 6 7 8 9

 DAW TRADEMARK REGISTERED
U.S. PAT. OFF. MARCA
REGISTRADA. HECHO EN U.S.A.

PRINTED IN U.S.A.

The
Big
Black
Mark

CHAPTER 1

Commander John Grimes, Federation Survey Service, should have been happy.

Rather to his surprise he had been promoted on his return, in the Census Ship *Seeker*, to Lindisfarne Base. He now wore three new, gleaming stripes of gold braid on his shoulder boards instead of the old, tarnished two and a half. Scrambled egg—the stylized comets worked in gold thread—now adorned the peak of his cap. And not only had he been promoted, from lieutenant commander to commander, he had been appointed to the command of a much bigger ship.

He should have been happy, but he was not.

The vessel, to begin with, was not a warship, although she did mount some armament. Grimes had served in real warships only as a junior officer, and not at all after he had reached the rank of lieutenant. As such he had commanded a Serpent Class courier, a little ship with a small crew, hardly better than a spacegoing mail van. Then, as a lieutenant commander. he had been captain of *Seeker*, and in her had been lucky enough to stumble upon not one, but two Lost Colonies. It was to this luck that he owed his promotion; normally it was the officers in the fighting ships, with the occasional actions in which to distinguish themselves, who climbed most rapidly up the ladder of rank.

Now he was captain of *Discovery*, another Census Ship.

And what a ship!

To begin with, she was old.

She was not only old; she had been badly neglected.

She had been badly neglected, and her personnel, who seemed to be permanently attached to her, were not the sort of people to look after any ship well. Grimes, looking down the list of officers before he joined the vessel, had recognized

7

several names. If the Bureau of Appointments had really tried to assemble a collection of prize malcontents inside one hapless hull they could not have done better.

Or worse.

Lieutenant Commander Brabham was the first lieutenant. He was some ten years older than Grimes, but he would never get past his present rank. He had been guilty of quite a few Survey Service crimes. (Grimes, too, had often been so guilty—but Grimes's luck was notorious.) He was reputed to carry an outsize chip on his shoulder. Grimes had never been shipmates with him, but he had heard about him.

Lieutenant Commander (E) MacMorris was chief engineer. Regarding him it had been said, in Grimes's hearing, "Whoever gave that uncouth mechanic a commission should have his head examined!" Grimes did not know him personally. Yet.

Lieutenant (S) Russell was the paymaster. Perhaps "paymistress" would have been a more correct designation. Ellen Russell had been one of the first female officers of the Supply Branch actually to serve aboard a ship of the Survey Service. From the very beginning she had succeeded in antagonizing her male superiors. She was known—not affectionately—as Vinegar Nell. Grimes had, once, been shipmates with her. For some reason or other she had called him an insufferable puppy.

Lieutenant (PC) Flannery was psionic communications officer. He was notorious throughout the Service for his heavy drinking. He owed his continuing survival to the fact that good telepaths are as scarce, almost, as hens' teeth.

So it went on. The detachment of Federation Marines was commanded by Major Swinton, known as the Mad Major. Swinton had faced a court-martial after the affair on Glenrowan. The court had decided, after long deliberation, that Swinton's action had been self-defense and not a massacre of innocent, unarmed civilians. That decision would never have been reached had the Federation not been anxious to remain on friendly terms with the king of Glenrowan, who had requested Federation aid to put down a well-justified rebellion.

Officers . . . petty officers.

Grimes sighed as he read. All were tarred with the same brush. He had little doubt that the ratings, too, would all be Federation's bad bargains. It occurred to him that his own superiors in the Service might well have put him in the same category.

The thought did not make him any happier.

"Those are your officers, Commander," said the admiral. "Mphm," grunted Grimes. He added hastily, "Sir."

The admiral's thick, white eyebrows lifted over his steely blue eyes. He frowned heavily, and Grimes's prominent ears flushed.

"Don't *grunt* at me, young man. We may be the policemen of the galaxy, but we aren't pigs. Hrrmph. Those are your ship's officers. You, especially, will appreciate that there are some people for whom it is difficult to find suitable employment."

The angry flush spread from Grimes's ears to the rest of his craggy, somewhat unhandsome face.

"Normally," the admiral went on, *"Discovery* carries on her books some twenty assorted scientists—specialist officers, men and women dressed as spacemen. But she is not a very popular ship, and the Bureau of Exploration has managed to find you only one for the forthcoming voyage."

Maggy Lazenby? Grimes wondered hopefully. Perhaps she had relented. She had been more than a little cold toward him since his affair with the cat woman, but surely she couldn't bear a grudge this long.

"Commander Brandt," the admiral went on. "Or Dr. Brandt, as he prefers to be called. Anthropologist, ethologist, and a bit of a jack-of-all-trades. He'll be under your orders, of course.

"And, talking of orders—" The admiral pushed a fat, heavily sealed envelope across his highly polished desk. "Nothing very secret. No need to destroy by fire before reading. I can tell you now. As soon as you are ready for Deep Space in all respects you are to lift ship and proceed to New Maine. We have a sub-Base there, as you know. That sub-Base will be your Base. From New Maine you will make a series of exploratory sweeps out toward the Rim. A Lost Colony Hunt, as you junior officers romantically put it. Your own two recent discoveries have stimulated interest, back on Earth, in that sort of pointless exercise. Hrrmph."

"Thank you, sir." Grimes gathered up his papers and rose to leave.

"Not so fast, Commander. I haven't finished yet. *Discov-*

ery, as I can see that you suspect, is not a happy ship. Your predecessor, Commander Tallis, contrived to leave her on medical grounds. The uniformly bad reports that he put in regarding *Discovery*'s personnel were partly discounted in view of his nervous—or mental—condition. Hrrmph.

"Now, Grimes, I'm going to be frank. There are many people in the Service who don't like you, and who did not at all approve of your last two promotions. I didn't altogether approve of them myself, come to that, although I do admit that you possess one attribute that just might, in the fullness of time, carry you to flag rank. You're lucky, Grimes. You could fall into a cesspit and come up not only smelling of roses but with the Shaara Crown Jewels clutched in your hot little hands. You've done it, figuratively, more than once.

"But I only hope that I'm not around when your luck runs out!"

Grimes started to get to his feet again.

"Hold it, Commander! I've some advice for you. Don't put a foot wrong. And try to lick that blasted *Discovery* into some sort of shape. If you do find any Lost Colonies play it according to the book. Let's have no more quixotry, none of this deciding, all by your little self, who are the goodies and who are the baddies. Don't take sides.

"That's all."

"You mean, sir," asked Grimes, "that this is some sort of last chance?"

"*You* said it, Commander. *You* said it. But just don't forget that the step from commander to captain is a very big one." The admiral shot out a big hand. Grimes took it, and was surprised and gratified by the warmth and firmness of the old man's grip. "Good hunting, Grimes. And good luck!"

CHAPTER 2

Grimes dismounted from the ground car at the foot of *Discovery*'s ramp. The driver, an attractive blonde spacewoman, asked, "Shall I wait for you, Commander?"

Grimes, looking up at the towering, shabby bulk of his new command, replied, "No, unfortunately."

The girl laughed sympathetically. "Good luck, sir."

"Thank you," he said.

He tucked his briefcase firmly under his arm, strode toward the foot of the ramp. He noted that the handrails were long unpolished, that a couple of stanchions were missing and that several treads were broken. There was a Marine sentry at the head of the ramp in a khaki uniform that looked as though it had been slept in. The man came to a rough approximation to attention as Grimes approached, saluted him as though he were doing him a personal favor. Grimes returned the salute with unwonted smartness.

"Your business, Commander?" asked the sentry.

"My name is Grimes. I'm the new captain."

The man seemed to be making some slight effort to smarten himself up. "I'll call Commander Brabham on the PA, sir."

"Don't bother," said Grimes. "I'll find my own way up to my quarters." He added, rather nastily, "I suppose the elevator is working?"

"Of course, sir. This way, sir."

Grimes let the Marine lead him out of the airlock chamber, along a short alleyway, to the axial shaft. The man pressed a button, and after a short interval, the door slid open to reveal the cage.

"You'll find all the officers in the wardroom, sir, at this time of the morning," volunteered his guide.

11

"Thank you." Then, "Hadn't you better be getting back
to your post?"

"Yes, sir. Of course, sir."

Grimes pushed the button for CAPTAIN'S FLAT.

During the journey up he was able to come to further con-
clusions—none of them good—about the way in which the
ship had been run. The cage was not quite filthy, but it was
far from clean. The gloss of the panel in which the buttons
were set was dulled by greasy fingerprints. On the deck
Grimes counted three cigarette butts and one cigarillo stub.
Two of the indicator lights for the various levels were not
working.

He got out at the Captain's Flat, the doughnut of accommodation that surrounded the axial shaft, separated from it
by a circular alleyway. He had a set of keys with him,
obtained from the admiral's office. The sliding door to the
day room opened as soon as he applied the appropriate strip
of magnetized metal. He went in.

An attempt, not very enthusiastic, had been made to clean
up after Commander Tallis' packing. But Tallis had not
packed his art gallery. This consisted of a score of calendars,
of the type given away by ship chandlers and ship-repair
firms, from as many worlds, utterly useless as a means of
checking day and date except on their planets of origin.
Evidently *Discovery*'s last census run had consisted of making the rounds of well-established colonies. Grimes stared at
the three-dimensional depiction of a young lady with two
pairs of overdeveloped breasts, indubitably mammalian and
probably from mutated human stock, turned from it to the
picture of a girl with less spectacular upperworks but with
brightly gleaming jewelry entwined in her luxuriant pubic
hair. The next one to catch his attention showed three people
in one pose.

He grunted—not altogether in disapproval—then found
the bell push labeled PANTRY over his desk. He used it. He
filled and lit his pipe. When he had almost finished it he
pushed the button again.

At last a spacewoman, in slovenly uniform, came in. She
demanded surlily, "Did you ring? Sir."

"Yes," answered Grimes, trying to infuse a harsh note into
his voice. "I'm the new captain. My gear will be coming
aboard this afternoon some time. Meanwhile, would you

mind getting this . . . junk disposed of?" He waved a hand to indicate the calendars.

"But if Commander Tallis comes back—"

"If Commander Tallis comes back, you can stick it all back up again. Oh, and you might give Lieutenant Commander Brabham my compliments and ask him to come to see me."

"The first lieutenant's in the wardroom. Sir. The PA system is working."

Grimes refrained from telling her what to do with the public-address system. He merely repeated his order, adding, "And I mean *now*."

"Aye, aye, sir, Captain, sir."

Insolent little bitch, thought Grimes, watching the twitching rump in the tight shorts vanishing through the doorway.

He settled down to wait again. Nobody in this ship seemed to be in any hurry about anything. Eventually Brabham condescended to appear. The first lieutenant was a short, chunky man, gray-haired, very thin on top. His broad, heavily lined face wore what looked like a perpetual scowl. His faded gray eyes glowered at the captain. The colors of the few ribbons on the left breast of his shirt had long since lost their brilliance and were badly frayed. Grimes could not tell what decorations—probably good attendance medals—they represented. But there were plenty of canteen medals which were obvious enough—smudges of cigarette ash, dried splashes of drinks and gravies—to keep them company. The gold braid on Brabham's shoulder boards had tarnished to a grayish green.

A gray man, thought Grimes. *A gray, bitter man.* He said, extending his hand, "Good morning, Number One."

"Good morning. Sir."

"Sit down, Number One." Grimes made a major operation out of refilling and lighting his pipe. "Smoke, if you wish." Brabham produced and ignited an acrid cigarette. "Mphm. Now, what's our condition of readiness?"

"Well, sir, a week at the earliest."

"A *week?*"

"This isn't an Insect Class Courier, sir. This is a *big* ship."

Grimes flushed, but held his temper in check. He said, "Any Survey Service vessel, regardless of size, should be ready, at all times, for almost instant liftoff."

"But, to begin with, there's been the change of captains. Sir."

"Go on."

"And Vinegar Nell—Miss Russell, I mean—isn't very co-operative."

"Mphm. Between ourselves, Number One, I haven't been impressed by the standard of efficiency of her staff." *Or, he thought, with the standard of efficiency of this ship in general. But I shall have to handle people with kid gloves until I get the feel of things.*

Brabham actually grinned. "I don't think that Sally was overly impressed by you, sir."

"Sally?"

"The captain's tigress. She used to be Commander Tallis' personal servant." Brabham grinned again, not very pleasantly. "Extremely personal, if you get what I mean, sir."

"Oh. Go on."

"And we're still trying to get a replacement for Mr. Flannery's psionic amplifier. He insists that only the brain of an Irish setter will do."

"And what happened to the old one?"

Brabham permitted himself a small chuckle. "He thought that it should share a binge. He poured a slug of Irish whiskey into its life-support tank. And then he tried to bring it around with black coffee."

"Gah!" exclaimed Grimes.

"Then he blamed the whiskey for the demise of the thing. It wasn't *real* Irish whiskey, apparently. It was some ersatz muck from New Shannon."

Grimes succeeded in dispelling the vision of the sordidly messy death of the psionic amplifier from his mind. He said firmly, "To begin with, Miss Russell will just have to pull her finger out. You're the first lieutenant. Get on to her."

"I'd rather not, sir."

Grimes glared at the man. "I'm not being funny, Mr. Brabham. Shake her up. Light a fire under her tail. And as for Mr. Flannery, he'll just have to be content with whatever hapless hound's brain the Stores Department can dig up—even if it comes from an English bulldog!"

"Then there are the engines, sir."

"The engines? What about them?"

"The chief has taken down both inertial drive-units.

There're bits and pieces strewn all over the engine room deck."

"Was the port captain informed of this immobilization?"

"Er, no, sir."

"And why not?"

"I didn't know what the chief had done until he'd already done it."

"In the captain's absence you were the officer in charge. You should have known. All right, all right, the chief should have come to you first. Apparently he didn't. But as soon as you knew that this rustbucket was immobile you should have reported it."

"I—I suppose I should, sir."

"You suppose! Why didn't you?"

A sullen flush spread over the grayish pallor of Brabham's face. He blurted, "Like the rest of us in this ship, MacMorris has been in quite enough trouble of various kinds. I didn't want to get him into any more. Sir."

Grimes repressed a sigh. It was obvious that this ship was a closed shop, manned by the No Hopers' Union, whose members would close ranks against any threatened action by higher authority, no matter how much they bickered among themselves. And what was he, Grimes? A No Hoper or a pillar of the Establishment? In his heart of hearts, which side was he on? While he was sorting out a reply to make to Brabham a familiar bugle call, amplified, drifted through and over the ship's PA system.

Brabham shifted uneasily in his chair.

"Are you coming down to lunch, sir?" he asked.

"No," decided Grimes. "You carry on down, and you can ask—no, *tell*—Miss Russell to send me some sandwiches and a pot of coffee up here. After lunch I shall see Lieutenant Commander MacMorris, Miss Russell, and Mr. Flannery, in that order. Then I shall see you again.

"That is all."

CHAPTER 3

It was the little blonde stewardess, Sally, who brought up Grimes's lunch. While he was eating it she set about stripping Tallis' calendars from the bulkheads, performing this task with a put-upon air and a great deal of waste motion. Grimes wondered if she had made the sandwiches and the coffee in the same sullenly slapdash way. No, he decided after the first nibble, the first sip. She must have gone to considerable trouble with the simple meal. Surely all the available bread could not have been as stale as the loaf that had been used. Surely it must have been much harder to spread butter so extremely thinly than in the normal manner. And where had she found that stringy, flavorless cold mutton? The coffeepot must have been stood in cold water to bring its weak contents to the correctly tepid stage.

"Will that be all? Sir?" she asked, her arms full of calendars.

"Yes," Grimes told her, adding, "Thank you," not that she deserved it. He decided that he would tell Miss Russell to let him have a male steward to look after him. Obviously this girl would give proper service only to those who serviced her, and she was too coarse, too shop-soiled for his taste, apart from the obvious disciplinary considerations.

Almost immediately after she was gone there was a knock at the door. A big man entered. He was clad in filthy, oil-soaked overalls. A smear of black grease ran diagonally across his hard, sullen face. More grease was mixed with his long, unruly yellow hair. His hot blue eyes glared down at Grimes.

"Ye wanted to see me, Captain? I'm a busy man, not like some I could mention."

"Lieutenant Commander MacMorris?"

"Who else?"

"Commander MacMorris, I understand that this ship is immobilized."

"Unless ye intend to take her up on reaction drive, she is that."

"By whose authority?" demanded Grimes coldly.

"Mine, o' course. Both the innies was playin' up on the homeward passage. So I'm fixin' 'em."

"Didn't you inform the first lieutenant before you started taking them down? He was in charge, in the absence of a captain."

"Inform *him?* He looks after whatever control room ornaments look after. I look after my engine room."

"As long as I'm captain of this ship," snapped Grimes, "it's *my* engine room. How long will it take you to reassemble the inertial drive-units?"

Grimes could almost read MacMorris' thoughts as the engineer stood there. Should he or should he not angrily protest the captain's assumption of proprietorial rights? He muttered at last, "If I do all that has to be done, a week."

"A week? Just to put things together again?"

"A week it will be."

"Normal in-port routine, I suppose, Commander MacMorris . . . 0800 to 1700, with the usual breaks . . . I see. But if you work double shifts . . . ?"

"Look, Captain, you're not suggesting—"

"No, Commander MacMorris. I'm not suggesting. I'm ordering."

"But we all have friends on the Base, and the last cruise was a long one."

"You will work double shifts, Chief, longer if necessary. I'll want this vessel ready for Space no more than three days from now."

MacMorris grunted wordlessly, turned to go.

"Oh, one more thing," said Grimes.

"Yes? Sir."

"In the future you are to ask me for permission before you immobilize the engines. That is all."

The engineer left sullenly. Grimes carefully filled and lit his battered pipe. What was it that somebody, some girl, had called it, some time ago? *The male pacifier.* Well, he needed pacifying. He disliked having to crack the whip, but there were occasions when it was unavoidable. MacMorris was known to be a good engineer—but he was one of those engineers to whom a ship is no more than a platform existing for the sole purpose of supporting machinery. Grimes thought, not for the first time, that captains had it much better in the days of sail. Even then there were technicians —such as the sailmaker—but a competent wind ship master would be able to repair or even to make a sail himself if he absolutely had to.

There was another knock at the door.

"Come in!" he called.

"I see you're still smoking that filthy thing!" sniffed Vinegar Nell.

She had hardly changed at all, thought Grimes, since when they had last been shipmates—and how many years ago was that? She was slim, still, almost to the point of thinness. Her coppery hair was scraped back severely from her broad brow. Green eyes still glinted in the sharp, narrow face. Her mouth was surprisingly wide and full. She could have been very attractive were it not for her perpetually sour expression.

Grimes said stiffly, "Must I remind you, Miss Russell, that I am the captain of this ship?"

"And so you are, sir. *And* a full commander. I never thought you'd make it."

"That will do, Miss Russell." Belatedly he remembered his manners. "Sit down, will you?" The legs displayed when her short uniform skirt rode up were excellent. "Now, Miss Russell, I want *Discovery* ready for Space in three days."

"You're asking a lot, Captain."

"I'm not, Paymaster. You know the regulations as well as I do. At least as well." He quoted, "All fleet units shall be maintained in a state of instant readiness."

"But there are provedore stores to be loaded. The farm needs a thorough overhaul; the yeasts in numbers two and three vats went bad on me last trip, and I'm not at all happy about the beef tissue culture. The pumping and filtration systems for the hydroponic tanks need a thorough clean out."

"You can write, can't you?"

"Write?" The fine eyebrows arched in puzzlement.

"Yes. Write. It's something you do on a piece of paper, such as an official form, with a stylus. Make out the necessary requisitions. Mark them *urgent*. I'll countersign them."

"Commander Tallis," she told him, "always wanted all repairs and maintenance carried out by the ship's personnel."

"One way of making sure that you get longer in port. But my name is Grimes, not Tallis. I don't like to loaf around Base until the stern vanes take root. Make out those requisitions."

"All right," she said flatly.

"Oh, and that stewardess . . . Sally, I think her name is."

"Your servant."

"My ex-servant. Have her replaced by a male steward."

A smile that was almost a sneer flickered over her full mouth as she looked around at the bulkheads, bare now, stripped of their adornment of blatantly bare female flesh. "Oh, I see. I never thought that you were *that* way in the old days, Captain."

"And I'm not now!" he snarled. "It's just that I don't like insolent sluts who can't even make a decent sandwich. On your way down, tell Mr. Flannery that I want him, please."

"Nobody wants Mr. Flannery," she said. "But we're stuck with him."

Flannery finally put in an appearance. He looked as though he had been dragged out from a drunken slumber. He was red-haired, grossly fat, and his unhealthily pale face was almost featureless. His little eyes were a washed-out blue, but so bloodshot that they looked red. The reek of his breath was so strong that Grimes, fearing an explosion, did not relight his pipe.

"Mr. Flannery?"

"An' who else would it be, Captain?"

"Mphm." The temperamental telepaths had always to be handled carefully and Grimes did not wish to provoke the man into insubordination, with its inevitable consequences. It would take much too long to get a replacement. Once the ship was up and away, however— "Mphm. Ah, Mr. Flannery, I believe that you're unable to get a suitable psionic amplifier to replace the one that, er, died."

"An' isn't that the God's truth, Captain? Poor Terence, he was more than just an amplifier for me feeble, wanderin' thoughts. He was more than just a pet, even. He was a brother."

"Mphm?"

"A dog from the Ould Sod, he was, a sweet Irish setter. They took his foine body away, bad cess to 'em, but his

poor, naked brain was there, in that jar o' broth, his poor,
shiverin' brain an' the shinin' soul o' him. Night after night
we'd sit there, out in the dark atween the stars, just the pair
of us, a-singin' the ould songs. The Minstrel Boy to the war
has gone. . . . *An' ye are that Minstrel Boy, Paddy,* he'd say
to me, he'd *think* to me, *an' you an' me is light-years from
the Emerald Isle, an' shall we iver see her again?*" Grimes
noted with embarrassed disgust that greasy tears were trickling from the piggy eyes. "I'm a sociable man, Captain, an'
I niver likes drinkin' alone, but I'm fussy who I drinks with.
So ivery night I'd pour a drop, just a drop, mind ye, just a
drop o' the precious whiskey into Terence's tank . . . he
liked it, as God's me guide. He loved it, an' he wanted it. An'
wouldn't ye want it if the sweet brain of ye was bare an'
naked in a goldfish bowl, a-floatin' in weak beef tea?"

"Mphm."

"An one cursed night me hand shook, an' I gave him
half the bottle. But he went happy, a-dreamin' o' green
fields an' soft green hills an' a blue sky with little, white
fleecy clouds like the ewe lambs o' God himself. . . . I only
hope that I go as happy when me time comes."

If you have anything to do with it, thought Grimes,
there's a very good chance of it.

"An' I've tried to get a replacement, Captain, I've tried,
an' I've tried. I've haunted the communications equipment
stores like a poor, shiverin' ghost until I thought they'd be
callin' one o' the Fathers to exorcise me. But what have they
got on their lousy shelves? I'll tell ye. The pickled brains o'
English bulldogs, an' German shepherds an'—ye'll niver believe me!—an Australian dingo! But niver an honest Irish
hound. Not so much as a terrier."

"You have to settle on something," Grimes said firmly.

"But you don't understand, Captain." Suddenly the heavy
brogue was gone and Flannery seemed to be speaking quite
soberly. "There must be absolute empathy between a telepath and his amplifier. And could *I* achieve empathy with an
English dog?"

Balls! thought Grimes. *I'll order the bastard to take the
bulldog, and see what happens.* Then a solution to the prob-
lem suddenly occurred to him. He said, "And they have a
dingo's brain in the store?"

"Oh, sure, sure. But—"

"But what? A dingo's a dog, isn't he? As a dog he possesses a dog's telepathic faculties. And he's a peculiarly Australian dog."

"Yes, but—"

"And what famous Australians can you call to mind? What about the Wild Colonial Boy? Weren't all the bush-rangers—or most of 'em—Irish?"

"Bejabbers, Captain, I believe ye've got it!"

"You've got it, Mr. Flannery. Or you will get it. And you can call it Ned, for Ned Kelly."

And so that's that, thought Grimes, when Flannery had shambled off. *For the time being, at least. It still remains to be seen if my departmental heads can deliver the goods.* But he was still far from happy. Unofficially and quite illegally a captain relies upon his psionic communications officer to keep him informed when trouble is brewing inside his ship. "Snooping" is the inelegant name for such conduct, which runs counter to the Rhine Institute's code of ethics.

For such snooping to be carried out, however, there must be a genuine trust and friendship between captain and tele-path. Grimes doubted that he could ever trust Flannery or that he could ever feel friendly toward him.

And, to judge by his experience to date, similar doubts applied to everybody in this unhappy ship.

CHAPTER 4

Surprisingly, the ship was ready for liftoff in three days.

Had the Survey Service been a commercial shipping line the refitting operations would have been uneconomical, with swarms of assorted technicians working around the clock and a wasteful use of materials. It was still a very expensive operation in terms of goodwill. *Discovery*'s people were robbed of the extra days at Lindisfarne Base to which they had all been looking forward, and the officers in charge of the various Base facilities grew thoroughly sick and tired of being worried by Grimes, all the time, about this, that, and the other.

But she was ready, spaceworthy in all respects, and then Grimes shook Brabham by saying that he was going to make an inspection.

"Commander Tallis only used to make inspections in Space," objected the first lieutenant.

"Damn Commander Tallis!" swore Grimes, who was becoming tired of hearing about his predecessor. "Do you really think that I'm mug enough to take this rustbucket upstairs without satisfying myself that she's not going to fall apart about my ears? Pass word to all departmental heads that I shall be making rounds at 1000 hours. You, Miss Russell, and Major Swinton will accompany me. Every other officer and petty officer will be standing by whatever he's responsible for."

"Ten hundred is morning smoko, sir."

"And so what? Smoko is a privilege, and not a right. Report to me at 1000 hours with Miss Russell and the major. Oh, and you might polish your shoes and put on a clean uniform shirt."

If looks killed, Brabham would have had to organize a funeral, not captain's rounds. Had he been too harsh? Grimes asked himself as the first lieutenant walked stiffly out of the day cabin. *No*, he thought. *No. This ship needs shaking up, smartening up.* He grinned. *And I've always hated those captains who pride themselves on a taut ship. But I don't want a taut ship. All I want is something a few degrees superior to a flag of convenience star tramp.*

Meanwhile his own quarters were, at least, clean. The steward who had replaced Commander Tallis' pet, Sally, was a taciturn lout who had to be told everything, but once he was told anything, he did it. And the service of meals in the wardroom had been improved, as had been the standard of cookery. Also, under Grimes's prodding, Brabham was beginning to take a little pride in his appearance and was even seeing to it that his juniors did likewise. MacMorris, however, was incorrigible. The first time that Grimes put in an appearance in the wardroom, for dinner on the evening of his first day aboard, the engineer was already seated at the table, still wearing his filthy coveralls. On being taken to task he told the captain that *he* had to work for a living. Grimes ordered him either to go and get cleaned up or to take his meal in the duty engineers' mess. Rather surprisingly, MacMorris knuckled under, although with bad grace. But was it, after all, so surprising? Like all the other people in this ship he was regarded as being almost unemployable. If he were paid off from *Discovery* he would find it hard, if not impossible, to obtain another spacegoing appointment in the Survey Service. In a ship, any ship, he was still a big frog in a small puddle and, too, was in receipt of the active-duty allowance in addition to the pay for his rank. As one of the many technicians loafing around a big Base he would be a not too generously paid nobody.

The steward brought in Grimes's coffee. It was the way that he liked it, very hot and strong. He poured a cup of the steaming brew, sipped it appreciatively. There was a knock at the door. It was Brabham, accompanied by Major Swinton and Vinegar Nell.

"Rounds, sir?" asked the first lieutenant.

Grimes glanced at the bulkhead clock. "A little early yet. Be seated, all of you. Coffee?"

"No, thank you, sir. We have just finished ours."

The three officers sat in a stiff line on the settee, the woman in the middle. Grimes regarded them over the rim of his cup. Brabham looked, he thought, like a morose bloodhound.

The Mad Major, with his wiry gray hair and bristling moustache, his hot yellow eyes, looked like a vicious terrier. Grimes had never liked terriers. And Vinegar Nell? More cat than dog, he decided. A certain sleekness . . . but sleek cats can be as bad tempered as the rougher ones. He finished his coffee, got to his feet, reached for his cap.

"All right," he said. "We'll get the show on the road."

They started in the control room. There was little to find fault with there. Lieutenant Tangye, the navigator, was a man who believed in maintaining all his instruments in a highly polished state. Whether or not Tangye was capable of using these instruments Grimes had yet to discover. Not that he worried much about it; he was quite prepared to do his own navigation. (He, while serving as navigator in a cruiser, had been quite notorious for his general untidiness, but no captain had ever been able to complain about any lack of ability to fix the ship's position speedily and accurately.)

The next deck down was Grimes's own accommodation, with which he was already familiar. He devoted more time to the two decks below in which the officers, of all departments, were accommodated. The cabins and public rooms were clean, although not excessively so. The furnishings were definitely shabby. Miss Russell said, before he could make any comment, "*They* won't supply anything new for this ship."

Perhaps They wouldn't, thought Grimes, but had anybody bothered to find out for sure?

The Marines' quarters were next, housing twenty men. Here, as in the control room, there was some evidence of spit and polish. Grimes decided that the sergeant, a rugged, hairless black giant whose name was Washington, was responsible. Whatever the crimes that had led to his appointment to *Discovery* had been, he was an old-timer, convinced that the space soldiers were superior to any mere spaceman, ships' captains included. The trouble with such men was that, in a pinch, they would be loyal only to their own branch of the Survey Service, to their own officers.

Petty officers' quarters next, with the bos'n—another old-timer—coming to stiff attention as the inspection party entered the compartment. Grimes decided that he wouldn't trust the man any farther than he could throw him—and, as the bos'n was decidedly corpulent, that would not be very far. Langer . . . yes, that was his name. Hadn't he been implicated in the flogging of ship's stores when the heavy cruiser *Draconis* had been grounded on Dingaan for Mannschenn Drive recalibration?

Provedore ratings, deck ratings, engine room ratings . . . everything just not quite clean, with the faint yet unmistakable taint of too-long-unwashed clothing and bedding permeating the ship's atmosphere.

Storerooms—now well stocked.

The farm decks, with their hydroponic tanks, the yeast and algae and tissue culture vats—everything looked healthy enough. Grimes expressed the hope that it would all stay that way.

The cargo hold, its bins empty, but ready for any odds and ends that *Discovery* might pick up during the forthcoming voyage.

The boat bays . . . Grimes selected a boat at random, had it opened up. He satisfied himself that all equipment was in good order, that the provisions and other supplies were according to scale. He ran the inertial drive-unit for a few seconds in neutral gear. The irregular beat of it sounded healthy enough.

Engine spaces, with the glowering MacMorris in close attendance. In the Mannschenn Drive room, ignoring the engineer's scowl, Grimes put out a finger to one of the finely balanced rotors. It began to turn at the slightest touch and the other rotors, on their oddly angled spindles, moved in sympathy. There was the merest hint of temporal disorientation, a fleeting giddiness. MacMorris growled, "An' does he want us all to finish up in the middle o' last week?" Grimes pretended not to have heard him.

The inertial drive room, with the drive-units now reassembled, their working parts concealed beneath the casings . . . reaction drive . . . nothing to see there but a few pumps. And there was nothing to see in the compartment that housed the hydrogen fusion power plant; everything of any importance was hidden beneath layers of insulation. But if MacMorris said that it was all right, it must be.

"Thank you," said Grimes to his officers. "She'll do." He thought, *She'll have to do.*

"You missed the dogbox, sir," Brabham reminded him, with ill-concealed satisfaction.

"I know," said Grimes. "I'm going there now. No, you needn't come with me."

Alone, he made his way to the axial shaft, entered the elevator cage. He pushed the button for the farm deck. It was there that the psionic amplifier was housed, for no other reason than to cut down on the plumbing requirements. Pumps and pipes were essential to the maintenance of the tissue culture vats; some of the piping and one of the pumps were used to provide the flow of nutrient solution through the tank in which floated the disembodied canine brain.

On the farm deck he made his way through the assemblage of vats and tanks and found, tucked away in a corner, a small, boxlike compartment. Some wit had taped a crudely printed notice to the door: BEWARE OF THE DOG. *Very funny*, thought Grimes. *When I was a first trip cadet it always had me rolling on the deck in uncontrollable paroxysms of mirth.* But what was that noise from inside the room? Someone singing? Flannery, presumably.

> *"I'll die but not surrender*
> *Cried the Wild Colonial Boy. . . ."*

Grimes grinned. It sounded as though the psionic communications officer had already established rapport with his new pet. But wouldn't a dingo prefer the eerie music of a didgeridoo? What if he were to indent for one? He grinned again.

He knocked at the door, slid it open. Flannery was sitting —sprawling, rather—at and over his worktable. There was a bottle, open, ready to hand, with a green label on which shone a golden harp. There was no glass. The PCO, still crooning softly, was staring at the spherical tank, at the obscene, pallid, wrinkled shape suspended in translucent brown fluid.

"Mr. Flannery!"

Flannery went on singing.

"Mr. Flannery!"

"Sorr!" The man got unsteadily to his feet, almost knocked himself down again with a flamboyant parody of a salute. "Sorr!"

"Sit down before you fall down!" Grimes ordered sharply. Flannery subsided gratefully. He picked up the bottle, offered it to Grimes, who said, "No, thank you," thinking, *I*

daren't antagonize this fat, drunken slob. I might need him.
He remarked, "I see you have your new amplifier."

"Indeed I have, Captain. An' he's good, as God's me witness. Inspired, ye were, when ye said I should be takin' Ned."

"Mphm. So you don't anticipate any trouble?"

"Indeed I do not. Ask me to punch a message through to the Great Nebula of Andromeda itself, an' me an' Ned'll do it."

"Mphm." Grimes wondered how he should phrase the next question. He was on delicate ground. But if he had Flannery on his side, working for him, he would have his own, private espionage system, the Rhine Institute's code of ethics notwithstanding. "So you've got yourself another pal. Ha, ha. I wonder what he thinks of the rest of us in this ship . . . me, for example."

"Ye want the God's own truth, Captain?"

"Yes."

"He hates you. If he had his teeth still, he'd be after bitin' you. It's the uniform, ye see, an' the way ye're wearin' it. He remembers the cowardly troopers what did for the Ned who's his blessed namesake."

"Not to mention the jolly swagman," growled Grimes. "But that's all nonsense, Mr. Flannery. You can't tell me that *that's* the brain of a dingo who was around when the Kelly Gang was brought to book!"

Flannery chuckled. "What d'ye take me for, Captain? I don't believe that, an' I'm not expectin' you to. But he's a dog, an' all dogs have this race memory, goin' back to the Dream Time, an' farther back still. And now, Captain, will ye, with all due respect, be gettin' out of here? Ye've got Ned all upset, ye have."

Grimes departed in a rather bad temper, leaving Flannery communing with the whiskey bottle and his weird pet.

CHAPTER 5

Six hours before liftoff time Grimes received Brandt, the only scientific officer who was making the voyage, in his day cabin. From the very start they clashed. This Dr. Brandt—he soon made it clear that he did not wish to be addressed as "Commander" and that he considered his Survey Service rank and uniform childish absurdities—was, Grimes decided, a typical case of small-man-itis. He did not need to be a telepath to know what Brandt thought about him. He was no more than a bus driver whose job it was to take the learned gentleman to wherever he wished to go.

And then Brandt endeared himself to Grimes still further by putting his thoughts into words. "It's a high time, Captain," said the little, fat, bald black-bearded man, "that contacts with Lost Colonies were taken out of the clumsy hands of you military types. You do irreparable damage with your interferences. *I* should have been on hand to make a thorough and detailed study of the New Spartan culture before you ruined it by aiding and abetting revolution."

"Mphm," grunted Grimes.

"And you did the same sort of thing on Morrowvia."

"Did I? I was trying to save the Morrowvians from Drongo Kane—who, in case you don't know, is a slave trader—and from the Dog Star Line, who wanted to turn the whole damn planet into a millionaires' holiday camp."

"Which it is now well on the way to becoming, I hear."

"The Morrowvians will do very nicely out of it. In any case, on neither occasion was I without scientific advice."

"Dr. Lazenby, I suppose you mean. Or Commander Lazenby, as she no doubt prefers to be called. Pah!"

"Wipe the spit off your beard, Doctor," admonished Grimes, his prominent ears flushing angrily. "And, as far as Commander Lazenby is concerned, the advice she gave me was consistently good."

28

"*You* would think so. An ignorant spaceman led up the garden path by a flashily attractive woman."

Luckily Brabham came in just then on some business or other, and Grimes was able to pass Brandt on to the first lieutenant. He sat down at his littered desk and thought, *That cocky little bastard is all I need.* He remembered a captain under whom he had served years ago, who used to exclaim when things went wrong, "I am surrounded by rogues and imbeciles!"

And how many rogues and imbeciles was he, Grimes, surrounded by? He began to make calculations on a scrap of paper.

Control room officers—six.

Electronic communications officers—two.

Psionic communications officer—one (and that was more than ample!).

Supply branch officers—two.

Engineer officers—six.

Medical officer—one.

Marine officer—one.

Scientific officer—one.

That made twenty, in the commissioned ranks alone.

Cooks—four.

Stewards—two.

Stewardesses—four.

That made thirty.

Marines, including the sergeant and corporal—twenty-two.

Fifty-two was now the score.

Petty officers—four.

General purpose ratings—twenty.

Total, seventy-six. Seventy-six people who must have ridden to their parents' weddings on bicycles.

Grimes had done his figuring as a joke, but suddenly it was no longer funny. Normally he enjoyed the essential loneliness of command, but that had been in ships where there was always company, congenial company, when he felt that he needed it. In this vessel there seemed to be nobody at all with whom he could indulge in a friendly drink and a yarn.

Perhaps things would improve.

Perhaps they wouldn't.

Growl you may, he told himself, *but go you must.*

CHAPTER 6

It is always an anxious moment when a captain has to handle a strange ship, with strange officers and crew, for the first time. Grimes, stolidly ensconced in the pilot's chair, tried, not unsuccessfully, to convey the impression that he hadn't a worry in the whole universe. He made the usual major production of filling and lighting his pipe while listening to the countdown routine. "All hands," Brabham was saying into the intercom microphone, "secure ship for liftoff. Secure ship. Secure ship." Lieutenant Tangye, the navigator, was tense in the co-pilot's seat, his hands poised over the duplicate controls. No doubt the slim, blond, almost ladylike young man was thinking that he could make a far better job of getting the old bitch upstairs than this new skipper. Other officers were standing by radar and radar altimeter, NST transceiver, drift indicator, accelerometer, and all the rest of it. It was unnecessary; all the displays were visible to both pilot and co-pilot at a glance—but the bigger the ship the more people for whom jobs must be found.

From the many compartments the reports came in. "All secure." "All secure for liftoff." "All secure." "All secure."

"Any word from Commander Brandt yet?" asked Grimes. "After all, he is a departmental head."

"Nothing yet, sir," replied Brabham.

"Shake him up, will you, Number One."

"Control to Commander Brandt. Have you secured yet? Acknowledge."

Brandt's voice came through the speaker. "*Doctor* Brandt here. Of course I'm secure. This isn't my first time in Space, you know."

Awkward bastard, thought Grimes. He said, "Lifting off."

"Lifting off," repeated Brabham.

At Grimes's touch on the controls the inertial drive, deep

30

in the bowels of the ship, muttered irritably. Another touch —and the muttering became a cacophonous protest, loud even through the layer after layer of sonic insulation. *Discovery* shook herself, her structure groaning. From the NST speaker came the bored voice of Aerospace Control. "You are lifting, *Discovery*. You are clear of the pad. *Bon voyage.*"

"Acknowledge," said Grimes to the radio officer. He didn't need to be informed that the ship was off the ground. His own instruments would tell him that if he bothered to look at them—but the *feel* of the ship made it quite obvious that she was up and clear, lifting faster and faster. In the periscope screen he could see the spaceport area—the clusters of white administration buildings, the foreshortened silvery towers that were ships, big and little, dropping away, diminishing. The red, flashing beacons marking the berth that he had just left were sliding from the center of the display, but it didn't matter. He had been expecting drift, the wind the way it was. If he had been coming in to a landing it would have been necessary to apply lateral thrust; during a liftoff all that was required was to get up through and clear of the atmosphere.

A hint of yaw—

Only three degrees, but Grimes corrected it, more to get the feel of the ship than for any other reason. With the same motivation he brought the red flashers back to the center of the periscope screen. Mphm. The old bitch didn't handle too badly at all. He increased acceleration from a half gee to one gee, to one and a half, to two.

The intercom speaker squawked. "Dr. Brandt, here. What the hell are you playing at up there?"

"Minding our own bloody business!" snapped Grimes into his microphone. "Might I suggest that you do the same?"

Brabham sniggered loudly.

"Emergency rocket drill," ordered Grimes quietly. That, as he had suspected it would, took the grin off the first lieutenant's face. But the reaction drive was here to be used, wasn't it? "Number One, pass the word."

"Attention, all hands," growled Brabham into the intercom. "Stand by for testing of reaction drive. Sudden variations in acceleration are to be expected. Stand by. Stand by."

Grimes pushed a button, looked down at his console. Under ROCKETS the READY light glowed vivid green. With all his faults, MacMorris kept every system in a state of go. Decisively Grimes cut the inertial drive. His stomach tried to push its way up into his throat as acceleration abruptly ceased. He brought a finger down to the FIRE button, pushed it down past the first, second, and third stops. He felt as well as heard the screaming roar as the incandescent gases rushed through the venturis, and then the renewal of acceleration pushed him downward into the thick padding of his chair.

"Aerospace Control to *Discovery*. Are those pyrotechnics really necessary?"

"Tell him testing, testing," said Grimes to the radio officer. He succeeded in restarting the inertial drive and cutting the rockets at exactly the same instant. The ship continued to drive upward with no reduction of velocity.

Brabham loudly sighed his relief. "You're lucky," he commented. "Sir. Come to that, we're all lucky."

"What do you mean, Number One?" demanded Grimes.

The first lieutenant laughed sourly. "This is the first time that the reaction drive has been tested within the memory of the oldest man. Commander Tallis would *never* use it."

"How many times must I tell you that I am not Commander Tallis?"

The intercom speaker crackled, then, "Dr. Brandt here. I'm speaking from my laboratory. What the hell is going on? Do you know that you've smashed thousands of credits worth of valuable equipment?"

"You saw it stowed?" Grimes asked Brabham.

"Yes, sir. There was no chance of its shifting."

Grimes signaled to Tangye to take over the controls. "Keep her going as she is, pilot." Then he said into his microphone, "Captain here, Dr. Brandt. Did anything shift?"

"No. But I heard glass breaking in the cases. Delicate apparatus can't stand up to your needlessly violent maneuvers."

"Did you see the stuff packed, Doctor?"

"Of course."

"Then might I suggest that next time you see that your bits and pieces are packed properly? There are excellent padding materials available."

"I hold you entirely responsible for the breakages, Captain."

"You knew that you were embarking in a spaceship, Doctor."

"Yes. I did. But rockets went out generations ago."

"Reaction drive is still fitted to all Survey Service vessels, as you should have known, *Commander* Brandt."

"Pah!"

Grimes returned his attention to ship handling, taking over from Tangye. Overhead—or forward—the sky seen through the control room dome was a dark purple, almost black. In the periscope screen Lindisfarne was assuming a spherical aspect. Outside the ship there was still atmosphere—but atmosphere in the academic sense of the word only. On the dial of the radar altimeter the decades of kilometers were mounting up steadily and rapidly.

There was nothing to do now but to run out and clear of the Van Allens, while the globe that was Lindisfarne dwindled steadily in the periscope screen, a diminishing half-moon, the sunlit hemisphere opalescently aglow.

The stars were bright and unwinking in the black sky, and the polarizers were automatically dimming the harsh glare of the Lindisfarne sun on the beam. Grimes looked at the magnetometer. The bright red warning light was dimming. It gave one last flicker, then turned to green.

"Clear of the Van Allens, sir," announced Tangye belatedly.

Slow reaction time, thought Grimes. He said, "So I see. Cut the inertial drive and line her up on the target star, will you?"

"Aye, aye, sir," replied the young man, smartly enough.

The engines grumbled to a stammering halt. Only then did Tangye busy himself with a star chart, looking through the ports frequently to check the relative positions of the constellations. Grimes refrained from pointing out the sun that he wanted to head for, a second magnitude luminary in the constellation of The Bunny, as this grouping of stars had been dubbed by the first settlers on Lindisfarne. There was, if one had a strong imagination, a suggestion of rabbit's ears and woman's breasts, thought Grimes while his navigator fumbled and bumbled. *If this were a* real *bunny,* he thought sardonically, *young Tangye'd be on target a damn sight sooner!* And how long would it be before Brandt, the obnoxious fool, started to whine about being kept too

long in a condition of free fall? Meanwhile, other people besides the navigator were exhibiting shortcomings.

"Number One," Grimes said mildly, "you didn't make the
usual announcement on the intercom. Stand by for free fall,
setting trajectory and all the rest of it."

"You never told me to, sir."

"It's part of your job to look after these details," snapped
Grimes.

"Commander Tallis didn't want announcements made every five minutes. Sir."

"Neither do I. But I want those announcements made
that are required by Survey Service regulations."

Then Brandt came through on the intercom. "Doctor
Brandt here. What *is* going on up there?"

"Stand by for setting trajectory," said Brabham sulkily
into his microphone.

"On target, sir," announced Tangye. "I mean, I've *found*
the target."

"Then get on to it."

The directional gyroscopes rumbled into motion. Slowly
the ship turned about her axes, centrifugal forces giving an
off-center surrogate of gravity. Grimes, looking up into the
cartwheel sight set into the dome, saw The Bunny swim slowly into view.

The gyroscopes stopped.

"On target, sir."

"Mphm. Have you allowed for galactic drift, Mr.
Tangye?"

"Eh . . . no, sir."

"Then please do so."

There was more delay while Tangye fumbled through the
ephemeris, fed data into the control room computer. *All
this should have been done before liftoff,* thought Grimes disgustedly. *Damn it all, this puppy couldn't navigate a plastic
duck across a bathtub!* He watched the nervous young man,
glowering.

"Allowance applied, sir." The gyroscopes restarted as the
navigator spoke.

"Being applied, you mean. And are you sure that you're
putting it on the right way? All right, all right. Leave it. *I*
worked it out roughly before we pushed off."

"On trajectory, sir."

"Thank you." Grimes himself announced over the PA

system that the Mannschenn Drive was about to be restarted and that acceleration would be resumed immediately
thereafter.

He pushed the button to start the interstellar drive. He
could imagine those shining rotors starting to turn, spinning
faster and faster, spinning, precessing at right angles to all
the dimensions of normal space, tumbling through the dark
infinities, dragging the ship and all aboard her with them as
the temporal precession field built up.

There was the disorientation in space and time to which
no spaceman ever becomes inured. There was the uncanny
sensation of *déjà vu*. There was, as far as Grimes was concerned, an unusually strong premonition of impending doom.
It persisted after everything had returned to normal—to
normal, that is, as long as one didn't look out through the
viewports at the contorted nebulosities that glimmered eerily
where the familiar stars had been. The ship, her restarted
inertial drive noisily clattering, the thin, high whine of the
Mannschenn Drive pervading every cubic millimeter of her,
was speeding through the warped continuum toward her
destination.

"Thank you, gentlemen," said Grimes heavily. (*Thank
you for what?*) "Normal Deep Space watches and routine,
Number One."

"Normal Deep Space watches and routine, sir," replied
Brabham.

Grimes unbuckled himself from his chair, got up and went
down to his quarters. He poured himself a stiff brandy. Even
if he hadn't earned it, he felt that he needed it.

CHAPTER 7

Nonetheless, Grimes was much happier now that the voyage had started.

The ship was back in her natural element, and so were her people. As long as she was in port—at a major naval base especially—the captain was not the supreme authority. On Lindisfarne, for example, Grimes had come directly under the orders of the officer-in-charge-of-surveys, and of any of that rear admiral's officers who were senior to himself. Too, any rating, petty officer or officer of his own who considered that he had a grievance, could run, screaming, to one or another of the various Survey Service personnel protection societies, organizations analogous to the several guilds, unions, and whatever representing merchant spacemen. Of course, any complaint had to be justifiable—but it was amazing how many complaints, in these decadent days, were held to be warranted. Had MacMorris not been in such bad odor with the officials of the Engineer Officers' Association his tales about Grimes's alleged bullying would have been listened to; had they been, *Discovery* would never have got away from Lindisfarne.

In Deep Space, everybody knew, a captain could do almost anything to anybody provided that he were willing to face a Board of Inquiry at some later date. He could even order people pushed out of the airlock without spacesuits as long as they were guilty of armed mutiny.

All in all, Grimes was not too displeased with his new command. True, she was an old ship—but as an old ship should be (and sometimes is) she was as comfortable as a well-worn shoe. She was not a taut ship; she never would be or could be that. All of her people were too disheartened by slow, even nonexistent promotion, by the knowledge that they had been passed over, would always be passed over. She was not a happy ship—but once she settled down to the old, familiar routine, once her crew realized that it was less trouble to do things Grimes's way than his predecessor's way, she was not actively unhappy.

Grimes did not mix much with his officers. He would pass the time of day with the watchkeeper when he went up to the control room, he would, naturally, meet people when he made rounds, he took his seat at the head of the senior officers' table at meals, occasions at which scintillating conversation was conspicuous by its absence.

Brabham was too morose, too full of his own woes. Mac-Morris was as he had been described more than once, an uncouth mechanic, incapable of conversation about anything but machinery. Vinegar Nell could have been good company—she was a highly intelligent, witty woman—but she could not forget that the last time she and Grimes had been shipmates she had been a lieutenant while Grimes was only a lowly ensign. The fact that he was now a commander and captain of a big ship she ascribed to sex and luck rather than ability.

The medical officer, Surgeon Lieutenant Commander Rath, was universally unpopular. He was barely competent, and in civil life his lack of a bedside manner would have militated against financial success. He was a tall, dark, thin (almost skeletal) man and his nickname, to all ranks, was The Undertaker. Nobody liked him, and he liked nobody.

And the Mad Major kept himself very much to himself. He was a Marine, and Marines were, in his opinion, the highest form of interstellar life.

All in all, Grimes began to think as the voyage wore on, the only interesting member of his crew was Flannery. But was it Flannery himself who was interesting—or was it that unfortunate dingo's brain in its tank of nutrient solution? The thing was fascinating—that alleged racial memory, for example. Was it genuine, or was it merely the product of Flannery's fertile, liquor-stimulated imagination? After all, Grimes only had Flannery's word for what Ned was thinking . . . and, according to Flannery, Ned's thoughts were fantastic ones.

"He thinks he remembers you, Captain," said the PCO one day when Grimes dropped in to see him after rounds.

"Mphm. Don't tell me that I'm a reincarnation of the original jolly swagman."

"Indeed ye're not, sorr! He's thinkin' o' you as Bligh!"

"I suppose I should be flattered," admitted Grimes. "But I'm afraid that *I* shall never finish up as an admiral *and* as a colonial governor."

"An' that's not what the black Captain Bligh was famous for, sorr!"

"The mutiny? His first one? But during that, as during the subsequent ones, he was more sinned against than sinning!"

"Not the way that Ned, here, recollects it, Captain."

"Come off it, Mr. Flannery. There weren't any dogs of any kind aboard the *Bounty*!"

The telepath stared at his grisly pet through bleary eyes, and his thick lips moved as he subvocalized his thoughts. Then: "Ned wasn't there himself, o' course, Captain, nor any of his blessed forefathers. But he still says as that was the way of it, that the wicked Captain Bligh drove his crew to mutiny, indeed he did."

"Indeed he did not!" snapped Grimes, who had his own ideas about what had happened aboard the ill-fated *Bounty*.

"If that's the way ye feel about it, Captain," murmured Flannery diplomatically.

"It *is* the way I feel about it." And then, a sudden, horrid suspicion forming in his mind: "What *is* all this about Bligh and the *Bounty*? Are you suggesting. . . ?"

"Indeed I'm not, Captain. An' as for Ned, here"—the waving hand just missed the tank and its gruesome contents—"would he be after tellin' ye, if he could? He would not. He would niver be on the side o' the oppressor."

"Good for him," remarked Grimes sardonically. He got up to leave. "And, Mr. Flannery, you might get this—this mess cleaned up a bit. I did mention it to Miss Russell, but she said that her girls aren't kennelmaids. Those empty bottles . . . and that . . . *bone*."

"But t'is only an old bone, Captain, with niver a shred o' meat nor gristle left on it. Poor Terry—may the blessed saints be kind to the soul of him—knew it was there, an' imagined it like it used to be. An' Ned's the same."

"So it is essential to the efficient working of the amplifier?"

"Indeed it is, sorr."

Grimes stirred the greasy, dog-eared playing cards, spread out on the table for a game of Canfield, with a gingerly forefinger. "And I suppose that these are essential to *your* efficient working?"

"Ye said it, Captain. An' would ye deprive me of an innocent game of patience? An' don't the watch officers in the control room, when ye're not around, set up games o' three-dimensional noughts an' crosses in the plottin' tank, just to while away the weary hours? Ye've done it yerself, like enough."

Grimes's prominent ears flushed. He could not deny it— and if he did this telepath would know that he was lying.

"An' I can do more wi' these than play patience, Captain. Did I iver tell ye that I have Gypsy blood in me veins? Back in the Ould Isle me great, great granny lifted her skirts to a wanderin' tinker. From him, an' through her, I have the gift." The grimy pudgy hands stacked the cards, shuffled them, and then began to rearrange them. "Would ye like a readin'? Now?"

"No, thank you," said Grimes as he left.

CHAPTER 8

Discovery came to New Maine.

New Maine is not a major colony; its overall population barely tops the ten million mark. It is not an unpleasant world, although, even on the equator, it is a little on the chilly side. It has three moons, one so large as to be almost a sister planet, the other two little more than oversized boulders. It is orbited by the usual system of artificial satellites—communication, meteorological, and all the rest of it. The important industries are fisheries and fish processing; the so-called New Maine cod (which, actually, is more of a reptile than a true fish) is a sufficiently popular delicacy on some worlds to make its smoking, packaging, and export worthwhile.

A not very substantial contribution to the local economy is made by the Federation Survey Service sub-Base, which is not important enough to require a high ranking officer-in-charge, these duties being discharged by a mere commander, a passed-over one at that. At the time of *Discovery*'s visit this was a Commander Denny, a flabby, portly gentleman who looked and acted older than he actually was and who, obviously, had lost all interest in the job long since.

Shortly after berthing at the small, badly run-down naval spaceport, Grimes paid the usual courtesy call on the officer-commanding-base. It was not an occasion demanding full dress, with fore-and-aft hat, frock coat, sword, and all the rest of the anachronistic finery; nonetheless an OCB is an OCB, regardless of his actual rank. The temperature outside the ship was 17°, cool enough to make what Grimes thought of as his "grown-up trousers" comfortable. He changed from his shipboard shorts and shirt into his brass-buttoned, gold-braided black, put on his cap with the scrambled egg on its peak still undimmed by time, made his way down to the after airlock. The Marine on gangway duty, he was pleased to note, was smartly attired; obviously Major Swinton had taken the hints regarding the appearance of his men and, equally obviously, Sergeant Washington had cooperated to the full with his commanding officer in this respect.

The man saluted crisply. "Captain, sir!"

Grimes returned the salute. "Yes?"

"Are you expecting a ground car, sir? If one hasn't been arranged, I'll call one."

"I'll walk," said Grimes. "The exercise will do me good."

Discovery's ramp was still battered and shabby, although a few repairs had been made before departure from Lindisfarne. The ship herself was still showing her many years, the ineradicable signs of neglect as well as of age. But even she, who on her pad at the Main Base had looked like an elderly poor relation, here had the appearance of a rich aunt come a-visiting. Nobody expects to be obliged to eat his meals off a spaceport apron—but there are minimal standards of cleanliness that should be maintained. These were certainly not being maintained here. It was obvious that during the night some large animals had wandered across the expanse of concrete and treated it as a convenience. It was equally obvious that they had done the same during the previous night, and the night before. In addition, there were tall, straggling, ugly weeds thrusting up through ragged cracks, with dirty scraps of plastic and paper piling up around them, entangled with them.

The block of administration buildings toward which Grimes was heading, treading carefully to avoid getting his well-polished shoes dirty, was plain, functional—and like most functional constructions would have been pleasant enough in appearance if only it had been clean. But the wide windows were dull with an accumulation of dust and the entire facade was badly stained. Were there, Grimes wondered, flying creatures on this world as big as the animals that had fouled the apron? He looked up at the dull sky apprehensively. If there were, he hoped that they came out only at night. As he elevated his regard he noticed that the flagstaff atop the office block was not quite vertical and that the Survey Service ensign, flapping lazily in the light breeze, was ragged and dirty, and was not right up to the truck.

The main doors, as he approached them, slid open reluctantly with a distinctly audible squeak. In the hallway beyond them an elderly petty officer, in shabby grays, got slowly up from his desk as Grimes entered. He was not wearing a cap, so he did not salute; but neither did he stiffen to attention.

He asked, "Sir?"

"I am Commander Grimes, captain of *Discovery*."

"Then you'll be wanting to see the old—" He looked at the smartly uniformed Grimes and decided to start again. "You'll be wanting to see Commander Denny. You'll find him in his office, sir." He led the way to a bank of elevators, pressed a button.

"Rather shorthanded, aren't you?" remarked Grimes conversationally.

"Oh, no, sir. On a sub-Base like this it isn't necessary to have more than the duty PO—which is me—manning Reception."

"I was thinking about policing the spaceport apron," said Grimes.

"Oh, *that!*" The petty officer's face did show a faint disgust.

"Yes. That."

"But there's nothing that we can do about the bastards, sir. They always did relieve themselves here, before there was a spaceport. They always will. Creatures of habit, like—"

"*They?*"

"The great snakes, sir. They're called great snakes, though they're not snakes at all, really. More of a sort of slug. Just imagine a huge sausage that eats at one end and—"

"I get the idea. But you could post guards, suitably armed."

"But the great snakes are protected, sir. There's only the one herd left on the entire planet."

"Then why not a force field fence, with a nonlethal charge."

"Oh, no, sir. That would never do. The Old Man's wife—I beg pardon, sir, the commander's wife—would never stand for it. She's the chairlady of the New Maine Conservationist Association."

"Mphm." At this moment the elevator, which had taken its time about descending, arrived. The door opened. Grimes got into the car as the petty officer said, "Seventh deck, sir." He pressed the right button and was carried slowly upward.

Commander Denny's office was as slovenly as his spaceport. Untidiness Grimes did not mind—he never set a good example himself in that respect—but real dirt was something else again. The drift of papers on Denny's desk was acceptable, but the dust-darkened rings on its long-unpolished surface left by mugs of coffee or some other fluids were not. Like his petty officer in Reception, Denny was wearing a shabby gray uniform. So were the two women clerks. Grimes thought it highly probable that it was the elderly, unattractive one who did all the work. The other one was there for decoration—assuming that one's tastes in decoration run to bold-eyed, plump, blonde, micro-skirted flirts.

The Base commander got slowly to his feet, extended a pudgy hand. "Commander Grimes?"

"In person."

The two men shook hands. Denny's grip was flabby.

"And these," went on Denny, "are Ensign Tolley"—the older woman favored Grimes with a tight-lipped smile—"and Ensign Primm." Miss Primm stared at the visitor haughtily. "But sit down, Grimes. You're making my control room—ha, ha—look untidy."

Grimes looked around. There were two chairs available in addition to those occupied by the clerks, but each of them held an overflow of paper.

"Sit down, man. Sit down. This is Liberty Hall. You can spit on the mat and call the cat a bastard."

"I don't see any cats," said Grimes. *Not of the four-legged variety, anyhow,* he thought. "And to judge by the state of your spaceport apron, somebody, or something, has already been . . . er . . . spitting on the mat!"

Surprisingly it was the elderly ensign who laughed, then got up to clear the detritus from one of the chairs. Neither Denny nor the younger woman showed any amusement.

"And now, Commander," asked Denny, "what can I do for you?"

"I shall require the use of your port facilities, Commander," Grimes told him. "I'll be wanting to replenish stores, and my chief engineer could do with some shore labor to lend a hand with his innies; he wants to take them down to find out why they're working, and then he'll have to put them together again. You know what engineers are."

"Yes. I know. And then you'll be off on your Lost Colony hunt, I suppose."

"That's what I'm being paid for. Have you heard any rumors of Lost Colonies out in this sector?"

"I'm just the OCB, Grimes. Nobody ever tells me anything."

And would you be interested if they did? Grimes wondered. He said, "Our lords and masters must have had something in mind when they sent me out this way."

"And who knows what futile thoughts flicker through their tiny minds? *I* don't."

And you've got to the stage where you don't much care, either, thought Grimes. But he could not altogether blame the man. This dreary sub-Base on a dull world was obviously the end of the road for Denny. Here he would mark time until he reached retirement age. And what about himself? Would this sort of job be his ultimate fate if some admiral or politician upon whose corns he had trodden finally succeeded in having him swept under the carpet and forgotten?

"Oh, Commander," said Denny, breaking into his thoughts.

"Yes, Commander?"

"You'll be getting an official invitation later in the morning. It's quite a while since we had one of our ships in here, so the mayor of Penobscot—that's where the commercial spaceport is—is throwing an official party tonight. Bum freezers and decorations. You and your officers are being asked."

"I can hardly wait."

"The master of *Sundowner* should be there, too, with his people."

"*Sundowner?*"

"She's at Port Penobscot, loading fish. She's a star tramp. Rim Worlds registry. She gets around."

"Mphm. It could be worthwhile having a yarn with him."

"It could be, Commander. These tramp skippers often stumble on things that our survey captains miss. Sometimes they report them, sometimes they don't."

"You can say that again, Commander. The last Lost Colony that I visited, Morrowvia, the Dog Star Line was trying to keep all to its little self. And it looks as though they'll be able to do just that." Grimes looked at his watch. Denny had made no move to offer him tea, coffee, or anything stronger, and it was past the time when he usually had his morning coffee aboard the ship. "I'd better be getting back to find out what disasters have been happening in my absence. And my departmental heads should have their requisitions ready for my autograph by now."

"I'll see you tonight, Commander," said Denny.

"See you tonight, Commander Denny," said Grimes.

As he let himself out he overheard the younger of the two women say, in a little-too-loud whisper, "Gawd save us all! What a stuck-up tailor's dummy! I hope he treads in something on the way back to his rustbucket!"

CHAPTER 9

The mayor sent a small fleet of ground cars to pick up *Discovery*'s officers. Grimes, resplendent in black and gold and stiff white linen, with his miniature decorations on their rainbow ribbons a-jingle on the left breast of his mess jacket, rode in the lead vehicle. He was accompanied by Brabham, Major Swinton, Dr. Brandt, and Vinegar Nell. The paymaster looked remarkably handsome in her severely cut, long-skirted evening dress uniform. Swinton, in his dress blue-and-scarlet, had transformed himself from a bad-tempered terrier into a gaudy and pugnacious psittacoid. Brabham (of course) was letting the side down. His mess uniform, when he extricated it from wherever it had been stowed, had proved to be unwearable, stained and creased and far too tight a fit. He had compromised by wearing a black bow tie, instead of one of the up-and-down variety, with his not-too-shabby double-breasted black outfit. And Brandt, of course, had never possessed a suit of mess kit. He was wearing civilian evening dress, with the sash of some obscure order—the sash itself was far from obscure, being bright purple edged with gold—stretched across his shirt front.

The electric cars sped swiftly along the road between the Base and Penobscot. Dusk was falling fast from a leaden sky, and little could be seen through the wide windows of the vehicles. Even in broad daylight there would have been little to see; this country was desolate moorland, only slightly undulant, with not so much as a tree or a hill or even a stony outcrop to break the monotony. Ahead, brighter and brighter as the darkness deepened and the distance diminished, glared the lights of the port city.

The motorcade swept past the spaceport where *Sundowner,* a stubby tower of metal, stood among the cargo-handling

46

gantries, a briefly glimpsed abstract of black shadows and garish, reflected light. Slowing down at last it skirted the harbor—Penobscot was a seaport as well as a spaceport—and the long quay where the big oceangoing trawlers were discharging their glittering catch.

The mayor's palace overlooked the harbor. It was a big, although not high, building, pseudo-classical, its pillared facade glowing whitely in the floodlights. The approach was along a wide avenue, lined with tall, feathery-leafed trees, in the branches of which colored glow-bulbs had been strung. Brabham muttered something in a sour voice about every day being Christmas on New Maine. Vinegar Nell told him tartly to shut up. The chauffeur said nothing, but Grimes could sense the man's resentment.

The car drew to a halt in the portico. The driver left his seat to open the door for his passengers—the sort of courtesy that was long vanished from Earth but that still persisted in many of the colonies. Grimes was first out, then assisted Vinegar Nell, who was having a little trouble with her unaccustomed long skirt, to the ground. Brabham dismounted, then Swinton, then Brandt. The chauffeur saluted smartly and returned to his driving seat in the car, which sped off in a spattering of fine golden gravel.

Grimes limped to the wide doorway—a tiny pebble had got inside his right shoe—followed by the others. Mingled music and light flowed out into the portico. Standing by a group of heroic statuary—well-muscled, naked women wrestling with some sort of sea serpent—was a portly individual whom Grimes took, at first, for a local admiral. This resplendently uniformed person bowed, albeit with more condescension than obsequiousness, and inquired smoothly, "Whom shall I announce, sir?"

"Commander Grimes, captain of the Survey Ship *Discovery*. And with me are Commander Brandt, of the scientific branch, Lieutenant Commander Brabham, my executive officer, Major Swinton, of the Federation Marines, and Lieutenant Russell, my paymaster."

The functionary raised a small megaphone to his mouth; with it he could compete quite easily with the buzz of conversation and the music from the synthesizer. "Captain Grimes . . . Commander Brandt . . ."

"*Doctor* Brandt!" snarled the scientist, but he was ignored.

"Lieutenant Commander Brabham . . . Major Swinton . . . Lieutenant Russell."

Grimes found himself shaking hands with a wiry little man in a bright green evening suit, with an ornate gold chain of office about his neck. "Glad to have you aboard, Captain!"

"Commander, Mr. Mayor," corrected Grimes. "Your majordomo seems to have promoted me."

"You're captain of a ship, aren't you?" The mayor grinned whitely. "Come to that, I always call Bill Davinas 'commodore.' I'll hand you over to him now while I greet your officers."

Grimes shook hands with Davinas, a tall, dark, black-and-gold uniformed man with four gold stripes on each of his epaulettes, who said, "I'm the master of *Sundowner*, Commander. You probably noticed her at the spaceport. I've been a regular trader here since Rim Runners pushed me off my old routes; the small, private owner just can't compete with a government shipping line."

"And what do I call you, sir? Commodore, or captain?"

"Bill, for preference." Davinas laughed. "That commodore business is just the mayor's idea of a joke. The Sundowner Line used to own quite a nice little fleet, but now it's down to one ship. So I'm the line's senior master—senior and only —which does make me a courtesy commodore of sorts. But I don't get paid any extra. Ah, here's a table with some good stuff. I can recommend these codfish patties, and this local rosé isn't at all bad."

While he sipped and nibbled Grimes looked around the huge ballroom. The floor was a highly polished black, reflecting the great, glittering electroliers, each one a crystalline complexity, suspended from the shallow dome of the ceiling, which was decorated with ornate bas-reliefs in a floral pattern. Along the white-pillared walls panels of deep blue, in which shone artificial stars set in improbable constellations, alternated with enormous mirrors. The overall effect was overpowering, with the crowd of gaily dressed people reflected and re-reflected to infinity on all sides. Against the far wall from the main doorway was the great synthesizer, an intricacy of transparent tubes through which rainbow light surged and eddied, a luminescent fountain containing within itself orchestra, choir, massed military bands —and every other form of music that Man has contrived to produce during his long history. The fragile blonde seated at the console—which would not have looked out of place in the control room of a Nova Class dreadnought—could certainly handle the thing. *Beauty and the beast,* thought Grimes.

"Jenkins' Folly," announced Davinas, waving an arm expansively.

"Jenkins' Folly?"

"This palace. The first mayor of Penobscot was a Mr. Jenkins. He'd got it firmly fixed in his thick head that New Maine was going to go the same way as so many—too many —other colonies. Population expansion. Population explosion. Bam! According to his ideas, this city was going to run to a population of about ten million. But it never happened. As you know, the population of the entire planet is only that. Once New Maine had enough people to maintain a technological culture with most of the advantages and few of the drawbacks the ZPG boys and girls took control. So this palace, this huge barn of a place, is used perhaps three times a year. Anniversary Day. New Year's Day. The Founder's Birthday. And, of course, on the very rare occasions when one of *your* ships, with her horde of officers, drops in."

"Mphm."

"Ah, here you are, Commander Grimes." It was Denny, looking considerably smarter than he had in his office, although the short Eton jacket of his mess uniform displayed his plump buttocks, in tightly stretched black, to disadvantage. "Clarice, my dear, this is Commander Grimes. Commander Grimes, meet the little woman."

Mrs. Denny was not a little woman. She was . . . vast. Her pale flesh bulged out of her unwisely low-cut dress, which was an unfortunate shade of pink. She was huge, and she gushed. "It's always good to see new faces, Commander, even though we are all in the same family."

"Ah, yes. The Survey Service."

She giggled and wobbled. "Not the Survey Service, Commander Grimes. The *big* family, I mean. Organic life throughout the universe."

If she'd kept it down to the mammalia, thought Grimes, looking with fascination at the huge, almost fully revealed breasts, *it'd make more sense.* He said, "Yes, of course. Although there are some forms of organic life I'd sooner not be related to. Those great snakes of yours, for instance."

"But you haven't *seen* them, Commander."

"I've seen the evidence of their passing, Mrs. Denny."

"But they're so sweet, and trusting."

"Mphm."

"She's playing our tune, dear," Denny put in hastily, extending his arms to his wife. He got them around her somehow, and the couple moved off to join the other dancers.

Grimes looked around for Davinas but the merchant captain had vanished, had probably made his escape as soon as the Denny couple showed up. He poured himself another glass of wine and looked at the swirling dancers. Some of them, most of them, were singing to the music of the synthesizer, which was achieving the effect of an orchestra of steel guitars.

> *Spaceman, the stars are calling,*
> *Spaceman, you live to roam,*
> *Spaceman, down light-years falling,*
> *Remember I wait at home. . . .*

Icky, thought Grimes. *Icky.* But he had always liked the thing, in spite of (because of?) its sentimentality. He started to sing the words himself in a not very tuneful voice.

"I didn't think you had it in you, Captain."

Grimes cut himself off in mid-note, saw that Vinegar Nell had joined him. It was obvious that the tall, slim woman had taken a drink—or two, or three. Her cheeks were flushed and her face had lost its habitually sour expression. She went on, "I'd never have dreamed that you're a sentimentalist."

"I'm not, Miss Russell. Or am I? Never mind. There are just some really corny things I love, and that song is one of them." Then, surprising himself at least as much as he did her: "Shall we dance?"

"Why not?"

They moved out onto the floor. She danced well, which was more than could be said for him. Normally, on such occasions, he was all too aware of his deficiencies—but all that he was aware of now was the soft pressure of her breasts against his chest, the firmer pressure and the motion of her thighs against his own. And there was no need for them to dance so closely; in spite of the illusory multitude moving in the mirrors the floor was far from crowded.

Watch it, Grimes, he admonished himself. *Watch it!*

And why the hell should I? part of him demanded mutinously.

That's why! he snarled mentally as one of his own officers, a junior engineer, swept past, holding a local lass at least as closely as Grimes was holding the paymaster. The young man leered and winked at his captain. Grimes tried to relax his grip on Vinegar Nell, but she wasn't having any. Her arms were surprisingly strong.

At last the music came to a wailing conclusion.

"I enjoyed that," she said.

"So did I, Miss Russell," admitted Grimes. "Some refreshment?" he asked, steering her toward one of the buffet tables.

"But I should be looking after you." She laughed.

It wasn't so much what she said, but the way that she said it. "Mphm," he grunted aloud.

Captain Davinas was already at the table with his partner, a tall, plain local woman. "Ah," he said, "we meet again, Commander."

Introductions were made, after which, to the disgust of the ladies, the men started to talk shop. The music began again and, with some reluctance, Vinegar Nell allowed herself to be led off by the Penobscot police commissioner, and the other lady by the first mate of *Sundowner.*

"Thank all the odd gods of the galaxy for that!" Davinas laughed. "I have to dance with her some of the time—she's the wife of my Penobscot agent—but she'll settle for one of my senior officers. Talking of officers—I'll swap my purser for your paymaster any day, John!"

"You don't know her like I do, Bill," Grimes told him, feeling oddly disloyal as he said it. He allowed Davinas to refill his glass, tried to ignore the beseeching glances of three young ladies seated not far from them. "Oh, well, I suppose we'd better find ourselves partners, especially since there seems to be a shortage of men here. But I'd sooner talk. Frankly, I'm sniffing around for information on this sector of space—but I suppose that can wait until tomorrow."

"Not unless you want a job as fourth mate aboard *Sundowner.* I lift ship for Electra bright and early—well, early —tomorrow morning."

"A pity."

"It needn't be. I'm not much of a dancing man. I'd sooner earbash and be earbashed over a cold bottle or two than be dragged around the floor by the local talent. And I was intending to return to my ship very shortly, anyhow. Why not come with me? We can have a talk on board."

CHAPTER 10

Davinas and Grimes slipped out of the ballroom almost unnoticed. A few cabs were waiting hopefully in the portico, so they had no difficulty in obtaining transport to the spaceport. It was a short drive only, and less than twenty minutes after they had left the palace Davinas was leading the way up the ramp to the after airlock of *Sundowner*.

It is impossible for a spaceman to visit somebody else's ship without making comparisons—and Grimes was busy making them. Here, of course, there was no uniformed Marine at the gangway, only a civilian night watchman supplied by the vessel's local agent, but the ramp itself was in better repair than *Discovery*'s, and far cleaner. It was the same inboard. Everything was old, worn, but carefully—lovingly, almost—maintained. Somehow the merchant captain had been able to instill in his people a respect—at least —for their ship. Grimes envied him. But in all likelihood Davinas had never been cursed with a full crew of malcontents, and would have been able to extract and dump the occasional bad apple from this barrel without being obliged to fill in forms in quintuplicate to explain just why.

The elevator cage slid upward swiftly and silently, came to a smooth stop. Davinas showed Grimes into his comfortable quarters. "Park the carcass, John. Make yourself at home. This is Liberty Hall; you can spit on the mat . . ."

". . . and call the cat a bastard," finished Grimes.

"Then why don't you?"

Grimes felt something rubbing against his legs, looked down, saw a large tortoiseshell tom. The animal seemed to have taken a fancy to him. He felt flattered. In spite of the affair on Morrowvia he still liked cats.

"Coffee?"

"Thanks."

53

Davinas poured two mugs from a large thermos container, then went into the office adjoining his dayroom. Grimes, while he petted the cat, looked around. He was intrigued by the pictures on the bulkheads of the cabin, holograms of scenes on worlds that were strange to him. One was a mountainscape—jagged peaks, black but snowcapped, thrusting into a stormy sky, each summit with its spume of ice particles streaming down wind like white smoke. He could almost hear the shrieking of the icy gale. Then there was one that could have been a landscape in Hell—contorted rocks, gaudily colored, half veiled by an ocher sandstorm.

Davinas came back, carrying a large folder. "Admiring the art gallery? That one's the Desolation Range on Lorn, my home world. And *that* one is the Painted Badlands on Eblis. Beats me why some genius doesn't open a tourist resort there. Spectacular scenery, friendly indigenes, and quite a few valleys where the likes of us could live quite comfortably."

"The Rim Worlds," murmured Grimes. "I've heard quite a lot about them, off and on. Somehow the Survey Service never seems to show the flag in that sector of space. I don't suppose I'll ever see them."

Davinas laughed. "Don't be so sure. Rim Runners'll take anybody, as long as he has some sort of certificate of competency and rigor mortis hasn't set in!"

"If they ever get me," declared Grimes, "that'll be the sunny Friday!"

"Or me," agreed Davinas. "When the Sundowner Line finally folds I'm putting my savings into a farm."

The two men sipped their good coffee. Davinas lit a long, slim cigar, Grimes his pipe. The cat purred noisily between them.

Then: "I hear that you're on a Lost Colony hunt, John."

"Yes, Bill. As a matter of fact, Commander Denny did mention that you might be able to give me a few leads."

"I might be. But, as a Rim Worlds citizen, I'm supposed to make any reports on anything I find to the Rim Worlds government. And to my owners, of course."

"But the Rim Worlds are members of the Federation."

"Not for much longer, they're not. Surely you've heard talk of secession lately." Davinas laughed rather unpleasantly. "But I'm not exactly in love with our local lords and masters. I've been in the Sundowner Line practically all my working life, and I haven't enjoyed seeing our fleet pushed off the trade routes by Rim Runners. *They* can afford to cut freights; they've the taxpayer's money behind them. And who's the taxpayer? Me."

"But what about your owners? Don't you report to them?"

"They just aren't interested anymore. The last time that I made a deviation, sniffing around for a possible new run for *Sundowner*, there was all hell let loose." He obviously quoted from a letter. " 'We would point out that you are a servant of a commercial shipping line, not a captain in the Federation Survey Service. . . .' Ha!"

"Mphm. So you might be able to help me?"

"I might. If you ask me nicely enough, I will." He poured more coffee into the mugs. "You carry a PCO, of course?"

"Of course. And you?"

"No. Not officially. Our head office now and again— only now and again, mind you—realizes that there is such a force as progress. They found out that one of the early Carlotti sets was going cheap. So now I have Carlotti, and no PCO. But—"

"But what?"

"My NST operator didn't like it. He was too lazy to do the Carlotti course to qualify in FTL radio. He reckoned, too, that he'd be doing twice the work that he was doing before, and for the same pay. So he resigned, and joined Rim Runners. They're very old-fashioned, in some ways. They don't have Carlotti equipment in many of their ships yet. They still carry psionic communication officers and Normal Space-Time radio officers."

"Old-fashioned?" queried Grimes. "Perhaps they still carry PCOs for the same reason as we do. To sniff things out."

"That's what I tried to tell my owners when they took away Farley's amplifier, saying that its upkeep was a needless expense. A few spoonfuls of nutrient chemicals each trip, and a couple of little pumps! But I'm getting ahead of myself. This Farley *was* my PCO. He's getting on in years, and knows that he hasn't a hope in hell of finding a job anywhere else. Unlike the big majority of telepaths he has quite a good brain and, furthermore, doesn't shy away from machinery, up to and including electronic gadgetry. He actually took the Carlotti course and examination, and qualified, and also qualified as an NST operator. So now he's my radio officer, NST, and Carlotti. It breaks his heart at times to have to push signals over the light-years by electronic means, but he does it. If they'd let him keep his beagle's brain in aspic he'd still be doing it the good old way, and the Carlotti transceiver would be gathering dust. But with no psionic amplifier, he just hasn't the range."

"No. He wouldn't have."

"Even so, if one passes reasonably close to a planet, within a few light-years, a good telepath can pick up the psionic broadcast, provided that the world in question has a sizable population of sentient beings."

"Human beings?"

"Not necessarily. But our sort of people, more or less. I'm told that there's no mistaking the sort of broadcast you get from one of the Shaara worlds, for example. Arthropods, however intelligent, just don't think like mammals."

"And you have passed reasonably close to a planet with an intelligent, mammalian population? One that's not on any of the lists?"

"Two of them, as a matter of fact. In neighboring planetary systems."

"Where?"

"That'd be telling, John. Nothing for nothing, and precious little for a zack. That's the way that we do business in the Sundowner Line!"

"Then what's the *quid pro quo*, Bill?"

Davinas laughed. "I didn't think that you trade school boys were taught dead languages! All right. This is it. Just let me know what you find. As I've already told you, the Sundowner Line's on its last legs; I'd like to keep us running just a little longer. A new trade of our own could make all the difference."

"There are regulations, you know," said Grimes slowly. "I can't go blabbing the Survey Service's secrets to any Tom, Dick, or Harry. Or Bill."

"Not even when they were Bill's secrets to begin with? Come off it. And I do happen to know that those same regulations empower you, as captain of a Survey Service ship, to use your own discretion when buying information. Am I right?"

"Mphm." Grimes was tempted. Davinas could save him months of fruitless searching. On the one hand, a quick conclusion to his quest would be to his credit. On the other hand,

or him to let loose a possibly unscrupulous tramp skipper
on a hitherto undiscovered Lost Colony would be to acquire
yet another big black mark on his record. But this man was
no Drongo Kane. He said, "You know, of course, that I
carry a scientific officer. He has the same rank as myself, but
if I do find a Lost Colony he'll be wanting to take charge,
and I may have to take a back seat."

"If he wants to set up any sort of Base," countered
Davinas, "he'll be requiring regular shipments of stores and
equipment and all the rest of it. Such jobs, as we both
know, are usually contracted out. And if I'm Johnny-on-the-
spot, with a reasonable tender in my hot little hand—"

It made sense, Grimes thought. He asked, "And will you
want any sort of signed agreement, Bill?"

"You insult me, and you insult yourself. Your word's
good enough, isn't it?"

"All right." Grimes had made up his mind. "Where are
these possible Lost Colonies of yours?"

"Farley picked them up," said Davinas, "when I was right
off my usual tramlines—*anybody's* usual tramlines, come to
that—doing a run between Rob Roy and Caribbea." He
pushed the coffee mugs and the thermos bottle to one side,
opened the folder that he had brought from his office on the
low table. He brought out a chart. "Modified Zimmerman
Projection." His thin forefinger stabbed decisively. "The Rob
Roy sun, here. And Sol, as the Caribbeans call their primary,
here. Between them, two G type stars, 1716 and 1717 in
Ballchin's catalog, practically in line, and as near as damnit
on the same plane as Rob Roy and Caribbea. Well clear of
the track, actually—but not too well clear."

"It rather surprises me," said Grimes, "that nobody has
found evidence of intelligent life there before."

"Why should it? When those old lodejammers were blown
away to hell and gone off course—assuming that these
worlds *are* Lost Colonies, settled by lodejammer survivors—
PCOs hadn't been dreamed of. When your Commodore
Slater made his sweep through that sector of space, PCOs
still hadn't been dreamed of. Don't forget that we had FTL
ships long before we had FTL radio, either electronic or
psionic."

"But what about the odd merchant ships in more recent
years, each with her trained telepath?"

"What merchant ships? As far as I know, *Sundowner* was the only one to travel that route, and just once, at that. I happened to be on Rob Roy, discharging a load of kippered New Maine cod, and the word got through to my agents there that one of the transgalactic clippers, on a cruise, was due in at Caribbea. She'd been chartered by some Terry outfit calling themselves The Sons of Scotia. And it seems that they were going to celebrate some Earth calendar religious festival—Burns Night—there."

"Burns?" murmured Grimes. "Let me see. Wasn't he a customs officer? An odd sort of chap to deify."

"Ha, ha. Anyhow, the Punta del Sol Hotel at Port of Spain sent an urgent Carlottigram to Rob Roy to order a large consignment of haggis and Scotch whiskey. I was the only one handy to lift it. I got it there on time, too, although I just about burned out the main bearings of the Mannschenn Drive doing it."

"And did they enjoy their haggis?" wondered Grimes.

"I can't say. *I* didn't. The shippers presented me with half a dozen of the obscene things as a token of their appreciation. Perhaps we didn't cook them properly."

"Or serve them properly. I don't suppose that *Sundowner* could run to a bagpiper to pipe them in to the messroom table."

"That could have been the trouble." Davinas looked at his watch. "I hate to hurry you up, John—but I always like to get my shut-eye before I take the old girl upstairs. But, before you go, I'd like to work out some way that you can let me know if you find anything. A simple code for a message, something that can't be cracked by the emperor of Waverley's bright boys. As you see from the chart, those two suns are practically inside Waverley's sphere of influence. I want to be first ship on the scene—after you, of course. I don't want to be at the tail end of a long queue of Imperial survey ships and freighters escorted by heavy cruisers."

"Fair enough," agreed Grimes. "Fair enough. Just innocent Carlottigrams that could be sent by anybody, to anybody. Greetings messages? Yes. Happy Birthday, say, for the first world, that belonging to 1717. Happy Anniversary for the 1716 planet. Signed 'John' if it's worth your while to persuade your owners to let you come sniffing around.

signed 'Peter' if you'd be well advised not to come within a hundred light-years.

"But you'll be hearing from me. I promise you that."

"Thank you," said Davinas.

"Thank *you*," said Grimes.

CHAPTER 11

Davinas phoned down to the night watchman to ask him to order a cab for Grimes. While they were waiting for the car he poured glasses of an excellent Scotch whiskey from Rob Roy. They were finishing their drinks when the night watchman reported that the car was at the ramp.

Grimes was feeling smugly satisfied when he left *Sundowner*. It certainly looked as though he had been handed his Lost Colony—correction, *two* Lost Colonies—on a silver tray. And this Davinas was a very decent bloke, and deserved any help that Grimes would be able to give him.

The ride back to the mayor's palace was uneventful. The party was still in progress in the huge ballroom; the girl at the synthesizer controls was maintaining a steady flow of dance music, although only the young were still on the floor. The older people were gathered around the buffet tables, at which the supplies of food and drink were being replenished as fast as they dwindled.

Grimes joined Brabham and Vinegar Nell, who were tucking into a bowl of caviar as though neither of them had eaten for a week, washing it down with locally made vodka.

"Be with us, sir," said Brabham expansively. "A pity they didn't bring *this* stuff out earlier. If I'd known this was going to come up, I'd not have ruined my appetite on fishcakes and sausage rolls!"

Grimes spread a buttered biscuit with the tiny, black, glistening eggs, topped it up with a hint of chopped onion and a squeeze of lemon juice. "You aren't doing too badly now. Mphm. Not bad, not bad."

"Been seeing how the poor live, sir?" asked the first lieutenant.

"What do you mean?"

"You went off with *Sundowner*'s old man."

"Oh, yes. He has quite a nice ship. Old, but very well looked after."

"Sometimes I wonder if I wouldn't have done better in the merchant service," grumbled Brabham. "Even the Rim Worlds Merchant Service. I was having a yarn with *Sundowner*'s chief officer. He tells me that the new government-owned shipping line, Rim Runners, is recruiting personnel. I've a good mind to apply."

"Nobody in the Survey Service would miss you," said Vinegar Nell. Then, before Brabham could register angry protest, she continued, "Nobody in the Survey Service would miss any of us. We're the square pegs, who find that every hole's a round one." She turned to Grimes, who realized that she must have been drinking quite heavily. "Come on, Captain! Out with it! What was in your sealed orders? Instructions to lose us all down some dark crack in the continuum, yourself included?"

"Mphm," grunted Grimes noncommittally, helping himself to more caviar. He noticed that the civilians in the vicinity had begun to flap their ears. He said firmly, "Things aren't as bad as they seem." He tried to make a joke of it. "In any case, I haven't lost a ship yet."

"There has to be a first time for everything," she said darkly.

"*Some* people are lucky," commented Brabham. "In the Survey Service, as everywhere else, luck counts for more than ability."

"Some people have neither luck *nor* ability," said Vinegar Nell spitefully. The target for this barbed remark was obvious—and Brabham, feared Grimes, would be quite capable of emptying the bowl of caviar over her head if she continued to needle him. And the captain of a ship, justly or unjustly, is held responsible for the conduct of his officers in public places. His best course of action would be to separate his first lieutenant and his paymaster before they came to blows.

"Shall we dance, Miss Russell?" he asked.

She produced a surprisingly sweet smile. "But of course, Captain."

The synthesizer was playing a song that he had heard before, probably a request from those of *Sundowner*'s people who were still at the party. The tune was old, very old, but the words were new, and Rim Worlders had come to regard it as their very own.

> *Good-bye, I'll run to find another sun*
> *Where I may find*
> *There are worlds more kind than the ones left behind. . . .*

Vinegar Nell, fitting into his arms as though she belonged there, had always belonged there, was singing softly as she danced. And was he, Grimes, dancing as well as he thought he was? Probably not, he admitted to himself, but she made him feel that he was cutting a fine figure on the polished floor. And she was making him feel rather more than that. He was acutely conscious of the tightness of the crotch of his dress trousers.

When the number was over he was pleased to see that Brabham had wandered off somewhere by himself, but he was not pleased when Commander Denny claimed Vinegar Nell for the next dance, and still less pleased when he found himself having to cope with Denny's wife. He suffered. It was like having to tow an unwieldy captive balloon through severe atmospheric turbulence. But then the Mayoress made a welcome change, although she chattered incessantly. After her, there were a few girls whose names he promptly forgot.

Vinegar Nell again, and the last dance.

> *Good night, ladies,*
> *Good night, ladies,*
> *Good night, ladies . . .*
> *We're bound to leave you now. . . .*

"But you don't have to leave *me*, John," she whispered.
Mphm?
And everybody was singing:

> *Merrily we roll along,*
> *Roll along, roll along,*
> *Merrily we roll along*
> *O'er the bright blue sea. . . .*

He said, "We have to roll along back to the ship, after we've said our good nights, and thanked the mayor for his party."

She said, her mood suddenly somber, "There's no place else to roll. Not for us."

The synthesizer emitted a flourish of trumpets, a ruffle of

drums. The dancers froze into attitudes of stiff—or not so stiff—attention. Blaring brass against a background of drum-beats, an attempt to make dreadfully trite melody sound important. It was one of those synthetic, utterly forgettable national anthems, the result, no doubt, of a competition, selected by the judges as the poor best of a bad lot. The words matched the music:

> *New Maine, flower of the galaxy,*
> *New Maine, stronghold of liberty. . . .*

Then: "Good night, Mr. Mayor. On behalf of my officers I must thank you for a marvelous party."

"Good night, Captain. It was a pleasure to have you aboard. Good night, Miss Russell. If the Survey Service had more paymasters like you, I'd be a spaceman myself. Ha, ha! Good night . . . good night."

"Good night."

The ground cars were waiting outside, in the portico. As before, Grimes rode in the lead vehicle with Vinegar Nell and Dr. Brandt. With them, this time, was the chief engineer.

"A waste of valuable time, these social functions," complained the scientist as they sped back toward the Base.

"Ye werenae darin' sae bad on the free booze an' tucker," pointed out MacMorris.

"And neither were you, Chief," put in Vinegar Nell.

"Ah'm no' a dancin' man, not like our gallant captain. An' as for the booze an' tucker—it's aye a pleasure to tak' a bite an sup wi'oot havin' you begrudgin' every mouthful!"

"I still say that it was a waste of time," stated Brandt. "Commander Grimes, for example, could have spent the evening going through the port captain's records to see if there are any reports of Lost Colonies."

"Mphm," grunted Grimes smugly, happily conscious of the folded copy of the chart that Davinas had given him, stiff in the inside breast pocket of his mess jacket.

They were approaching the Base now. There stood *Discovery*, a tall metal steeple, dull-gleaming in the wan light of the huge, high, lopsided moon. And there were great dark shapes, sluglike, oozing slowly over the concrete apron of the spaceport.

"Filthy brutes!" exclaimed the driver, breaking the morose

silence that he had maintained all the way from the mayor's palace.

"Great snakes?" asked Grimes.

"What else, Captain? Whoever decided that those bloody things should be protected should have his bloody head read!"

"You, man!" snapped Brandt. "Take us in close to one of them! Put your spotlight on it!"

"Not on your bloody life, mister! If anything scares those bastards, they *squirt*. And they squirt all over what scares 'em! I have to keep this car clean, not you. Now, here you are, lady and gentlemen. I've brought you right back to your own front door. A very good night to you—what's left of it!"

They got out of the car, which had stopped at the foot of *Discovery*'s ramp. The air was heavy with the sweet-sour stench of fresh ordure. Something splattered loudly not far from them. Their vehicle, its motor whining shrilly, made a hasty departure.

"Are you waiting outside to study the great snakes at close quarters, Doctor?" asked Grimes. "I'm not." He started up the ramp, as hastily as possible without loss of dignity, Vinegar Nell beside him. MacMorris came after and then, after only a second's hesitation, Brandt. At the outer airlock door the Marine sentry came to attention, saluted. Grimes wondered if the man would be as alert after Major Swinton was back safely on board.

The elevator cage was waiting for them. They got into it, were lifted through the various levels. Vinegar Nell, Brandt, and MacMorris got out at the officers' deck. Grimes carried on to Control, found the duty officer looking out through the viewport at the lights of the cars still coming in from Penobscot.

"Oh, good morning, sir." Then, a little wistfully, "Was it a good party?"

"It was, Mr. Farrow. Quite good." Grimes yawned. "If any of those . . . *things* try to climb up the side of the ship to do their business, let me know. Good night, or good morning, or whatever."

He went down to his quarters. He did not, he realized with some surprise, feel all that tired. He subsided into an armchair, pulled out from his pocket the copy of the star chart, unfolded it. Yes, it was certainly a good lead, and Captain Davinas was entitled to some reward for having given it to him.

There was a knock at the door.

"Come in!" he called, wondering who it could be. Not Brabham, he hoped, with some trifling but irritating worry that could well wait until a more civilized hour.

It was Vinegar Nell. She was carrying a tray upon which were a coffeepot, a cup—no, *two* cups—and a plate of sandwiches. She had changed out of her evening dress uniform into something that was nothing much over nothing at all. Grimes had seen her naked often enough in the sauna adjoining the ship's gymnasium, but this was . . . different. The spectacle of a heavily perspiring female body is not very aphrodisiac; that same body suggestively and almost transparently clad *is*.

She said, "I thought you'd like a snack before turning in, John."

"Thank you—er—Miss Russell."

She stooped to set the tray on the coffee table. The top of her filmy robe fell open. Her pink-nippled breasts were high and firm.

"Shall I pour?" she asked.

"Er, yes. Please."

She handed him a steaming cup. He was uncomfortably aware of the closeness of her, and fidgeted in his chair. He was relieved when she retired to a chair of her own.

She said, "It was a good night, wasn't it?"

"Yes."

She went on, "I've known you for *years*, haven't I? When was it that we were first shipmates? In the old *Aries*, wasn't it?"

"Yes."

"You know, John, I didn't much like you then."

"You didn't much like any of us in the wardroom. After all, you were the very first spacegoing female officer of the Supply Branch, and you were . . . prickly."

She laughed. "And you, a bright young lieutenant junior-grade, took pity on me, and made a pass at me out of the kindness of your heart."

Grimes's prominent ears were burning painfully. He could recall that scene all too well, could feel that stinging slap on his face and hear her furious voice: *Take your mucky paws off me, you insufferable puppy!*

He thought, *And a commander, the captain of a ship, doesn't have mucky paws, of course. But whatever sort of paws I do have, now, I'm keeping them to myself. Why, oh why, you stupid bitch, did you have to rake up that particular episode from the murky past?*

She was smiling softly. "We've come a long way since then, haven't we, John?"

"Mphm. Yes. Excellent coffee, this, Miss Russell. And these are very good sandwiches."

"Yes. You always liked your belly."

Again the memories: *You swaggering spacemen think that you're the Lord's anointed, but you aren't worth your keep, let alone your salaries.*

"Gutsy Grimes, the stewards and stewardesses used to call you."

"Oh. Did they?" Grimes put down a sandwich half eaten.

"Gutsy Grimes, the human garbage chute," she reminisced sentimentally.

"Fascinating."

And what was that perfume that she was wearing? Whatever it was, he decided that he didn't like it. He looked at his watch. "A spot of shut-eye is indicated. We have a busy day ahead of us tomorrow. Today, I mean."

She rose slowly to her feet, stretched and yawned like a lazy, graceful cat. Her robe fell open. Under the UV lamps in the ship's sun room she always freckled rather than tanned, and the effect was far from displeasing—yet Grimes, perversely, forced himself to think disparagingly of mutant leopards.

He yawned himself, then decisively drained his cup, set it down on the tray with a clatter. He said, "Thanks for the supper. I enjoyed it."

"I did, too."

Then, very firmly, "Good night, Miss Russell."

She flushed all over her body. *"Good night?* You don't mean . . . ?"

"I do mean. I'm turning in. By myself. Good night."

Without looking again at her he went through into his bedroom. He was afraid that she would (would not?) follow him. She did not. As he undressed he heard a vicious clattering as she put the remaining supper things back on the tray, then heard the outer door open and close behind her.

You bloody fool! he admonished himself. *You bloody, bloody fool!* But he thought (he hoped) that he had acted wisely. Vinegar Nell, as a *de facto* Captain's Lady, would very soon try to assume *de facto* command of the ship. On the other hand, because of his out-of-character puritanism, he could have made a dangerous enemy.

He did not sleep at all well.

CHAPTER 12

Discovery did not stay long on New Maine, although most of her people, who had speedily made friends locally, would have welcomed a longer sojourn on that planet.

Grimes feared that some ship, deviating from the usual route might stumble upon Davinas' Lost Colonies at any moment. He had been given access to the up-to-the-minute Lloyd's Register in the Penobscot port captain's office and had discovered that the majority of the ships of the Waverley Royal Mail had not yet made the change-over from psionic Deep Space communications to the Carlotti system. And Ballchin 1716 and 1717 were almost within the territorial space of the Empire of Waverley. The ruling emperor—as was known to Grimes, as a naval officer of the Federation—was not averse to the expansion of his already considerable dominions.

Discovery did not stay long on New Maine, which meant that her crew did not enjoy the shore leave that they had been expecting. It meant too that all hands, the senior officers especially, were obliged to dedigitate. Brabham, of whom it had been said that he had only two speeds, Dead Slow and Stop, was resentful. MacMorris, who had been looking forward to an orgy of taking apart and putting together, was resentful. Brandt, who had been given the run of the extensive library of the University of New Maine, was resentful. Vinegar Nell was resentful for more reasons than the short stay at the sub-Base.

"Commander Grimes," complained Brandt, "even though *you* are doing nothing to turn up possible leads, *I*, in the little time that I shall be given, am sifting through *years* of records."

But Grimes kept Davinas' information to himself. He knew what would happen if it leaked, just as Davinas himself had

known. There would be an urgent Carlottigram from New
Maine—where the empire maintained a trade commissioner—to Waverley, and long before *Discovery* arrived off
those Lost Colonies some Imperial cruiser would have
planted the thistle flag.

Brabham sulked, MacMorris sulked, Brandt sulked, Swinton snarled, and Vinegar Nell was positively vicious. "I
suppose you know what you're doing, Captain." "I hope you
realize the consequences if the algae tanks go bad on us,
Captain." "I suppose you know that it's practically impossible
to replenish the beef tissue culture in the time you've given
me, Captain." "I'm afraid that I just can't accept responsibility if things go wrong in my department, Captain."

At least, Grimes consoled himself, he had one satisfied
customer. That was Denny. The elderly commander clearly
did not approve of the flurry of activity into which his
normally sleepy Base had been plunged. He knew that this
flurry would continue as long as *Discovery* was sitting on
the apron. He knew, too—Mrs. Denny made sure that he
knew—that the outsiders were interfering with the local
ecology. They had attached hoses to *his* hydrants and washed
down the entire spaceport area. They had rigged a wire
fence with a carefully calculated low voltage trickling
through it on a wide perimeter about their vessel. When
Denny had objected, Grimes had told him that his crew did
not like working in a latrine and that, furthermore, the
materials used for the fence came from ship's stores, and the
current in the wires from the ship's generators.

"I shall report this to Lindisfarne Base, Commander
Grimes," said Denny stiffly.

"I shall be making *my* report too," Grimes told him.
"And so will my medical officer. Meanwhile, my chief engineer tells me that he's not getting much help from your
workshops."

"I'll see that he gets all the help he wants," promised
Denny. His manner suddenly softened. "You're not married,
Commander, but you will be. Then you'll find out what it's
like, especially if your wife has a weird taste in pets."

"One man's pets are another man's pests," cracked Grimes.

"One woman's pets are, strictly between ourselves, her
husband's pests. Rest assured that I shall get your rustbucket
off my Base as soon as is humanly possible. Anything for a
quiet life."

And so the activity continued, with work around the clock.

"There's hardly been any shore leave, sir," complained Brabham.

"Growl you may, but go you must," countered Grimes cheerfully.

"But what's the *hurry*, sir?"

"There is a valid reason for it, Number One," Grimes told him.

"More sealed orders, I suppose," said Brabham, with as near to a sneer as he dared.

"Maybe, maybe not," replied Grimes, with what he knew must be infuriating smugness. There were times when he did not quite like himself, and this was one of them—but his officers were bringing out the worst in him. "Just take it from me that I know what I'm doing, and why. That's all."

"Very good, sir," said Brabham, conveying the impression that, as far as he was concerned, it wasn't.

Rather to Grimes's surprise the target date was met.

A cheerless dawn was breaking over the Base as the ramp was retracted, as the last of *Discovery*'s airtight doors sighed shut. The old ship was as spaceworthy as she ever would be, and she had somewhere to go.

Grimes, in the control room, spoke into the microphone. "*Discovery* to New Maine Aerospace Control. Request outward clearance. Over."

"All clear for your liftoff, *Discovery*. No air traffic in vicinity of Base. No space traffic whatsoever. Good hunting. Over."

"Thank you, Aerospace Control. Over."

"Base to *Discovery*." This was Denny's voice. "Good hunting. Over."

"Thank you, Commander Denny. Give my regards to the great snakes. They can have their public convenience back now. Over."

"I wish you were taking the bastards with you, Grimes. Over."

Grimes laughed, and started the inertial drive. *Discovery* shuddered, heaving herself clear of the apron. She clambered upward like an elderly mountaineer overburdened with equipment. No doubt MacMorris would complain that he should have been given more time to get his innies into proper working order. Then the beat of the engines became louder, more enthusiastic. Grimes relaxed a little. He took a side-wise glance at Tangye, in the co-pilot's seat. This time, he noted, the navigator had done his sums before departure; a loosely folded sheet of paper was peeping out of the breast pocket of his uniform shirt. And what target star would he have selected? Hamlet, probably, in the Shakespearean System, out toward the Rim Worlds. It was a pity that *Discovery* would not be heading that way.

The ship pushed through the low overcast as though she really meant it, emerged into the clear stratum between it and the high cirrus. Blinding sunlight, almost immediately dimmed as the viewports automatically polarized, smote through into the control room, and, outside, made haloes of iridescence in the clouds of ice particles through which the vessel was driving. She lifted rapidly through the last tenuous shreds of atmosphere.

"Clear of the Van Allens, sir," reported Tangye at last.

"Thank you, pilot," acknowledged Grimes. Then, to Brabham, "Make the usual announcements, Number One. Free fall, setting trajectory, all the rest of it."

"Take over now, sir?" asked Tangye, pulling the sheet of notes from his breast pocket.

Grimes grinned at him. "Oh, I think I'll keep myself in practice, pilot. It's time I did some work."

The ship was in orbit now, falling free about New Maine. Grimes produced his own sheet of paper, glanced at it, then at the constellations patterned on the blackness outside the viewports. He soon found the one that he was looking for, although why the first settlers on this planet had called it The Mermaid he could not imagine. Their imaginations must have been far more vivid than his. His fingers played over the controls and the directional gyroscopes began to spin, and the hull turned about them.

"Sir," said Tangye urgently. "Sir!"

"Yes, pilot?"

"Sir, Hamlet's in The Elephant. From here, that is—"

"How right you are, Mr. Tangye. But why should we be heading toward Elsinore?"

"But, sir, the orders said that we were to make a sweep out toward the Rim."

"That's right," put in Brabham.

"I have steadied this ship," said Grimes coldly, "on to

Delta Mermaid. We shall run on that trajectory until further orders—orders from myself, that is. Number One, pass the word that I am about to start the Mannschenn Drive."

"As you say, sir," replied Brabham sulkily.

Deep in the bowels of the vessel the gleaming rotors began to turn, to spin and to tumble, to precess out of normal space-time, pulling the ship and all her people with them down the dark dimensions, through the warped continuum. There was the usual fleeting second or so of temporal disorientation, while shapes wavered and colors sagged down the spectrum, while all sound was distorted, with familiar noises either impossibly high in pitch or so low as to be almost inaudible.

There was, as always, the uncanny sensation of *déjà vu.*

Grimes experienced no previsions but felt, as he had when setting trajectory off Lindisfarne, a deep and disturbing premonition of impending doom.

Perhaps, he thought, he should adhere to his original orders. Perhaps he should observe the golden rule for modest success in any service: Do what you're told, and volunteer for nothing.

But whatever he did, he knew from harsh experience, he always ran into trouble.

CHAPTER 13

The ship settled down into her normal Deep Space routine—regular watches, regular mealtimes, regular exercise periods in the gymnasium, and regular inspections. In many ways, in almost all ways, she was like any other ship; what made her different, too different, was the resentment that was making itself felt more and more by her captain. The short stay on New Maine, with hardly any shore leave, was in part responsible. But there was more than that. Everybody aboard knew what Grimes's original orders had been—to use New Maine as a base and to make a sweep out toward the Rim without intruding into what the Rim Worlds already were referring to as *their* territorial space. (It was not Federation policy to do anything that might annoy those touchy colonials, who, for some time, had been talking loudly about secession.) And now everybody aboard knew that *Discovery* was headed not toward the Rim but in the general direction of the Waverley sector. Grimes, of course, was the captain, and presumably knew what he was doing. Grimes was notoriously lucky—but luck has a habit of running out. If this cruise, carried out in contravention to admiralty orders—vague though those orders had been—turned out to be fruitless, Grimes would have to carry the can back—but his officers, none of them at all popular with high authority, would be even less likely to achieve any further promotion.

Grimes could not help overhearing snatches of conversation. *The old bastard is putting us all up Shit Creek without a paddle.* And, *He's always been fantastically lucky, but he's bound to come a real gutser one day. I only hope that I'm not around when he does!* And, *He must think that he's a reincarnation of Nelson—turning a blind eye to his orders!* With the reply, *A reincarnation of Bligh, you mean!*

73

This last, of course, was from Brabham.

And if Bligh, thought Grimes, had carried a trained and qualified telepath aboard *Bounty* he might have been given warning of the mutiny that was brewing. He, Grimes, did have such a telepath aboard *Discovery*—but was Flannery willing to bend the Rhine Institute's ethical code? If he were, it would be far easier to keep a finger on the pulse of things. But Flannery . . . his loyalties, such as they were, were to his shipmates, much as he disliked them all, rather than to the ship and her commander. He was bred of stock with a long, long record of rebellion and resentment of all authority. Even his psionic amplifier—one that Grimes, ironically enough, had persuaded the telepath to accept—seemed to share its master's viewpoint.

Yet Grimes did not dislike the whiskey-swilling psionic communications officer and did not think that Flannery actively disliked him. Perhaps, carefully handled, the man might be induced to spill a bean or two. In any case, Grimes would have to spill the beans to him, would have to tell him about Davinas and the suspected Lost Colonies. But did Flannery know already? PCOs were not supposed to pry, but very few of them were able to resist the temptation.

He made his way down to the farm deck, to the squalid cubbyhole where Flannery lived in psionic symbiosis with his amplifier. The man was more or less sober, having, over the years, built up a certain immunity to alcohol. He was playing patience—and, Grimes noted, cheating—between sips from a tumbler of whiskey.

"Ah, top o' the mornin' to ye, Captain! Or is it mornin'? Or evenin'? Or last St. Patrick's Day?"

"Good morning, Mr. Flannery."

"A drop on the real peat elixir for ye, Captain?"

Grimes hesitated, then accepted. Irish whiskey was not among his favorite tipples, but he wanted to keep Flannery in a good mood. He wondered how long it was since the glass into which his drink was poured had been washed.

"Thank you, Mr. Flannery. Mind if I sit down?"

"Not at all, not at all, Captain. This is Liberty Hall. Ye can spit on the mat an'—"

"Call Ned a bastard? He mightn't like it."

"He wouldn't be mindin' at all, at all. T'is a term o' endearment where *he* comes from. An' it was about Ballchin

1716 and 1717 ye were wantin' to see me, wasn't it?"

"You've been . . . snooping," accused Grimes.

"Snoopin', Captain? There was no need to. I'd have to blank me mind off entoirely not to pick up your broadcasts on *that* subject! An' if ye're askin' me now, I've picked up nary a whisper yet from the planets o' those two suns. But I'm listenin'. An' Ned—bless the sweet soul o' him—is listenin'."

"Thank you. Mphm. Oh, and there was something else."

"Ye're not after askin' me *that*, Captain, are ye? To pry on me mates?"

"Well, it is done, you know," said Grimes defensively. "When justified by the circumstances, that is."

"Niver by me it isn't, Captain. The Rhine Institute licensed me, an' I abide by its rules."

When it suits you, thought Grimes.

Flannery grinned, showing his mottled teeth. Grimes might just as well have spoken aloud. "I'll tell ye what," said the telepath cheerfully. "I'll tell ye what . . . I'll give ye a readin'. On the house, as the wee dog said." His grubby hands swept the cards into an untidy pile, stacked them. "Seein' as how we're aboard a starship I'll be usin' the Mystic Star."

"Mphm?" grunted Grimes dubiously.

Flannery riffled through the cards, selected one, laid it face upward on the dirty tabletop. "The King of Clubs," he announced. "That's you. Our leader, no less."

"Why the King of Clubs?"

"An' why not, Captain? Ye're a decent enough boyo under the gold braid an' brass buttons. The King o' Gravediggers, standin' for the military leader, is not for the likes o' you. Ye're not a bad enough bastard."

"Thank you."

"An' now take the pack. Shuffle it. Let the—the *essence* o' ye seep through yer hands into the Devil's Prayerbook."

Grimes felt that the reverse was taking place, that the uncleanliness of the cards was seeping through his skin into him, but he did as he was told.

"An' now, with yer left hand, put the cards down. Face down. Cut the pack. An' again, so we have three piles."

Grimes obeyed.

"An' now, the Indicator."

Flannery turned over the first stack, revealing the nine of

diamonds, then the second, to show the eight of the same suit, then the third, exposing the two of spades.

"Ah, an' what have we here? The unexpected gift, an' the journey that's made possible. The cards don't lie, Captain. Didn't the man Davinas give ye that star chart? An' the eight o' sparklers—a lucky card for the explorer. But what's this mean? The deuce o' gravediggers. Could it be that yer famous luck is goin' to turn sour on ye? Change, disruption, an' voyages to far places. What are ye runnin' from, Captain? Are ye runnin' away, or are ye bein' thrown out from somethin'? Good luck, an' bad luck, an' isn't that the way with ivery mother's son of us? But with you—the good outweighin' the bad."

Rubbish, thought Grimes, not quite convincing himself. "Go on," he said.

"Ye're in this too." Flannery swept the cards, with the exception of the King of Clubs, back into one pack. "Take 'em, Captain. Shuffle again. Now give 'em back to me."

Working widdershins, Flannery placed eight cards around the King in the form of an eight-pointed star. Then he gave the pack back to Grimes, telling him to put two more cards on each of the eight points.

"An' now," he said, "we shall see what we shall see." He turned up the three cards at the top of the star. "Aha! The King o' Sparklers, the four o' blackberries, an' the seven o' gravediggers. Someone's workin' against ye, Captain. A military man, a soldier, an' there's the warnin' o' danger ahead, an' another warnin', too. A woman could land ye in the cactus."

"It wouldn't be the first time," grunted Grimes.

"An' now—" Flannery turned up the three cards to the left of the first three: the four and the six of spades, the two of clubs. "Good an' bad again—but that's life. Loss, an' poverty, an' jealousy, an' envy a-destroyin' of yer success—but good luck again when it's all over. The Odd Gods o' the Galaxy alone know how ye do it, but always ye come to the top. Not at once, mind ye. It takes time. But remember this —when all the cards are on the table there's but the one man in the universe ye can trust. Yerself.

"Now—" the telepath turned up the third trio of cards: five of clubs, four of hearts, and six of diamonds. He chuckled. "A foine mixture, this! The cards say as how ye're to take things as they come, marriage wise. It'll all turn out wrong in the end, anyhow. Did I iver tell ye that I was married once? Anyhow—play yer cards right for a wealthy marriage says *this* one, an' *this* one says that ye're the last o' a long line o' bachelors. An' *this* one—an early, romantic marriage *an'* an unlucky second marriage. So ye *did* have fun, or ye're goin' to have fun, or ye never did have nor ever will have any fun at all. Take yer choice.

"Aha!" The next set of three was flipped over. "The King an' the Queen o' Gravediggers, an' the trey o' diamonds. The King's another captain, who's going to get in yer hair in the nearish future. And would it be yer old pal Commander Delamere?"

"What do you know about him?" snapped Grimes.

"Only what flickered through yer mind when I turned up the card. An' the Queen? Sorry, Captain, I can't place her. She's nobody ye know—*yet*. But ye'll be gettin' quite a handful. An' that little three? Oh, all sorts o' fun an' games, an' I have a feelin' that the King'll be playin' a part in 'em. He doesn't like you at all, at all.

"An' now, what have we? Six an' eight o' blackberries, seven o' sparklers. Goodish, goodish—but not all that good when ye remember all that's come before, an' all that's to come. Good for *business?* Ha! Ye're not a shopkeeper, Captain. An', come to that, ye're not a merchant skipper. Your ship doesn't have to show a profit. An' the other two cards warn ye against gamblin'. But isn't all life a gamble? Aren't we gamblin' with our lives ivery time that we liftoff planet, or come in for a happy landin'? And when ye gamble ye must always expect the odd run o' bad luck."

He turned over the sixth set of three. "Eight o' spades, two an' three o' hearts. Ah, overcome resistance, it says. Ye always do that, don't ye? But what about traitors? What about them as'd stab ye in the back?"

"What about them?" demanded Grimes sharply.

"*I* said nothin', Captain, nothin' whativer. T'was the cards said it—an' surely ye, of all men, wouldn't be after payin' attention to silly pieces o' plastic? Or would ye?" He chuckled, prodding the cards with a thick forefinger. "But the deuce an' the trey—don't they cancel out sweetly? Success, an' good fortune, an' everything ye wish yerself—but *when?* This week, next week, sometime, never. An' agin that there's the risk o' unwise choices, an' leapin' afore ye look, an' all the rest of it. So—look first, leap second—if at all.

"Nine an' ten o' hearts, nine o' spades. Two o' one, one o' t'other. Hearts an' flowers the first two, love and roses all the way—*but,* if that black bastard of a nine is telling the truth, only if ye come through the troubles that are waitin' for ye. There's a crisis brewin', Captain. Beware o' the night o' the long knives. Keep yer back to the bulkhead."

I do have enemies, bad ones, thought Grimes.

"An' don't ye ever!" There was a note of admiration in Flannery's voice. "But now we'll see what the last point o' the star has to tell us. Nine o' clubs. Two o' spades, an' the ten o' the same. Black, black, black. Really, ye should ha' stayed in bed in the BOQ on Lindisfarne. Battle, murder, an' sudden death. Disasters by land an' by sea an' in deep space. If it wasn't for the very last card of all I'd be wishin' meself that I'd gone sick on New Maine an' been left behind."

"The ten of spades?" asked Grimes. "But that's unlucky too, surely."

"Think yerself lucky that it's not the Gravedigger itself, the Ace. Do ye really want to know what it means?"

"Yes," Grimes told him firmly.

Flannery laughed. "Beware o' false prophets. That's its meanin'. So, decide for yerself, Captain. Do ye trust the cards, or don't ye?"

And do I trust you? wondered Grimes.

"The cards say to trust *nobody,*" Flannery told him.

CHAPTER 14

Grimes did not believe the card reading, of course. Nonetheless it added to his growing uneasiness, and when he was uneasy he tended to snarl. He knew that his officers and crew resented his attempts to maintain minimal standards of smartness aboard the ship, and that the scientist, Dr. Brandt, regarded him as a barely necessary evil. He refused to admit that in taking command of *Discovery* he had bitten off more than he could chew, but he was coming to realize, more and more, that his predecessor had taken the easy way out, had made arrangements for his own comfort and then allowed the vessel to run herself in her own bumbling, inefficient way.

Meanwhile, as the ship steadily narrowed the distance between herself and the first of the two possible stars, Flannery, with all his faults, was pulling his weight. Straining his telepathic faculties, he had begun to pick up what could be construed as indications of intelligent life on one of the worlds in orbit about that sun.

"The skipper of *Sundowner* was right, Captain," he said. "There's somethin' there, all right. Or, even, somebody. There's—there's a sort o' murmur. Ye can't hear it, of course, but Ned's hearin' it, an' I'm hearin' it." He grinned. "T'is a real Irish parliament. Everybody talkin', an' nobody listenin'."

"Except you," said Grimes.

"Exceptin' me—an' Ned," agreed the PCO.

"Human?" asked Grimes.

"That I couldn't be sayin', Captain. T'is too early yet. But humanoid, for sure. Somethin' with warm blood an' breathin' oxygen."

"Or its equivalent," suggested Grimes doubtfully. "After

all, the essential physiology of chlorine breathers is very similar to our own."

"A bridge we'll cross when we come to it, Captain. But even if *they,* whoever they might be when they're up an' dressed, ain't human, ye'll still have discovered a new world for the Federation—may all the Saints preserve it—an' that'll be a feather in yer cap!"

"I suppose so." Somehow the prospect did not cheer Grimes, as it should have done. "I suppose so."

He got up to return to his own quarters, where he was to preside over a meeting of his senior officers and petty officers.

He sat behind his desk, facing the others.

Brandt was there, sitting by himself, a compact ball of hostility. Brabham, Swinton, and Vinegar Nell shared a settee—sullen bloodhound, belligerent terrier, and spiteful cat. Dr. Rath was wrapped in his own private cloud of funereal gloom. MacMorris, too, was keeping himself to himself, obviously begrudging the time that he was being obliged to spend away from his precious engines. Langer, the bos'n, and Washington, the sergeant of Marines, formed a two-man conspiracy in a corner, ostentatiously holding themselves aloof from the commissioned officers.

"Gentlemen," began Grimes. "And Miss Russell," he added. "Mphm." He answered their not very friendly stares with one of his own. "Mr. Flannery assures me that there is life, intelligent life, very probably our sort of life, on one of the worlds of Ballchin 1717, the star that we are now approaching."

"So your luck is holding, sir," said Brabham.

"What exactly do your mean, Number One?"

"Even you, sir, would have found it hard to justify this deviation from the original plan if you'd found nothing."

"We have only the word of a drunken telepath that anything *has* been found," huffed Brandt. "And it still might not be a Lost Colony."

"Even if it is," grumbled MacMorris, "I doubt if there'll be any machine shops. I'm still far from happy about my innies."

"You never are," remarked Brabham.

"We didn't have enough time on New Maine to get

anything fixed up properly," complained Vinegar Nell, fa-voring Grimes with a hostile glare.

"At least," stated Swinton, "*my* men, as always are ready for anything."

"There probably will be some civilians for you to mas-sacre," murmured Vinegar Nell sweetly.

Swinton flushed hotly and Grimes spoke up before a quarrel could start. "Gentlemen. Miss Russell. If you wish to squabble, kindly do so elsewhere than in my quarters. I have called you here to discuss our course of action."

"To begin with," said Brandt, "there must be the minimal interference with whatever culture has developed on that world."

"If we're shot at," snapped Swinton, "we shoot back!"

"You tell 'em, Major!" murmured Sergeant Washington.

"That will do," said Grimes coldly. Then, "To begin with, I shall advise you all of my intentions. This original plan will be subject to modification as required by changing circumstances and, possibly, as suggested by your good selves.

"The vessel will continue on her present trajectory. Mr. Flannery will maintain his listening watch, endeavoring to learn as much as possible of the nature of the inhabitants. We are also, of course, maintaining a Carlotti listening watch, although it is doubtful if we shall pick anything up. The Carlotti system had not been dreamed of at the time of the Second Expansion, the heyday of the lodejammers. And, in any case, any station using it must, of necessity, be a well-established component of today's network of interstellar communications. We can't listen on NST radio, of course, until we shut down the Mannschenn Drive and reemerge into normal space-time.

"We shall endeavor to home on the source of psionic emission. With the interstellar drive shut down, we shall establish ourselves in orbit about the planet. We shall ob-serve, listen, and send down our unmanned probes. And then we come in to a landing."

"Not in the ship," said Brandt flatly.

"And why not?" countered Grimes coldly.

"Have you considered," asked the scientist, "the effect that a hulking brute of a vessel like this might—no, *would!*—have on a people who have reverted to savagery, who are painfully climbing back up the hill to civilization?"

"If I'm going to be a stranger on a strange world," Grimes told him, "I prefer to be a stranger with all the resources of my own culture right there with me, not hanging in orbit and all too likely to be on the wrong side of the planet when I want something in a hurry!"

"I agree with the captain," said Brabham.

"And I," said Swinton.

"It is high time that the real command was put in the hands of the scientists," growled Brandt.

"If it ever is," Brabham snarled, "my resignation goes in."

"That will do, gentlemen," said Grimes firmly. "Whether we land in the ship, or whether we send down small parties in the boats, will be decided when we know more about 1717—but I can say, now, that the second course of action is extremely unlikely. Needless to say, the actual site of our landing will have to be decided upon. *If* the civilization has attained or reattained a high standard of technology, then there is no reason why we should not set down close to a large center of population, in broad daylight. If the people reverted to savagery after their own first landing, and stayed that way, then caution on our part is indicated."

"Putting it bluntly, Commander Grimes," said Brandt unpleasantly, "you are dithering."

"Putting it shortly," retorted Grimes, "I shall be playing by ear. As I always do. As I always have done." He was exaggerating, of course. Before any operation he always worked out his course of action in every smallest detail—but he was ever alert to changing circumstances, always ready to abandon his elaborate plan of campaign and to improvise.

He went on, "I want all of you carefully to consider the problems that are liable to confront us. I want all of you to work out your own ways of dealing with them. I am always open to suggestions. Don't forget that we are a team." (Did he hear a faint, derisive, *Ha, ha!?*) "Don't forget that we are a team, and remember that this is a Federation vessel and not a warship of the Waldegren Navy, whose kapitan would have you pushed out of the airlock for speaking out of turn." (And who was it who whispered in mock incredulity, *Oh, no?*) "Be ready for anything—and, above all, be ready for the things for which you aren't ready. Mphm." He carefully filled and then lit his pipe.

"Very enlightening, Commander Grimes," commented Brandt condescendingly.

Brabham said nothing, merely looked wooden. Swinton said nothing and looked skeptical. Vinegar Nell permitted herself a slight sneer. Dr. Rath looked like an undertaker counting the dead for whom he would have to provide a free funeral. The burly Langer raised his hand, looking like an oversized schoolboy. "Captain?"

"Yes, Bos'n?"

"Speaking on behalf of the men, sir, I hope that you will allow shore leave. We had precious little back at Main Base, and precious little on New Maine."

"This is not a pleasure cruise, Bos'n," said Grimes.

"You can say that again!" whispered somebody, not quite inaudibly.

CHAPTER 15

Star 1717 in the Ballchin Catalog was a Sol-type sun.

Somehow it and its planetary family had, to date, escaped close investigation by the survey ships of the Interstellar Federation, the Empire of Waverley (although it was almost in the Imperial back yard), or the Duchy of Waldegren, to name the major human spacefaring powers; neither had it attracted the attention of the far-ranging Seeker-Queens of the Shaara Galactic Hive. One reason for its being ignored was that it lay well away from the regular trade routes. Another reason was that nobody—at the moment—was acutely short of *lebensraum*. There were other reasons—economic, political, and whatever—but Grimes, a mere Survey Service commander, knew nothing of these, and would know nothing of such matters until, if at all, he wore gold braid up to the elbow and a cap whose peak was one solid encrustation of scrambled egg.

The planetary system of 1717 consisted of six worlds, easily observed as *Discovery*, her own time out of kilter with the *real* time of the universe, cautiously approached the star, running on interstellar drive, from well to the north of the plane of the ecliptic. The planets showed as wavering bands of luminescence about the shapeless, quivering iridescent blob that was their primary. After the Mannschenn Drive had been shut down they were, of course, far harder to locate—but Flannery, one of those telepaths capable of psionic direction-finding, was able to guide the ship in toward the world that harbored intelligent life.

Of 1717's six planets, the outermost three were gas giants. Of the innermost three, one was far too close to the sun for life, of any kind, to have developed. The other two were within the biosphere. The third one was almost another Earth, a resemblance that became more and more striking

84

as *Discovery* approached it. There were seas and continents, mountain ranges, polar ice caps, and a cloudy atmosphere. On the night side were sparkling clusters of lights that had to be cities. And there were networks of unnaturally straight lines crisscrossing the landmasses that could be roads, or railways, or canals.

There was no doubt that 1717 III was inhabited. The people of 1717 III had achieved, it seemed certain, some kind of industrial civilization. But until an actual landing was made little could be known about them, although Flannery was doing his best to pick up information. He said to Grimes, who had taken to haunting the PCO's squalid office, "T'is like the roarin' o' the crowd at a football game, Captain. Niver a single voice that ye can make out what it's sayin' . . . just jabber, jabber, jabber. Oh, there's a power o' people down there all right, an' they're after thinkin' what people always do be thinkin'—that it's too hot, or too cold, or that it's almost dinnertime, or that it's a dreadful long time atween drinks. Which reminds me—" He reached for a full bulb of whiskey. "An' how long are ye keepin' us in free fall, Captain? I mislike these baby's feedin' bottles."

Grimes ignored this. "But are they thinking in Standard English?" he demanded. "Or in any other human language?"

"Now ye're askin'. An' the answer is—I don't know. Trouble is, there's niver a *real* telepath among the bunch of 'em. If there was, he'd be comin' in loud and clear at this range, and I'd be able to tell ye for sure." Flannery grinned. "Am I to take it that the opposition hasn't brought ye any joy? That the bould Sparkses—bad cess to 'em!—haven't been able to raise anythin' on their heathenish contraptions?"

"You know damn well they haven't!" huffed Grimes. "We weren't expecting anything on the Carlotti—but there's been nothing on the NST either, nothing but static."

"So ye haven't found a Lost Colony after all Captain. But ye've discovered a new world with new people. An' isn't that better?"

"A new world? How do you make that out?"

"A Lost Colony'd be makin' its start with all the books an' machinery an' know-how aboard the ship, wouldn't it? 'Less they went all the way back to the Stone Age they'd be keepin' the technology they started with, an' improvin' on it."

"Mphm. But perhaps, for some reason, our friends down there prefer landlines to radio."

"Ye've somethin' there, Captain. But—there's altogether too many o' the bastards. That world has a powerful big population. Could the crew an' passengers o' just *one* ship—one flyin' fridge, perhaps, or one o' the lodejammers still not accounted for—have done so well, even if they bred like rabbits? Historically speakin', the Deep Freeze ships o' the First Expansion were only yesterday, an' the Second Expansion was no more than a dog watch ago."

"But you forget," Grimes told him, "that the later Deep Freeze ships, and *all* the lodejammers, carried big stocks of fertilized ova, together with the incubating machinery. One ship would have the capability to populate a small—or not so small—continent within a few decades after the first landing."

"Ye've almost convinced me, Captain. But I can't pick up any clear thinkin' at all, at all. All I can tell ye is that *they*—whoever or whatever *they* are—are mammals, an' have two sexes an' a few o' the in-betweens, an' that most of 'em are runnin' hard to keep up in some sort o' rat race . . . like us. But *how* like? Now ye're askin', an' I can't tell ye. Yet."

"So we just have to wait and see," said Grimes, getting up to return to the control room.

The planet 1717 III loomed huge through the planetward viewports, a great island in the sky along the shores of which *Discovery* was coasting. Like all prudent explorers in Man's past Grimes was keeping well out from the land until he knew more of what awaited him there. Like his illustrious predecessors he would send in his small boats to make the first contact—but, unlike them, he would not be obliged to hazard the lives of any of his crew when he did so.

"Number one probe ready," reported Brabham.

"Thank you," said Grimes.

He glanced around the control room. Tangye was seated at the console, with its array of instruments, from which the probe would be operated. Brandt was looking on, obviously sneering inwardly at the amateurishly unscientific efforts of the spacemen. The officer of the watch was trying to look busy—although, in these circumstances, there was very little for him to do. The radio officers were hunting up and down the frequencies on the NST transceiver, bringing in nothing but an occasional burst of static.

"Launch the probe, sir?" asked Brabham.

"I'll just check with Mr. Tangye first, Number One." Then, to the navigator, "You know the drill, pilot?"

"Yes, sir. Keep the probe directly below the ship to begin with. Bring it down slowly through the atmosphere. The usual sampling. Maintain position relative to the ship unless instructed otherwise."

"Good. Launch."

"Launch, sir."

The muffled rattle of the probe's inertial drive was distinctly audible as, decks away below and aft, it nosed out of its bay. It would not have been heard had *Discovery*'s own engines been running, it was little more than a toy, but the big ship, in orbit, was falling free. Needles on the gauges of Tangye's console jerked and quivered, the traces in cathode ray tubes began their sinuous flickering; but as yet there was nothing to be seen on the big television screen tuned to the probe's transmitter that could not be better observed from the viewports.

"Commander Grimes," said Brandt, "I know that you are in charge, but might I ask why you are not adhering to standard procedure for a first landing?"

"What do you mean, Dr. Brandt?"

"Aren't first landings supposed to be made at dawn? That tin spy of yours will be dropping down from the noon sky, in the broadest daylight possible."

"And anybody looking straight up," said Grimes, "will be dazzled by the sun. The real reason for a dawn landing—a manned landing, that is—is so that the crew has a full day to make their initial explorations. That does not apply in this case."

"Oh. This, I take it then, is yet another example of your famous playing by ear."

"You could put it that way," said Grimes coldly.

Shuffling in his magnetic-soled shoes, he went to stand behind Tangye. Looking at the array of instruments, he saw that the probe had descended into an appreciable atmosphere and that friction was beginning to heat its skin. He said, "Careful, pilot. We don't want to burn the thing up."

"Sorry, sir."

Clouds on the screen—normal enough high cirrus.

More clouds below the probe—an insubstantial but solid-seeming mountainscape of cumulus. A break in the cloud-floor, a rift, a wide chasm, and through it the view of a vast plain, and cutting across it a straight ribbon, silver-gleaming against the greens and browns of the land.

"Oxygen . . . nitrogen . . . carbon dioxide . . ." Tangye was reciting as he watched the indicators on the console.

"Good," murmured Grimes. Then, "Never mind the analysis for now. It's all being recorded. Watch the screen. Bring the probe down to that . . . canal."

"How do you know it's not a road or a railway?" asked Brandt.

"I don't. But it *looks* like water."

The probe was now losing altitude fast, plunging down through the rift in the clouds, dropping below the ceiling. Beneath it spread the great plain, the browns and yellows and greens of it now seen to be in regular patterns—crops as yet unripe, crops ready for harvesting, crops harvested? There were roads between the fields, not as distinct as the canal, but definite enough. There was motion—dark cloud shadows drifting with the wind, a ripple over the fields that subtly and continuously changed and shifted the intensities of light and shade and color. And there was other motion, obviously not natural—a tiny black object that crawled like a beetle along the straight line of the canal, trailing a plume of white smoke or steam.

"Home on that boat," ordered Grimes.

"That . . . *boat*, sir?"

"That thing on the canal." Grimes could not resist a little sarcasm. "The word 'boat,' Mr. Tangye, was used long before it was applied to the small craft carried by spaceships. Home on the boat."

"Very good, sir," responded Tangye sulkily.

As the probe descended, details of the boat could be make out. It was a barge, self-propelled, with its foredeck practically all one long hatch, with a wheelhouse-cum-accommodation-block aft, just forward of the smoking stovepipe funnel. Suddenly a head appeared at one of the open wheelhouse windows, looking all around, finally staring upward. That was the main drawback of the probes, thought Grimes. With their inertial drive-units running they were such noisy little brutes. He could imagine the bewilderment of the bargemen when they heard the strange clattering in the sky, louder than the steady thumping of their own engines, when they looked up to see the silvery flying torpedo with its spiky efflorescence of antennae.

The crew member who had looked up withdrew his head suddenly, but not before those in *Discovery*'s control room had learned that he was most definitely nonhuman. The neck was too long, too thin. The eyes were huge and round. There was no nose, although there was a single nostril slit. The mouth was a pouting, fleshy-lipped circle. The skin was a dark olive-green. The huge ears were even more prominent than Grimes's own.

The water under the stern of the barge—which, until now, had been leaving only a slight wake—boiled into white foam as the revolutions of the screw were suddenly increased. Obviously the canal vessel was putting on a burst of speed to try to escape from the thing in the sky. It could not, of course; Tangye, with a slight adjustment to the probe's remote controls, kept pace easily.

"No need to frighten them to death," said Grimes. "Make it look as though you're abandoning the chase."

But it was too late. The barge sheered in toward the bank and the blunt stem gouged deeply into the soft soil, the threshing screw keeping it firmly embedded. The wheelhouse erupted beings; seen from the back they looked more human than otherwise. They ran along the foredeck, jumped ashore from the bows, scurried, with their long arms flailing wildly, toward the shelter of a clump of trees.

"Follow them, sir?" asked Tangye.

"No. But we might as well have a close look at the barge, now. Bring the probe down low over the foredeck."

Steel or iron construction, noted Grimes as the probe moved slowly from forward to aft. *Riveted plates . . . no welding. Wooden hatch boards, as like as not, under a canvas—or something like canvas—hatch cover.*

He said, "Let's have a look in the wheelhouse, pilot. Try not to break any windows."

"Very good, sir."

It was not, strictly speaking, a wheelhouse, as steering was done by a tiller, not a wheel. There was, however, what looked like a binnacle, although it was not possible to see, from outside, what sort of compass it housed. There was a voicepipe—for communication with the engine room? Probably.

Grimes then had Tangye bring the probe to what had to be the engine room skylight, abaft the funnel. Unfortunately both flaps were down, and secured somehow from below so that it was impossible for the probe's working arms to lift them.

"Well," commented Grimes at last, "we have a fair idea of the stage their technology has reached. But it's odd, all the same. People capable of building and operating a quite sophisticated surface craft shouldn't bolt like rabbits at the mere sight of a strange machine in the sky."

"Unless," sneered Brandt, "other blundering spacemen have made landings on this world and endeared themselves to the natives."

"I don't think so, Doctor," Grimes told him. "Our intelligence service, with all its faults, is quite efficient. If any human ships had made landings on this planet we should have known. And the same would apply in the case of nonhuman spacefarers, such as the Shaara and the Hallicheki. Mphm. Could it be, do you think that they have reason to fear flying machines that do not bear their own *national* colors? Mightn't there be a war in progress, or a state of strained relations liable to blow up into a war at any moment?"

Brandt laughed nastily. "And wouldn't that be right up your alley, Commander Grimes? Gives you a chance to make a snap decision as to who are the goodies and who the baddies before taking sides. I've been warned about that unfortunate propensity of yours."

"Have you?" asked Grimes coldly. Then, to Tangye, "Carry on along the canal until you come to the nearest town or city. Then we'll see what happens."

CHAPTER 16

Swiftly along the canal skimmed the probe, obedient to Tangye's control. It hovered for a while over a suspension bridge—an affair of squat stone pylons and heavy chain cables—and turned its cameras on to a steam railway train that was crossing the canal. The locomotive was high-stacked, big-wheeled, belching steam, smoke, and sparks, towing a dozen tarpaulin-covered freight cars. The engine crew did not look up at the noisy machine in the sky; as was made evident by the probe's audio pickups their own machinery was making more than enough racket to drown out any extraneous mechanical sounds.

The train chuffed and rattled away serenely into the distance, and Grimes debated with himself whether or not to follow it—it had to be going somewhere—or to carry on along the canal. He ordered Tangye to lift the probe and to make an all-around scan of the horizon. At a mere two kilometers of altitude a city came into full view, on the canal, whereas the railway line, in both directions, lost itself in ranges of low hills. The choice was obvious.

He ordered the navigator to reduce altitude. From too great a height it is almost impossible to get any idea of architectural details; any major center of habitation is no more than a pattern of streets and squares and parks. It was not long before the city appeared again on the screen—a huddle of towers, great and small, on the horizon, bisected by the gleaming straight edge of the canal. It was like an assemblage of child's building bricks—upended cylinders and rectangular blocks, crowned with hemispheres or broad-based cones. The sun came out from behind the clouds and the metropolis glowed with muted color—yellows and browns and russet reds. Without this accident of mellow light striking upon and reflected from surfaces of con-

91

trasting materials the town would have seemed formidable, ugly, even—but for these moments at least it displayed an alien beauty of its own.

There was traffic on the canal again, big barges like the one of which the crew had been thrown into such a panic. There were three boats outbound from the city. These, sighting the thing in the sky, turned in a flurry of reversed screws and hard-over rudders, narrowly escaping ramming one another, scurried back to the protection of the high stone walls. The probe hovered and allowed them to make their escape unpursued.

And then, surging out from between the massive piers of a stone bridge, the watergate, came a low black shape, a white bone in its teeth, trailing a dense streamer of gray smoke. It had a minimal funnel and a heavily armored wheelhouse aft, a domed turret forward. Through two parallel slits in the dome protruded twin barrels. There was little doubt as to what they were, even though there was a strong resemblance to an old-fashioned observatory. "Those sure as hell aren't telescopes!" muttered Brabham.

The barrels lifted as the dome swiveled.

"Get her upstairs, pilot!" ordered Grimes. "Fast!"

Tangye stabbed in fumbling haste at his controls, keeping the probe's camera trained on the gunboat, which dwindled rapidly in the screen as the robot lifted. Yellow flame and dirty white smoke flashed from the two muzzles—but it was obvious that the result would not be even a near miss. Antiaircraft guns those cannon might well be, but their gunners were not used to firing at such a swift moving target.

"All right," said Grimes. "Hold her at that, Mr. Tangye. We can always take evasive action again if we have to. I doubt if those are very rapid-fire guns."

"I—I can't," mumbled the navigator.

In the screen the picture of the city and its environs was dwindling fast.

"You *can't?*"

Tangye, at his console, was giving an impersonation of an overly enthusiastic concert pianist. The lock of long fair hair that had flopped down over his forehead aided the illusion. He cried despairingly, "She—she won't answer."

"Their gunnery must have been better than we thought," remarked Brabham, with morose satisfaction.

"Rubbish!" snapped Swinton. "I watched for the shell

bursts. They were right at the edge of the screen. Nowhere near the target."

"Mr. Brabham," asked Grimes coldly, "did you satisfy yourself that the probe was in good working order? A speck of dust in the wrong place, perhaps . . . a drop of moisture . . . a fleck of corrosion."

"Of course, sir," sneered Brabham, "all the equipment supplied to *this* ship is nothing but the best. I don't think!"

"It is *your* job, Number One," Grimes told him, "to bring it up to standard."

"I'm not a miracle worker. And I'd like to point out, sir, that this probe that we are—sorry, *were*—using—"

"I'm still using it!" objected Tangye.

"After a fashion." Then, to Grimes again: "This probe, Captain, has already seen service aboard *Pathfinder, Wayfarer,* and, just before *we* got it, *Endeavor*—all of them senior ships to this, with four ring captains."

"Are you insinuating," asked Grimes, "that mere commanders get captains' leavings?" (He had thought the same himself, but did not like Brabham's using it as an excuse.)

"Sir!" It was Tangye again. "The screen's gone blank. We've lost the picture!"

"And the telemetering?"

"Still working—most of it. But she's going up like a rocket. I can't stop her. She's— Sir! She's had it! She must have blown up!"

Grimes broke the uneasy silence in the control room. "Write off one probe," he said at last. "Luckily the taxpayer has a deep pocket. Unluckily I'm a taxpayer myself. And so are all of you."

"One would never think so," sneered Brandt.

"Send down the other probe, sir?" asked Brabham sulkily.

"What is its service history?" countered Grimes.

"The same as the one Mr. Tangye just lost."

"It lost itself!" the navigator objected hotly.

Grimes ignored the exchange. He went on, "It has, I suppose, received the same loving attention aboard this ship as its mate?"

Brabham made no reply.

"Then it stays in its bay until such time as it has been subjected to a thorough—and I mean *thorough*—overhaul. Meanwhile, I think that we shall be able to run a fair preliminary survey of this planet if we put the ship into a circumpolar orbit. We might even be able to find out for sure if there are any wars actually in progress at this moment. I must confess that the existence of readily available antiaircraft artillery rather shook me."

"What are you saying in your preliminary report to Base, Commander Grimes?" asked Brandt.

"There's not going to be one," Grimes told him.

"And why not?" demanded the scientist incredulously.

One reason why not, thought Grimes, *is that I'm not where I'm supposed to be. I'll wait until I have a* fait accompli *before I break radio silence.* He said, "We're far too close to the territorial limits of the Empire of Waverley. If the emperor's monitors pick up a signal from us and learn that there are Earth-type planets in their back yard we shall have an Imperial battle cruiser squadron getting into our hair in less time than it takes to think about it."

"But a coded message—" began Brandt.

"Codes are always being broken. And the message would have to be a long one, which means that it would be easy to get a fix on the source of transmission. There will be no leakage of information insofar as this planet is concerned until we have a cast-iron treaty, signed, sealed, and witnessed, with its ruler or rulers. And, in any case, we still have another world to investigate. Mphm."

He turned to the executive officer. "Commander Brabham, you will organize a working party and take the remaining probe down completely. You will reassemble it only when you are quite satisfied that it will work the way it should." Then it was the navigator's turn. "Mr. Tangye, please calculate the maneuvers required to put us in the circumpolar orbit. Let me know when you've finished doing your sums."

He left the control room, well aware that if the hostile eyes directed at his back were laser projectors he would be a well-cooked corpse.

Back in his own quarters he considered sending an initial message to Captain Davinas, then decided against it, even though such a code could never be broken and it would be extremely difficult for anybody to get a fix on such a short transmission. He would wait, he told himself, until he saw which way the cat was going to jump.

CHAPTER 17

It was an unexpected cat that jumped.

It took the form of suddenly fracturing welding when the old ship was nudged out of her equatorial orbit into the trajectory that, had all gone well, would have been developed into one taking her over north and south poles while the planet rotated beneath her. With the rupturing of her pressure hull airtight doors slammed shut, and nobody was so unfortunate as to be caught in any of the directly affected compartments. But atmosphere was lost, as were many tons of fresh water from a burst tank. Repairs could be carried out in orbit, but the air and water could be replenished only on a planetary surface.

A landing would have to be made.

A landing—and a preliminary report to Base?

A preliminary report to Base followed, all too probably, by the arrival on the scene of an Imperial warship with kind offers of assistance and a cargo of Waverley flags to be planted on very available site.

So there was no report.

Meanwhile, there was the landing place to select. Grimes wanted somewhere as far as possible from any center of population, but with a supply of fresh water ready to hand. He assumed that the seas of this world were salt and that the rivers and lakes would not be. That was the usual pattern on Earth-type planets, although bitter lakes were not unknown.

There was a large island in one of the oceans, in the northern hemisphere, well out from the coastline of its neighboring continent. By day lakes and rivers could be seen gleaming among its mountains. By night there were no lights to be seen, even along the shore, to indicate the presence of cities, towns, or villages—and *Discovery*'s main telescope could have picked up the glimmer of a solitary candle. With a little bit of luck, thought Grimes, his descent through the atmosphere would go unheard and unobserved. It should be possible to replenish air and water without interference by the natives—and, even more important, without being obliged to interfere with them.

The repairs were carried out while the ship was still in orbit; Grimes had no desire to negotiate an atmosphere in a ship the aerodynamic qualities of which had been impaired. This essential patching up meant that there was no labor to spare to work on the remaining probe—but in these circumstances a landing would have to be made without too much delay. The closed ecology of the ship had been thrown badly out of kilter by the loss of water and atmosphere, and would deteriorate dangerously if time were spent on preliminary surveys.

The landing was timed so that touchdown would be made shortly after sunrise. This meant that there would be a full day in which to work before nightfall—and as it was summer in the northern hemisphere the hours of daylight would be long. Also, a low sun casts long shadows, showing up every slightest irregularity in the ground. A spaceship, descending vertically and with tripedal landing gear, can be set down on quite uneven surfaces; nonetheless the vision of a disastrous topple recurs in the nightmares of every survey ship captain.

During her slow, controlled fall *Discovery* was bathed in bright sunlight while, until the very last few minutes, the terrain directly below her was still in darkness. To the east of the terminator, where there was full daylight, the sea was a glowing blue and, dark against the oceanic horizon, in silhouette against the bright, clear sky, lifted the mountains of the distant mainland.

Night fled to the west and the rugged landscape beneath the ship took on form and color. Yes, there was the lake, an amoeboid splotch of liquid silver almost in the center of the periscope screen, its mirrorlike surface broken by a spattering of black islets. The northern shore was cliffy, and inland from the escarpments the forested hillside was broken by deep gullies. To the south, however, there was a wide, golden beach fronting a grassy plain, beautifully level, although there were outcrops of what seemed to be large boulders. There was an area, however, that seemed to be reasonably clear of the huge stones with their betraying shadows and, applying lateral thrust, Grimes maneuvered his ship until she was directly above it.

"Why not land on the beach, sir?" asked Brabham.

"Sand can be treacherous," Grimes told him.

"But it will be a long way to lug the hoses," complained the first lieutenant.

Isn't that just too bad, thought Grimes.

He concentrated on his piloting. He might have let the navigator handle a landing at a proper spaceport, with marker beacons and the certainty of a smooth, level surface to sit down on, but Tangye's reaction times were far too slow to cope with emergencies that might suddenly arise in these circumstances. Tangye was sulking, of course, as was Brabham, and as the bos'n would be when he and his men had to drag the hoses all the way to the lake.

There was little wind at this time of the day, and no lateral drift. Grimes found it easy to keep the ship dropping toward the spot that he had selected as his target. He could make out details in the periscope screen now, could see the long grass (it *looked* like grass) flattening, falling into patterns like iron filings in a magnetic field as the downward thrust of the inertial drive was exerted against blades and stems. There were tiny blue flowers, revealed as the longer growth was pushed down and away. There was something like an armored lizard that scuttled frantically across the screen as it ran to escape from the great, inexorably descending mass of the ship. Grimes hoped the creature made it to safety.

The numerals of the radar altimeter, set to measure distance from the pads of the landing gear to the ground, were flickering down the single digits. Seven . . . six . . . five . . . four . . . three . . . only three meters to go. But it would still be a long way down, as far as those in the control room were concerned, if the ship should topple. Two . . . one . . . a meter to go, and a delicate balance of forces achieved, with the rate of descent measured in fractions of a millimeter a second.

"I wish the old bastard'd get a move on," whispered somebody. Grimes could not identify the voice. Not that it mattered; everybody was entitled to his own opinions. Until he had coped with a landing himself he had often been critical of various captains' shiphandling.

Zero!

He left the drive running until he felt secure, then cut it. *Discovery* shuddered, complained, and the great shock absorbers sighed loudly. She settled, steadied. The clinometer indicated that she had come to rest a mere half degree from the vertical. What was under her must be solid enough. Grimes relaxed in his chair, filled and lit his pipe.

He said, "All right, Number One. Make it 'finished with engines,' but warn the chief that we might want to get upstairs in a hurry. After all, this *is* a strange and possibly hostile planet. In any case, he'll be too busy with his pumps to be able to spare the time to take his precious innies apart."

"I hope," muttered Brabham.

"Then make sure he knows that he's not to. Mphm. Meanwhile, I shall require a full control room watch at all times, with main and secondary armament ready for instant use. You can man the fire control console until relieved, Major Swinton."

"Open fire on anything suspicious, sir?" asked the Marine, cheerfully and hopefully.

"*No*," Grimes told him. "You will not open fire unless you get direct orders from myself."

"But, sir, we must make the natives respect us."

"What natives? I sincerely hope there aren't any on this island. In any case, there are other and better ways of gaining respect than killing people. Don't forget that *we* are the aliens, that *we* have come dropping down on this planet without so much as a by-your-leave. And Dr. Brandt—I hope—is the expert on establishing friendly relations with indigenes."

"I should hope so, Commander Grimes!" huffed Brandt.

"And if you go shooting at anything and everybody, Major Swinton," went on Grimes, "you'll be making the good doctor's job all the harder." He grinned. "But I don't think I shall be needing the services of either of you."

"Then," said Swinton sourly, "I may as well cancel my orders to Sergeant Washington to provide an escort for the hose parties. Sir."

"You will do nothing of the kind, Major. There may be dangerous wild animals on this planet. An uninhabited island like this is the very sort of place to find them."

"Then I and my men have permission to shoot *animals,* sir?"

"Yes!" snapped Grimes, but he was beginning to relent. After all, the major was only doing the job for which he had been trained. He turned to Brandt. "I suppose you'd like some specimens, Doctor? Geological, botanical, and so on?"

"I certainly would, Commander Grimes."

"Then you have my permission to call for volunteers from such personnel as aren't already employed. And you, Major, can tell the sergeant to lay on escorts for them as well as for the working parties."

"I can't spread the few men I have that thinly, sir."

"Mphm. Then you and your volunteers, Dr. Brandt, are to stay close to the hose crews at all times. You are not to stray out of sight of the ship. Oh, Number One—"

"Sir?" acknowledged Brabham.

"Pass the word to everybody going ashore that they are to return *at once* if the alarm siren is sounded."

"Very good, sir. All right to carry on down to get things organized?"

"Yes. Carry on."

Grimes felt a twinge of envy. He would have liked to have gone ashore himself, to stretch his legs, to feel grass under his feet and sunlight on his skin, to breathe air that had not been cycled and recycled far too many times. But in these circumstances his place was here, in the control room, the nerve center of his ship.

He got up from his chair and tried to pace up and down, like an old-time surface ship captain walking his bridge. But control rooms are not designed for taking strolls in. Swinton and the officer of the watch regarded him with poorly concealed amusement. He abandoned his attempt at perambulation, made his way through the clutter of chairs and consoles to the viewports overlooking the lake.

The working parties, under the bos'n, were running the ends of long hoses out to the water. Brabham slouched along beside them, his hands in his pockets, moodily kicking at tufts of grass. A young steward, one of Brandt's volunteers, was tap-tap-tapping at an outcrop of chalky rock with a hammer. A stewardess was gathering flowers. Among them, around them, in full battle armor, men walking like robots, were Swinton's Marines.

Already there was a small party on the beach—young

Tangye, three of the junior engineers, and Vinegar Nell. And what were *they* doing? Grimes asked himself. He lifted the binoculars that he had brought with him to his eyes. The men and the women were undressing. Oh, well, he thought, there was nothing wrong with that; a *real* sunbath after the weeks of unsatisfactory, psychologically speaking, exposure to the rays of the ship's UV lamps. But surely Brabham should have found jobs for these people.

The idlers were naked now, were sprawling on the fine sand. Grimes envied them. Then Vinegar Nell got up and walked slowly and gracefully into the water. She was followed by Tangye. The junior engineers got to their feet, obviously about to follow the paymaster and the navigator.

Grimes growled angrily, ran to the transceiver handling ship-to-shore communication. "Commander Brabham!" he barked.

He saw Brabham raising his wrist radio to his mouth, taking far too long about it, heard, at last, "Brabham here."

"Get those bloody fools out of the water. At once!"

Vinegar Nell was well away from the beach now, swimming strongly. Tangye was splashing after her. The engineers were already waist-deep in the shallows.

"Major Swinton," ordered Grimes, "tell Sergeant Washington to get his men down to the water's edge, and to keep their eyes skinned for any dangerous life-forms." Swinton spoke rapidly into the microphone of his own transceiver, which was hanging about his neck. "Commander Brabham, get a move on, will you?" Grimes went on, into his own microphone.

"Oh, all right, all right." That irritable mutter was not meant to be heard, but it was.

Brabham was down to the beach at last, had his hands to his mouth and was bawling out over the water. The engineers, who had not yet started to swim, turned, waded slowly and reluctantly back to the sand. But Vinegar Nell and Tangye either would not or could not hear the first lieutenant's shouts.

"May I, sir?" asked Swinton. There was a nasty little grin under his moustache.

"May you what, Major?"

"Order my men to drag them out."

No, Grimes was about to say, *no*—but he saw an ominous

swirl developing a little way out from the swimmers. "Yes!"
he said.

Four Marines plunged into the lake. *They* were safe
enough. Full battle gear has been described, variously, as
armored tanks on legs, as battle cruisers on legs and, even,
as submarines on legs. They streaked out toward Vinegar
Nell and Tangye, boiling wakes astern of them as they actuated their suit propulsion units. Two of them converged
on the paymaster, two on the navigator. There was a flurry
of frail naked limbs among the ponderous metal-clad ones.
Ignominiously the swimmers were dragged to the shore,
carried out onto the dry land. It looked like a scene from
somebody's mythology, thought Grimes, watching through
his powerful glasses—the naked man and the naked woman
in the clutches of horrendous scaly monsters.

"Have them brought up here," he said to the major.

He assumed that they would be allowed to dress, but he
did not give any orders to that effect, thinking that such
would be unnecessary. He should have known better. Vinegar Nell, in a flaming temper, was splendid in her nudity.
Tangye, with his unsightly little potbelly, was not. Tangye
was thoroughly cowed. Vinegar Nell was not.

"I demand an explanation, Captain!" she flared. "*And* an
apology. "Was it you who ordered these"—she gestured with
a slim, freckled arm toward the armored Marines—"en-
listed men to attack me?"

"To save you," said Grimes coldly, "from the consequences
of your own stupidity." He grinned without humor. "Your
job is to provide meals for the personnel of this vessel, not
for whatever carnivores are lurking in the lake."

"Ha!" she snorted. "Ha!" She brushed past Grimes to
stand at the viewport. "What carnivores?"

The surface of the water was placid again. But there had
been something there.

"Sir!" called the officer of the watch suddenly, "I have a
target on the radar. Bearing 047. Range thirty kilometers.
Bearing steady, range closing."

"Sound the recall," ordered Grimes. He went to the intercom. "Captain here. Mr. Flannery to the control room. At
once."

CHAPTER 18

Flannery came into the control room, trailing a cloud of whiskey fumes, as Vinegar Nell and Tangye were hastily leaving. He guffawed, "An' what's goin' on, Captain? An orgy, no less!"

"Out of my way, you drunken bum!" snarled the paymaster, pushing past him.

Grimes ignored this. Vinegar Nell and Tangye would keep until later, as could the junior engineers who had followed their bad example. Looking out through the ports he saw that the last members of the shore parties were almost at the foot of the ramp, with Sergeant Washington and his Marines chivying them like sheepdogs. But the end of one hose had been placed in the lake; there was no reason why the pump should not be started. He told the officer of the watch to pass the order down to the engine room.

"Ye wished for me, Captain?" the telepath was asking.

"Yes, Mr. Flannery. Something, some kind of flying machine, is approaching."

"Bearing 047. Range twenty. Closing," reported the OOW.

"It must be an aircraft," went on Grimes. "The mountains cut off our line of sight to the sea. Could you get inside the minds of the crew? Are their intentions hostile?"

"I'll do me best, Captain. But as I've told ye an' told ye —these people must be the lousiest telepathic transmitters in the entoire universe!"

"All hands on board, sir," reported Brabham, coming into the control room. "Shall we reel in the hoses?"

"No. I've already told the engineers to start pumping. If I want to get upstairs in a hurry I shall be using the rockets, and I'll want plenty of reaction mass. But you can retract the ramp and close the after airlock door." Tangye—clothed, sheepish—made a reappearance. "Pilot, put the engines—

inertial drive *and* reaction drive—on standby. Warn the chief that I may be wanting them at any second."

"Range fifteen. Closing."

Grimes raised his glasses to his eyes and looked along the 047 bearing. Yes, there it was in the sky, a black spot against a backdrop of towering, snowy cumulus. An aircraft, all right—but what sort of aircraft? Friendly or hostile? And how armed?

"All possible weaponry trained on target, sir," reported Swinton.

"Thank you, Major. What do you have to report, Mr. Flannery?"

"I'm tryin', Captain, indeed I'm tryin'. T'is like lookin' for truth at the bottom of a well full o' mud. The odd thought comes bubblin' up through the ooze—an' then it bursts, like a bubble, when I try to get ahold of it. But—but I'm gettin' somethin'. They're a bit scared—an' why shouldn't they be? They're a bit scared, but they're determined. They mayn't look much like us—but they're *men.*"

"Range ten. Closing."

"Ship buttoned up, apart from the hoses," reported Brabham.

"All engines on standby," said Tangye. "Enough reaction mass in the tanks for limited use."

"How limited?" demanded Grimes testily.

"He didn't say, sir. But the pump is still sucking in water."

"They're comin' on," muttered Flannery, "although they're not likin' the idea of it at all, at all. But—but they—they trust? Yes. They trust us, somehow, not to swat 'em down out o' the sky like flies."

"Ha!" barked Swinton, hunched eagerly over his fire control console.

"Watch it, Major!" warned Grimes sharply.

"Range five. Closing."

Grimes studied the thing in the visual pickup screen, which gave far greater magnification than his binoculars. It looked like a big balloon, with a car hanging from the spherical gas bag. But a balloon would never be capable of that sort of speed. Then the thing turned to make a circuit of the valley, presenting its broadside to the human observers. The shape of it made sense—a long, fabric-covered torpedo with a control cabin forward, a quartet of engine pods aft.

The outlines of frames and longerons were visible through the covering. *A rigid airship*, thought Grimes. *A dirigible*.

"They're havin' a good look at us," said Flannery unnecessarily. "They know that we're from . . . outside."

The airship flew in a circle with *Discovery* at its center, maintaining its distance but well within the range of the spaceship's weaponry. Perhaps its crew, knowing only the capabilities of their own artillery, thought they were out of range.

"Another target," reported the officer at the radar. "Bearing 047. Range thirty-five. Closing."

"Holdin' the first one's hand, like," volunteered Flannery.

Swinton, tracking the dirigible within visual sight, complained, "The bloody thing's making me dizzy."

"It's stopped," said Brabham. "No. It's turning. Toward us."

Toward, or away? wondered Grimes. Yes, toward it was.

"They've made their minds up," whispered Flannery. "They're thinkin'—may the Saints preserve 'em!—that there's no harm in us."

The airship drove in steadily. On its new course it would pass directly over *Discovery*. It approached with a stately deliberation. Then, suddenly, from the gondola, a half dozen relatively tiny objects fell in succession.

Swinton cried out—in exultation, not fear. And Flannery screamed, "No! No!" Grimes, belatedly recognizing the falling things for what they were, shouted, "Check! Check! Check!" But the major ignored the order to hold his fire. The slashing, stabbing beam of his laser was a ghostly, almost invisible sword. Each of the falling bodies exploded smokily, even as the parachutes started to blossom above them, and as they did so there was the deafening rattle of *Discovery*'s forty millimeter battery and a torrent of bright tracer. The airship disintegrated, her twisted, black skeleton in brief silhouette against the fireball of blazing hydrogen. The blast rocked the spaceship on her landing gear and a strip of burning fabric drifted down across her stem, blotting out the control room viewports with writhing blue and yellow flames.

"You bloody pongo murderer!" screamed Flannery, beating at the major with his fists.

"Call this lunatic off me," shouted Swinton, "before I have to kill him!"

Grimes grabbed the telepath by the shoulder, yanked him away from the Marine. He said, trying to keep his voice under some sort of control, "You bloody murderer, Swinton. You'll face another court-martial when we get back to Base!"

"I saved the ship!" Swinton was on his feet now. "I saved your precious ship for you. I call upon you all as witnesses. That was a stick of bombs."

"Bombs don't explode the way those bodies did," said Grimes coldly. "But living flesh does, when a laser beam at wide aperture hits it. The parachutes were just starting to open when you killed the poor bastards wearing them."

"Parachutists, then," admitted the major. "Paratroopers."

"Emissaries," corrected Flannery. "Comin' in peace, wantin' to make our acquaintance. An' didn't they just, you murtherin' swine?"

"Target number two," said the officer at the radar in a shaky voice, "bearing 047. Range twenty, opening. Twenty-one, opening . . . twenty-two . . . twenty-three."

"They know now what to expect from Earthmen," said Flannery bitterly.

CHAPTER 19

There had been an unfortunate misunderstanding, and men had died because of it, but Grimes was still responsible for the safety of his own ship, his own crew. He ordered that the replenishment of essential air and water be resumed as soon as the wreckage of the dirigible was cleared from around *Discovery*. He allowed Brandt, assisted by a squad of Marines, to pick over the charred remains of the airship and her hapless people—a filthy, gruesome task but, viewed cold-bloodedly and scientifically, a most useful one. One of the least badly damaged bodies—it did not look as though it had ever been a living, sentient being, but it exuded the sickly smell of death—was brought on board for dissection at some later date. The other corpses were interred in a common grave, marked by an almost intact four-bladed wooden airscrew. "We'll try to show these people that we're civilized," growled Grimes to the giant, black sullen Sergeant Washington, who had been ordered to take charge of the burial and who had protested that his men weren't gravediggers. "Although it's rather late in the day for that."

It was obvious that the man resented having to take orders from anybody but his own officer, even from the ship's captain, but Major Swinton had been suspended from duty and sent down to his quarters in disgrace. Brabham had taken over fire control, and managed to convey the impression that he hoped he would not be required to function as gunnery officer. Tangye had the radar watch.

Grimes stayed in the control room, taking his sandwich lunch there, although the other officers were relieved for their meal. He continually refilled and rekindled a pipe that became ever fouler and fouler. He listened patiently to Brandt when the scientist reported on the findings that he, aided by the ship's technical staff, had made. There had been very little metal in the structure of the airship, he said. The framework, control cabin, and engine pods had been made from a light but very strong wood. Stays and control cables, however, were of stranded wire, indicative of a certain degree of technological sophistication. The engines, which had survived the crash almost intact, seemed to be similar to Terran diesels. Unfortunately no fuel remained, but analysis of the deposits in the cylinders would provide clues as to the nature of what had been burned in them.

The pieces of the jigsaw puzzle were beginning to fall into place—and Grimes regretted that he would not be able to complete the picture. After Swinton's trigger-happy effort any and all visitors to this world would be received with hostility. It was a pity, as this would have been an interesting planet for detailed study, a world upon which the industrial revolution had taken place or was, at the very least, well under way. And there were political and sociological aspects as well as the technological ones which Grimes would have liked to have investigated. That obvious state of war—or, at least, a warmish cold war—between nations. Anti-aircraft artillery and a willingness to use it—as witness the reception of *Discovery*'s probe outside that city. But at least one of the powers, whoever it was that had owned the ill-fated airship, was less apt to shoot first and ask questions afterward. Or, he told himself glumly, they had been less apt to shoot first and ask questions afterward. Now they had learned their lesson. *That bloody, bloody Swinton!*

"Of course," said Brandt, with whom Grimes had been talking things over, "the major ruined everything."

"He's ruined himself as well, this time!" snapped Grimes. "I told the man, before witnesses, not to open fire unless ordered by myself to do so." He laughed grimly. "I'm afraid you won't get the chance to give away your picture books and educational toys on this planet, Doctor. Thanks to the Mad Major we got off on the wrong foot."

He pushed himself up from his chair, made a circuit of the viewports. Shadow was creeping over the valley from the west, but the rugged country to the east of the tarn was still brightly illuminated by the slowly setting sun—the pearly gray and glowing ocher of the cliffs, the static explosions of vividly green foliage, spangled with the scarlet and purple of huge gaudy blossoms.

Where every prospect pleases, he thought, *but only Man is vile. Man, with a large, black, capital "M."*

"Target," called Tangye suddenly. "Aerial. Bearing 050. Range thirty-five."

"General standby," ordered Grimes. Then, more to himself than to anybody else, "I'll not make it 'action stations' yet. If I do, the work'll never get finished. I doubt if that gas bag'll be keen to close us." He turned to Brabham. "If it does, Number One, you can pump a few rounds of HETF across its bows, as a deterrent. You will not, repeat not, shoot to hit."

Brabham gave him a sour look of acknowledgment, as though to say, *You don't need to tell me my job!*

Grimes looked down at the hoses, still out, still writhing rhythmically as the pumps drew in water from the lake. He thought, *I'll let the old bitch drink her fill.* He watched the sullen Marines, ash-bedaubed, still at their grisly work, their morbid scavenging. He rather regretted that he had not put Major Swinton in personal charge of the operation.

"Bearing 050. Range thirty. Closing," intoned Tangye.

"The poor brave, stupid bastards!" whispered Grimes. That flimsy ship, flammable as all hell, against *Discovery*'s weaponry. He went to the intercom, called for Flannery.

"An' what would ye be wantin', Captain?" asked the telepath when he reported to the control room.

"Don't waste my time!" snapped Grimes testily. "You know damn well what I'm wanting!"

"Then I'll be tellin' ye, Captain. I'm receivin' 'em—loud, but not all that clear. Just raw emotions, like. Frightenin', it is. Hate. Revenge. Anybody'd think ye were the black Cromwell himself, payin' another visit to the Emerald Isle."

"But what can they hope to do against us?" demanded Grimes.

"I can't tell ye. But they are hopin' to do something that'll not be improvin' the state of our health."

"Range twenty-five. Closing."

Grimes called the engine room. "Captain here, Chief. How's that water coming in?"

"Only number six tank to top up now—an' it's almost full."

"Then stop the pumps. Reel in the hoses." He put down the telephone. "Commander Brambham—sound the recall."

The wailing of the siren was deafening, but above it

Tangye's voice was still audible. "Range twenty. Closing."

"We can reach them easily with a missile, sir," suggested Brabham.

"Then don't!" snarled Grimes.

The hoses were coming in, crawling over the grass like huge worms. The Marines were mounting the ramp, herded by Sergeant Washington.

"Liftoff stations," ordered Grimes quietly. He knew that he could be up and clear, especially with the reaction drive assisting the inertial drive, long before the airship, even if she attempted kamikaze tactics, could come anywhere near him. And if the dirigible were armed with missiles—which could hardly be anything more advanced than solid fuel rockets—*Discovery*'s anti-missile laser would make short work of them.

"Range fifteen. Closing."

The control room was fully manned now, the officers waiting for their captain's orders. But the hoses had stopped coming in; some mechanical hitch must have developed. But there was yet, thought Grimes, no urgency. He could well afford to wait a few more minutes. He had no wish to jettison equipment that could not be replaced until return to a Base.

"Range ten. Holding, holding, holding." There was relief in Tangye's voice.

The airship was well within sight now. It just hung there in the sky, from this angle looking like a harmless silver ball, a balloon, glittering with reflected light.

"And what do you pick up now, Mr. Flannery?" asked Grimes.

"Nothin' new at all, Captain. They're still hatin' us, still wantin' their revenge."

"They'll not be getting it at that range!" remarked Grimes cheerfully. He was certain that the natives' airborne weaponry would be unable to touch him. And he would soon be getting off this world, where things had gone so disastrously wrong. The sooner he was back in Deep Space the better. He said, "Once the hoses are in, I'll lift ship."

He went to the big binoculars on their universal mount, and the officer who had been using them made way for him. The instrument was already trained on the dirigible. He knew there would be nothing fresh to see—he was just passing the time—but then his attention was caught by a bright, intermittent flickering. A weapon? Hardly. It did not look like muzzle flashes, and surely these people did not yet have laser. The reflection of the sunlight from a control cabin window? Probably. He realized that he was trying to read the long and short flashes as though they were Morse, and laughed at himself for making the futile attempt.

"Hoses in, sir."

"Good." Grimes started to walk back to his control chair —and stopped in mid-stride as a violent explosion from somewhere outside shook the ship. "In the lake!" somebody was shouting. "The lake!" Over the suddenly disturbed water a column of spray, intermingled with dirty yellow smoke, was slowly subsiding. And something big and black and glistening had surfaced, was threshing in its death throes. But nobody could spare the time to look at it to determine what manner of beast it was. There was a second burst, a flame-centered eruption of sand and water on the beach itself, closer to the ship than the first one had been.

Suddenly that flickering light from the dirigible made sense to Grimes. It was either a heliograph or a daylight signaling lamp, and the function of the airship was not to attack but to spot for a surface vessel with heavy long-range guns, hidden from *Discovery*'s view, just as *Discovery* was hidden from hers. And what was she doing? he wondered. Laddering, or bracketing? The question was an academic one.

A third projectile screamed in—this one much too close for comfort. Fragments of stone, earth, and metal rattled against the spaceship's hull and she shuddered and complained, rocking in her tripedal landing gear. There was no time for normal liftoff procedure—the ritual countdown, the warning to all hands over the intercom to secure for space. There was no time, even, for Grimes to adjust himself properly in his chair. The inertial drive was ready, as was the auxiliary reaction drive. He slammed the controls of each straight from Standby to Maximum Lift, hoping desperately that at this time, of all times, the temperamental engines would not decide to play up. The violent acceleration pushed him deep into the padding of his seat; others, not so lucky, were thrown to the deck. *Discovery* did not have time to complain about the rough handling. (Normally she was the sort of ship that creaks and groans piteously at the least provocation.) She went up like a shot from a gun

—and a real shot, from a real gun, blew a smoking crater into the ground upon which she, only a split second before, had been resting.

Upward she roared on her column of incandescent steam, with the overworked inertial drive deafeningly cacophonous. Already the island was showing as a map in the periscope screen. Off the northern coast, a gray slug on the blue water, stood the warship. There was a scintillation of yellow flashes as her guns, hastily elevated, loosed off a wild, futile salvo, and another, and another. The shell bursts were all well below the rapidly climbing *Discovery*.

Laboriously Grimes turned his head, forcing it around against the crushing weight of acceleration, looked through the viewports. The airship was closer now, driving in at its maximum speed. But it did not matter. *Discovery* would be well above the dirigible by the time the courses intersected, at such an altitude that the down-licking exhaust would be dissipated, would not ignite the hydrogen in the gas cells. He bore the aviators no grudge, felt only admiration for them.

Admiration, and . . . helpless pity.

He stared, horror-stricken, into the periscope screen as the airship, now almost directly beneath *Discovery*, was caught in the turbulence of the spaceship's wake. Giant, invisible hands caught the fragile craft, wrenched her, twisted her, wrung her apart. But there was buoyancy still in the sundered bow and stern sections, there was hope yet for her crew.

There was hope—until chance sparks, friction engendered, ignited the slowly escaping hydrogen. She blossomed then into a dreadful flower of blue and yellow flame from the center of which there was a spillage of wreckage, animate and inanimate.

Grimes cut the reaction drive. He did not wish to blow away all the water that had been purchased at too great a cost. He continued his passage up through the atmosphere on inertial drive only. It was time that he started to think about the casualties among his own people—the sprains, contusions, and abrasions, if nothing worse. He told Brabham to get hold of Dr. Rath and to find out how things were. Luckily nobody in the control room was badly hurt; everybody there had seen what was happening, had been given a chance to prepare for what was going to happen.

Grimes pushed the ship up and out, looking with regret at the dwindling world displayed in the screen. There was so much that could have been learned about it and its people, so much that should have been learned.

But, as far as he was concerned, it was no more than a big black mark on his service record.

CHAPTER 20

So he was back in Deep Space again and the planet, the native name of which he had never learned, was no more than a tiny shapeless blob of luminescence, barely discernible to one side of the greater (but fast diminishing) blob that was its primary, Star 1717 in the Ballchin Catalog. He was back in Deep Space, and trajectory had been set for 1716, and *Discovery* had settled down, more or less, to her normal Deep Space routine.

More or less.

Officers and ratings were doing their jobs as usual and—also as usual—in a manner that wasn't quite grossly inefficient. The ship was even less happy than she ever had been. Cases of minor insubordination were all too common, and all too often the insubordination had been provoked.

Perhaps, hoped Grimes, things would be better after planetfall had been made on the most likely world of Star 1716. Perhaps that world would prove to be the home of a Lost Colony, with genuinely human inhabitants. Perhaps it would be possible to make an unopposed landing and to establish amicable relations with the people at once, in which case everybody (including, eventually, the Lords Commissioners of the Admiralty) would be happy.

Meanwhile, he did not forget his promise to Captain Davinas. He made out the message, using the simple code that he and the tramp master had agreed upon. *To: Davinas, d/s/s Sundowner. Happy Birthday. Peter.* There would be little chance of such a short transmission being picked up by the Waverley monitors. It was transmitted on a tight beam, not broadcast, directed at the Carlotti relay station on Elsinore. There it would be picked up and immediately and automatically retransmitted, broadcast, at regular intervals, until it was acknowledged by *Sundowner*. Davinas would

113

know from whom it came and what it meant. The Elsinore station would know the exact direction from which it had been beamed—but the straight line from *Discovery* to Elsinore was a very long one, stretching over many light-years. In the unlikely event of the broadcast's being received by any station within the Empire of Waverley it would be utterly meaningless.

The message on its way, he started to write his report on the happenings on and around the unlucky planet of 1717. It would be a long time before this report was handed in, he knew, but he wanted to get it on paper while the events were still fresh in his memory. It would not be, he was well aware, the only report. Brandt would be putting one in, probably arguing during the course of it that expeditions such as this should be under the command of scientists, not mere spacemen. The disgraced Swinton would be writing his, addressed to the General Officer Commanding Federation Space Marines, claiming, most certainly, that by his prompt action he had saved the ship. And officers, petty officers, and ratings would be deciding among themselves what stories they would tell at the inevitable Court of Inquiry when *Discovery* returned to Lindisfarne Base.

Grimes was still working on his first, rough draft when his senior officers—with the exception of the Mad Major—came to see him.

"Yes?" he demanded, swiveling his chair away from the paper-strewn desk.

"We'd like a word with you, sir," said Brabham. The first lieutenant looked as morose as ever, but Grimes noted that the man's heavy face bore a stubbornly determined expression.

"Take the weight off your feet," Grimes ordered, with forced affability. "Smoke, if you wish." He set the example by filling and lighting his pipe.

Brabham sat stiffly at one end of the settee. Vinegar Nell, her looks matching her nickname, took her place beside him. Dr. Rath, who could have been going to or coming from a funeral on a cold, wet day, sat beside her. MacMorris, oafishly sullen, lowered his bulk into a chair. The four of them stared at him in hostile silence.

"What is it you want?" snapped Grimes at last.

"I see you're writing a report, sir," said Brabham, breaking the ominous quiet.

"I am writing. And it is a report, if you must know."

"I suppose you're putting the rope around Major Swinton's neck," sneered Vinegar Nell.

"If there's any rope around his neck," growled Grimes, "he put it there himself."

"Aren't you being . . . unfair, Captain?" asked Brabham.

"Unfair? Everybody knows the man's no more than a uniformed murderer."

"Do they?" demanded MacMorris. "He was cleared by that court-martial."

And a gross miscarriage of justice that *was*, thought Grimes. He said, "I'm not concerned with what Major Swinton did in the past. What I'm concerned about is what he did under my command, on the world we've just left."

"And what did he do?" persisted Brabham.

"Opened fire against my orders. Murdered the entire crew of an airship bound on a peaceful mission."

"He did what he thought best, Commander Grimes. He acted in the best interests of the ship, of us all. He deserves better than to be put under arrest, with a court-martial awaiting him on Lindisfarne."

"Does he, Lieutenant Commander Brabham?"

"Yes. Damn it all, sir, all of us in this rustbucket are in the same boat. We should stick together."

"Cover up for each other?" asked Grimes quietly. "Lie for each other, if necessary? Present a united front against the common enemy, the Lords Commissioners of the Admiralty?"

"I wouldn't have put it quite in those words, Captain, but you're getting the idea."

"Am I?" exploded Grimes. "Am I? This isn't a matter of bending Survey Service regulations, Brabham! This is a matter of crime and punishment. I may be an easygoing sort of bastard in many ways, too many ways—but I do like to see real criminals, such as Swinton, get what's coming to them!"

"And is Major Swinton the only *real* criminal in this ship?" asked Vinegar Nell coldly.

"Yes, Miss Russell—unless some of you are guilty of crimes I haven't found out about yet."

"What about yourself, Commander Grimes?"

"What about myself?"

"I understand that two airships were destroyed. One by the major, when he opened fire perhaps—perhaps!—a little prematurely. The second by . . . yourself. Didn't you maneuver this vessel so that the backblast of your rockets blew the airship out of the sky?"

Grimes glared at her. "You were not a witness of the occurrence, the accident, Miss Russell."

"I know what I've been told," she snapped. "I see no reason to disbelieve it."

"It was an accident. The airship was well beneath us when it crossed our trajectory. It was not backblast that destroyed it, but turbulence." He turned to Brabham. "You saw it happen."

"I saw the airship go down in flames," said Brabham. He added, speaking very reasonably, "You have to admit, sir, that you're as guilty—or as innocent—as the major. You acted as you thought best. If you'd made a normal liftoff, using inertial drive only, there wouldn't have been any backblast. *Or* turbulence. But you decided to get upstairs in a hurry."

"If I hadn't got upstairs in a hurry," stated Grimes, "I'd never have got upstairs at all. None of us would. The next round—or salvo—would have been right on."

"We are not all gunnery experts, Captain," said Dr. Rath. "Whether or not we should have been hit is a matter for conjecture. But the fact remains that the airship was destroyed by your action."

"Too right it was!" agreed MacMorris. "An' the way you flogged my engines it's a miracle this ship wasn't destroyed as well."

"Gah!" expostulated Grimes. Reasonable complaints he was always prepared to listen to, but this was too much. He would regret the destruction of the second dirigible to his dying day, but a captain's responsibility is always to his own vessel, not to any other. Nonetheless he was not, like Swinton, a murderer.

Or was he?

"You acted as you thought best," murmured Brabham. "So did the major."

"Major Swinton deliberately disobeyed orders," stated Grimes.

"I seem to remember, Captain," went on Brabham, "that *you* were ordered to make a sweep out toward the Rim."

"If you ever achieve a command of your own," Grimes told him coldly, "you will discover that the captain of a ship is entitled—expected, in fact—to use his own discretion. It was suggested that I make my sweep out toward the Rim—but the Admiralty would take a very dim view of me if I failed to follow up useful leads taking me in another direction."

"All that has been achieved to date by this following of useful leads," said Rath, "is the probable ruin of a zealous officer's career."

"Which should have been ruined before he ever set foot aboard this ship!" flared Grimes.

"Then I take it, sir," said Brabham, "that you are not prepared to stretch a point or two in the major's favor."

"You may take it that way," agreed Grimes.

"Then, sir," went on the first lieutenant, speaking slowly and carefully, "we respectfully serve notice that we shall continue to obey your legal commands during the remainder of this cruise, but wish to make it clear that we shall complain to the proper authorities regarding your conduct and actions as soon as we are back on Lindisfarne."

"The inference being," said Grimes, "that if Swinton is for the high jump, I am too."

"You said it, Commander Grimes," put in Vinegar Nell. "The days when a captain was a little—or not so little—tin god are long dead. You're only a human being, like the rest of us, although you don't seem to think so. But you'll learn, the hard way!"

"Careful, you silly cow!" growled MacMorris.

Grimes forced himself to smile. "I am all too aware of my fallible humanity, Miss Russell. I'm human enough to sympathize with you, and to warn you of the consequences of sticking your necks out. But what puzzles me is why you're doing it for Major Swinton. The Marines have always been a pain in the neck to honest spacemen, and Swinton has all a Marine's faults and precious few of the virtues. And I know that all of you hate his guts."

"He *is* a son of a bitch," admitted the woman, "but he's *our* son of a bitch. But you, Commander Grimes, are the outsider aboard this ship. Lucky Grimes, always on the winning side, while the rest of us, Swinton included, are the born losers. Just pray to all the Odd Gods of the Galaxy that your luck doesn't run out, that's all!"

"Amen," intoned Rath, surprisingly and sardonically.

Grimes kept his temper. He said, "This is neither the time

nor the place for a prayer meeting. I suggest that you all return to your duties."

"Then you won't reconsider the action you're taking against the major, Captain?" asked Brabham politely.

"No."

"Then I guess this is all we can do," said the first lieutenant, getting up to leave.

"For the time being," added Vinegar Nell.

They left, and Grimes returned to his report writing. He saw no reason why he should try to whitewash Swinton, and regarding the destruction of the second airship told the truth, no more and no less.

CHAPTER 21

Grimes went down to the farm deck to see Flannery.

He could have sent for the telepath, but did not like to have the man in his quarters. He was always filthy, and around him hung the odors of stale perspiration, cheap whiskey, and organic fertilizers. Possibly this latter smell came from the nutrient solutions pumped into the hydroponic tanks—at times the atmosphere in the farm deck was decidedly ripe—and possibly not.

The PCO, as always, was hunched at his littered table, with the inevitable whiskey bottle and its accompanying dirty glass to hand. He was staring, as he usually was, at the spherical tank in which was suspended the obscenely naked canine brain, which seemed to be pulsating slowly (but surely this was an optical illusion) in the murky life-support fluid. His thick lips were moving as he sang, almost inaudibly, to himself, or to his weird pet.

> *"Now all you young dukies an' duchesses,*
> *Take warnin' from what I do say;*
> *Be sure that you owns what you touchesses*
> *Or ye'll jine us in Botany Bay!"*

"Mphm!" Grimes grunted loudly.

Flannery looked up, turned slowly around in his chair. "Oh, it's you, Captain Bligh. Sorry, me tongue slipped. Me an' Ned was back in the ould days, when the bully boys, in their pretty uniforms, was ridin' high an' roughshod. An' what can I be doin' for ye, Captain?"

"What were you getting at when you called me Captain Bligh?" demanded Grimes.

"Not what ye were thinkin'. Yer officers an' crew haven't decided to put ye in the long boat, with a few loyalists an'

119

the ship's cat . . . yet. Not that we have a cat. But ye're not loved, that's for sure. An' that murtherin' major's gettin' sympathy he's not deservin' of. Ned has *him* taped, all right. He doesn't like him at all, at all. He can remember the really bad bastards who were officers in the ould New South Wales Corps, floggin' the poor sufferin' convicts with nary a scrap o' provocation, an' huntin' down the black fellows like animals."

"I still don't believe that dingo of yours had a racial memory," said Grimes.

"Suit yersélf, Captain. Suit yerself. But he has. An' he has a soft spot for ye, believe it or not, even though he thinks o' ye as a latter-day Bligh. Even—or because. He remembers that it was Bligh who stood up for the convicts against the sodgers when he was governor o' New South Wales. After all, that was what the Rum Rebellion was all about."

"You're rather simplifying," said Grimes.

"No more than the descendants o' those New South Wales Corps officers who've been blackenin' Bligh's memory to try to make their own crummy forebears look like plaster saints by comparison." His voice faded, and then again he started to sing softly.

> *"Singin' tooral-i-ooral-i-addy,*
> *Singin' tooral-i-ooral-i-ay,*
> *Singin' tooral-i-ooral-i-addy,*
> *An' we're bound out for Botany Bay. . . ."*

"I didn't come down here for a concert," remarked Grimes caustically.

Flannery raised a pudgy, admonitory hand. "Hould yer whist, Captain. That song niver came from me. It came from outside."

"Outside?"

"Ye heard me. Quiet now. T'is from far away . . . but I could be there, whereiver *there* is. They're a-sittin' around a fire an' a-singin', an' a-suppin' from their jars. T'is a right ould time they're afther havin'. They're a-sendin' . . . oh, they're transmittin', if it's the technicalities ye want, but they're like all o' ye half-wits—beggin' your pardon, Captain, but that's what *we* call ye—ye can transmit after a fashion, but ye can't receive. I'm tryin' to get through to someone, anyone, but it's like tryin' to penetrate a brick wall."

"Mphm."

"Tie me kangaroo down, sport, tie me kangaroo down. . . ."

"Must you try to sing, Mr. Flannery?"

"I was only jinin' in, like. T'is a good party, an' Ned an' me wishes we was there."

"But where is it?"

"Now ye're askin'. There should be a bonus for psionic dowsin', there should. Ye've no idea, not bein' a telepath yerself, how it takes it out of yer. But I'll try."

Grimes waited patiently. It would be useless, he knew, to try to hurry Flannery.

At last: "I've got it, Captain. That broadcast—ye can call it that—comes from a point directly ahead of us. How far? I can't be tellin' ye, but t'is not all that distant. An' I can tell ye, too, that it comes from our sort o' people, humans."

"I somehow can't imagine aliens singing 'Botany Bay,'" said Grimes. And many of the lodejammers were out of Port Woomera, in Australia."

"I've found yer Lost Colony for ye," said Flannery smugly.

CHAPTER 22

So Grimes ordered the splicing of the mainbrace, the issue of drink to all hands at the ship's expense. He sat in the wardroom with his officers, drinking with them, and drinking to the Lost Colony upon which they would be making a landing before too long. He did not need to be a telepath to sense the change of mood. They were behind him, with him again, these misfits and malcontents. He responded, smiling, when Brabham toasted, "To Grimes's luck!" He clinked glasses with Vinegar Nell, even with the Mad Major. He joined in heartily when everybody started singing *"Botany Bay."*

Botany Bay.

He rather hoped that this would be the name given by the colonists to this chance-found world circling Star 1716 in the Ballchin Catalog. It might well be; such colonies as had been founded by the crews and passengers of the gauss-jammers of the New Australian Expansion tended to run to distinctively Australian names.

He left when the party began to get a little too rowdy. He did not retire at once, but sprawled in his easy chair, his mind still active. When people recovered from this letting off of steam, he thought, he would have to discuss his plan of campaign with the senior officers, the departmental heads. Then, suddenly but quietly, the outer door of his day cabin opened. He was somehow not surprised when Vinegar Nell came in. She was (as before) carrying a tray, with coffee things and a plate of sandwiches. But this time she was still in uniform.

Grimes gestured toward the supper as she set it down on the low table. "So you still think of me as Gutsy Grimes?" he asked, but he smiled as he spoke.

"Lucky Grimes," she corrected, smiling back, a little lopsidedly. "And I hope, John, I really hope that your luck rubs off on the rest of us."

"I do, too," he told her.

She straightened up after she had put the supper things down, standing over him. Her legs were very long, and slightly apart, her skirt very short. One of her knees was exercising a gentle but definite pressure on Grimes's outstretched thigh, but with a considerable effort he managed to keep his hands to himself. Then she stooped again as she poured him his coffee. The top two buttons of her shirt were undone and he glimpsed a nipple, erect, startlingly pink against the pale tan of the skin of her breast.

He whispered huskily, "Miss Russell, would you mind securing the door?"

She replied primly, "If you insist, Commander Grimes."

She walked slowly away from the table, away from him, shrugging out of her upper garment, letting it float unheeded to the deck. He heard the sharp *click* of the lock as it engaged. She turned, stepping out of her brief skirt as she did so. The sheer black tights that were all she was wearing beneath it concealed nothing. She walked past him into the bedroom, not looking at him, a faint smile on her face, her small breasts jouncing slightly, her round buttocks smoothly working, gleaming under the translucent material. He got up, spilling his coffee and ignoring it, following her.

She must have been fast. She was already completely naked, stretched out on the bunk, waiting for him, warmly glowing on the dark blue bedspread. In the dim light her hair glinted like dusky gold against the almost black material of the coverlet, in aphrodisiac contrast to the pale, creamy tan of her upper thighs and lower abdomen. She was beautiful, as only a desirous and desirable woman, stripped of all artifice, can be.

Grimes looked down at her and she looked up at him, her eyes large and unwinking, her lips slightly parted. He undressed with deliberate slowness, savoring the moment, making it last. He even put his shirt on a hanger and neatly folded his shorts. And then he joined her on the couch, warm, naked skin to warm, naked skin, his mouth on hers. It was as though he had known her, in the Biblical sense of the word, for many, many years.

She murmured, as they shared a cigarillo, "Now you're one of us."

"Is that why . . . ?" he started, hurt.

"No," she assured him. "No. That is not why I came to you. We should have done this a long time ago. A long, long time—"

He believed her.

CHAPTER 23

The people of Botany Bay—this was, in fact, the name of the Lost Colony—did not, of course, run to such highly sophisticated communications equipment as the time-space-twisting Carlotti radio. Had they possessed it they would not have stayed lost for long. But it had yet to be invented in the days of the gaussjammers—as had, too, the time-space-twisting Mannschenn Drive. It had been making a voyage, as passenger, in one of the timejammers that had started Luigi Carlotti wondering why, when ships could exceed the speed of light (effectively if not actually) radio messages could not. So Botany Bay did not possess Carlotti radio. Neither was there, as on most other Man-colonized worlds, a corps of trained telepaths; Flannery spoke with some authority on that point, maintaining that somehow psionic talent had never developed on the planet. But there was, of course, Normal Space-Time radio, both audio and visual, used for intraplanetary communications and for the broadcasting of entertainment.

It did not take long for the ship's radio officers to find this out once *Discovery* had reentered the normal continuum, shortly thereafter taking up a circumpolar orbit about the planet. It was no great trouble to them to ascertain the frequencies in use and then to begin monitoring the transmissions. Grimes went down to the main radio office—its sterile cleanliness made a welcome change from Flannery's pig pen—to watch the technicians at work and to listen to the sounds issuing from the speakers. Barbham accompanied him.

There were what sounded like radio telephone conversations. At first these seemed to be in some quite familiar yet unknown language—and then, as soon as Grimes's ear became accustomed to the peculiarly flat intonation of the voices—they suddenly made sense. The language, save for its accent, had survived almost unchanged, was still understandable Standard English. It became obvious that what was being picked up was an exchange of messages between a ship and some sort of traffic control authority.

"Duchess of Paddington," Grimes heard, "to Port Ballina. My ETA is now 0700 hours. What's the weather doin' at your end? Over."

"Port Ballina to *Duchess*. Wind west at ten kiph. No cloud. Visibility excellent. The moorin' crowd'll be waitin' for yer, Skip. Over."

"Sounds like a surface ship, Captain," commented Brabham.

"Mphm?" grunted Grimes dubiously.

The voice came from the speaker again. *"Duchess of Paddington* to Port Ballina. Please have one 'A' helium bottle waitin' for me. I'd a bastard of a slow leak in one o' my for'ard cells. Over."

"Wilco, *Duchess*. Will you be wantin' the repair mob? Over."

"Thanks muchly, but no. Got it patched meself, but I lost quite a bit o' buoyancy an' I've had to use the heaters to maintain altitude an' attitude. See you. Over."

"More ruddy airships!" growled Brabham. "I hope—" His voice trailed off into silence.

"You hope what?" asked Grimes coldly.

"Well, sir, there seems to be a sort of jinx on the things as far as we're concerned."

"There'd better not be *this* time," Grimes told him.

"Sir!" called one of the radio officers. "I think I'm picking up a treevee transmission, but I just can't seem to get any sort of picture."

Grimes shuffled slowly to the receiver on which the young man was working; with the ship now in free fall it was necessary to wear magnetic-soled shoes and, after the long spell under acceleration, to move with caution. He stared into the screen. It was alive with swirling color, an intermingling of writhing, prismatic flames and subtle and everchanging shades of darkness, an eddying opalescence that seemed always about to coalesce into a picture, yet

never did. The technician made more adjustments and suddenly there was music—from a synthesizer, thought Grimes
—with the effect of ghost guitars, phantom violins, and
distant drums. The ever-changing colors in the screen matched
the complex rhythms drifting from the speaker.

"Damn it!" muttered the radio officer, still fiddling with
the controls. "I still can't get a picture."

"Perhaps you aren't supposed to," murmured Grimes.

A final crash of guitars, scream of violins and rattle of
drums, an explosive flare of light and color, fading into
darkness . . . and then, at last, a picture. A young woman,
attractive, with deeply tanned skin and almost white-blonde
hair, stood with one slim hand resting on the surface of a
table. She was simply clad in a long white robe, which somehow hid no smallest detail of her firm body. She said—and it
was a pity that her voice, with its flat intonation, did not
match her appearance—"An' that was Damon's *Firebird
Symphony*, played to you by the composer himself. I hope
y'all liked it. An' that's it from this station for today. We'll
be on the air again at the usual time termorrer with our
brecker program, commencin' at 0600 hours. Nighty-night
all, an' good sleepin'.''

She faded slowly from the screen and the picture of a
flag replaced her—a familiar (to Grimes) ensign, horizontal
and rippling in a stiff breeze, dark blue, with a design of
red, white, and blue crosses superimposed upon each other
in the upper canton, a five-starred, irregularly cruciform
constellation in the fly. And there was music—also familiar.

"Once a jolly swagman," sang Grimes, softly but untune-
fully, "camped by a billabong. . . ."

"Do you *know* it, sir?" asked one of the radio officers.

Grimes looked at the young man suspiciously, then remembered that he was from New Otago, and that the
New Otagoans are a notoriously insular breed. He said,
"Yes. 'Waltzing Matilda,' of course. Wherever Aussies have
gone they've taken her with them."

"Who was Waltzing Matilda?" persisted the officer. "Some
old-time dancing girl?"

Brabham sniggered, and Grimes said, "Not exactly. But
it's a bit too complicated to explain right now."

And whose ghosts, he wondered, would be haunting the
billabongs (if there were billabongs) of this world upon

which they would soon be landing? The phantom of som
swagman, displaced in time and space, or—*Damn you
Flannery,* he thought, *stop putting ideas into my mind!*—
or, even, of the mutiny-prone Bligh?

CHAPTER 24

"We have to let them know we're here," said Grimes.

"The probe is in in good working order, sir," said Brabham.

"Not the probe," Grimes told him. He did not want a repetition of all that had happened the last time a probe had been used. He went on, "These people are human. They have maintained a reasonably high standard of technology."

"With *airships,* sir?" asked Brabham.

"Yes. With airships. It has never ceased to amaze me that so many human cultures have not persisted with their use. Why waste power just to stay up before you even think about proceeding from Point A to Point B? But never mind the airships. They also have radio." He turned to one of the technicians. "Did you note the time when the station closed down, Lieutenant? Good. And the blonde said that she'd be resuming transmission at 0600 hours tomorrow."

"Local time, sir," pointed out Brabham. "Not ship's time."

"When she whispered her sweet good nights," said Grimes, "I managed to tear my eyes away from her face long enough to notice a clock on the wall behind her. A twenty-four-hour clock. It was registering midnight. And we already know, from our own observations, that Botany Bay has a period of rotation of just over twenty-five Standard Hours. I assume—but, of course, I could be wrong—that there are people in this ship, besides myself, capable of doing simple sums."

Brabham scowled. The radio officers sniggered.

"So," went on Grimes, "I want to make a broadcast myself on that station's frequencies when it starts up again with the"—he made a grimace of distaste—*"brecker* program. I think we have the power from our jennies to override

129

anything they may be sending. I shall want a visual transmission as well as sound. There people will have as much trouble with our accent as we had with theirs. I'll leave you to work out the details. I'm going to prepare a series of cards, from which I shall be speaking. Do you think you'll be able to set up your end of it in the time?"

"Of course, sir," the senior radioman assured him.

"Their spelling's probably nothing at all like ours," muttered Brabham.

"It shouldn't have changed all that much," said Grimes hopefully. "And luckily, the blonde bombshell wasn't delivering her spiel in Hebrew or Chinese. Well, I'll leave you to it, gentlemen. You know where to find me if anything fresh crops up."

He went back to his quarters and set to work with sheets of stiff white paper and a broad-tipped stylus.

They were ready for him when he returned to the radio office. He stood where he was told, with the camera trained on him, watching the monitor screen, which was still blank. Suddenly he realized that he had omitted to change into his dress uniform and put on a cap—but, he told himself, it didn't matter.

The screen came alive. Again there was the flag, bravely flying, and again there was music—but, this time, it was "Botany Bay." When it was over the picture became that of an announcer. It was not—to the disappointment of Grimes and the others—the spectacular blonde. It was a young man, comfortably clad in colorful shirt, extremely short shorts, and sandals. Like the girl he was fair haired and deeply tanned. He was far more cheerful than he had a right to be at what must be, to him, an ungodly hour of the morning.

"Mornin', all—those of yer who're up, that is. An' you lucky bastards who're still in yer scratchers can get stuffed. Anyhow, this is Station BBP, the Voice of Paddo, openin' transmission on this bright an' sunny mornin' o' December nineteenth, Thursday. I s'pose yer wantin' the news. Now what have we to make yer day for yer?" He looked down at a sheet of paper in his right hand.

Grimes signaled with his own right hand to the senior radio officer. The lights in the radio office flickered and dimmed, except for the one trained on Grimes. The picture in the monitor screen faded—as must also have done the pictures in the screens of all the receivers tuned to that station. It was replaced by the image of Grimes himself, looking (he realized) very important, holding at chest level the first of his cards. He read from it, trying to imitate the local accent, "I am the captain of the Earth Survey Ship *Discovery*." He changed cards. "My ship is at present in orbit about your planet." He changed cards again. "I am about to cease transmission. Please make your reply. Over."

The picture of the announcer came back into the screen. The young man's pallor under his tan gave his complexion a greenish tinge. At last he spoke. "Is this some bloody hoax?" And somebody not in the screen said, "I could see the bastard in the monitor plain enough. T'aint nobody *we* know—an' we know everybody who is anybody in the radio trade!" "Get on the blower to the observatory, Clarry," ordered the announcer. "Tell the lazy bludgers ter get their useless radio telescope on the job." Then, facing his audience—those on the planet and those in space—"Orright, Captain whatever-yer-name-is. It's over ter you again." He grinned. "At least you've saved me the trouble o' readin' the bloody news!"

Grimes reappeared in the screen, holding another card. He read, "Can you understand me? Over."

The announcer came back. "Yair—though Matilda knows where yer learned yer spellin'. An' yer sound like you've a plum in yer mouf." He mimicked Grimes's way of speaking. "And whom have I the honor of addressing, Captain, sir?" He grinned again, quite convincingly. "I used to act in historical plays before I was mug enough to take this job. Over."

"My name is Grimes, Commander Grimes of the Federation Survey Service. I am, as I've already told you, captain of the Survey Ship *Discovery*. I was ordered to make a search for Lost Colonies. Over."

"An' you've sure found one, ain't yer? We're lorst orright. An' we thought we were goin' ter stay that way. Hold on a sec, will yer? Clarry's got the gen from the observatory."

The unseen Clarry's voice came from the speaker. "T'aint a hoax, Don. The bastards say there is somethin' up there, where somethin' shouldn't be."

"So yer for real, Commander Grimes. Ain't yer supposed ter say, 'Take me to yer leader'? Over."

"Take me to your leader," said Grimes, deadpan. "Over."

"Hold yer horses, Skip. This station'll be goin' up in flames at any tick o' the clock, the way the bleedin' phones are runnin' hot. Her Ladyship's on the way ter the studio now, s'matter o' fact. Over."

"Her Ladyship? Over."

"The mayor o' Paddo, no less. Or Paddington, as I s'pose you'd call our capital. Here she is now."

The announcer bowed, backed away from the camera at his end. He was replaced by a tall, ample woman, silvery haired and with what seemed to be the universal deep tan. She was undeniably handsome, and on her the extremely short dress with its gay floral pattern did not look incongruous —and neither, somehow, did the ornate gold chain that depended from her neck. She said—and even the accent could not entirely ruin her deep contralto—"'Ow yer doin', Skip? Orright?" Then, turning to address the announcer, "Wot do I say now, Don? 'Over,' ain't it? Orright. Over."

"I'm honored to meet you, Your Ladyship. Over."

"Don't be so bloody formal, Skipper. I'm Mavis to me mates—an' any bastard who's come all the way from Earth's a mate o' mine. When are yer comin' down ter meet us proper? Do yer have ter land at one o' the magnetic poles same as *Lode Wallaby* did? Or do yer use rockets? If yer do, it'll have ter be some place where yer won't start a bushfire. Wherever it is, there'll be a red carpet out for yer. Even at the bloody North Pole." Then, as an afterthought, "Over."

"I have rocket drive," said Grimes, "but I won't be using it. My main drive, for sub-light speeds, is the inertial drive. No fireworks. So I can put down on any level surface firm enough to bear my weight. Over."

"You don't look all that fat ter me, Skip. But you bastards are all the same, ain't yer? No matter what yer ship is, it's *I, I, I* all the time." She grinned whitely. "But I guess the Bradman Oval'll take the weight o' that scow o' yours. Havin' you there'll rather bugger the current test series but the landin' o' the first ship from Earth is more important than cricket. Never cared for the game meself, anyhow. Over."

"I'll make it the Bradman Oval, then, Your . . . sorry.

Mavis. Once we get some less complicated radio telephone system set up your technicians can go into a huddle with mine. I'd like a radio beacon to home on, and all the rest of it." He paused, then went on. "Forgive me if I'm giving offense, but do you speak for your own city only, or for the whole planet? Over."

"I speak for me own city-state. The other mayors speak for their city-states. An' it so happens that at the moment I *am* President of the Council of Mayors. So I do speak for Botany Bay. That do yer, Skip? Over."

"That does me, Mavis. And now, shall we leave all the sordid details to our technicians? Over."

" 'Fraid we have to, Skip. I can't change a bloody fuse, meself. Be seein' yer. Over."

"Be seeing you," promised Grimes.

CHAPTER 25

Grimes had several more conversations with the mayor of Paddington before the landing of *Discovery*. The radio experts on the planet and in the ship had not taken long to set up a satisfactory two-way service, and when this was not being used for the exchange of technical information the spaceship's crew was continuously treated to a planetary travelogue. Botany Bay was a *good* world, of that there could be no doubt. There was neither overpopulation nor pollution. There was industry, of course, highly automated—but the main power sources were the huge solar energy screens set up in what would have otherwise been useless desert areas, and wind- and water-drive turbo-generators. There were oil wells and coal mines—but the fossil fuels merely supplied useful chemicals. The only use of radioactives was in medicine. Airships, great and small, plied the skies, driven by battery-powered motors, although there were a few jets, their gas turbines burning a hydrogen-oxygen mixture. On the wide seas the sailing vessel was the commonest form of ship—schooners mainly, with auxiliary engines and with automation replacing man-power. Efficient monorail systems crisscrossed the continents—but the roads, surprisingly, seemed to be little more than dirt tracks. There was a reason for this, the spacemen soon discovered. *Lode Wallaby* had carried among other livestock the fertilized ova of horses—and horses were used extensively for private transport, for short journeys.

Botany Bay, in the main, enjoyed an almost perfect climate, its continents being little more than large islands, the oceans exercising a tempering effect from the tropics to the poles. The climate had not been so good when the first colonists landed, destructive hurricanes being all too common. Now, of course, there was a planetwide weather watch, and fast aircraft could be dispatched at short notice to a developing storm center to drop anti-thermal bombs.

Botany Bay, throughout, could boast of almost unspoiled scenery. In all industrial establishments ugliness had been avoided. In the cities there had been a deliberate revival of architectural styles long vanished, except in isolated cases, from Earth. Paddington, for example, was a greatly enlarged, idealized version of the Terran Paddington, maintained as a historical curiosity in the heart of sprawling Sydney. There were the narrow, winding streets, tree lined, and the terrace houses, none higher than three stories, each with its balconies ornamented by metal railings cast in intricate floral designs. It was all so archaic, charmingly so. Grimes remembered a party to which he had been invited in the original Paddington. The host, when accused of living in a self-consciously ancient part of Sydney, had replied, "We Australians don't have much history—but, by any deity you care to name, we make the most of what we have got!"

This Paddington, the Botany Bay Paddington, was a city, not a mere inner suburb. It stood on the western shore of the great, natural harbor called Port Jackson. Its eastern streets ran down to the harbor beaches. To the west of it was the airport, and also the Bradman Oval. To the south and east were the port facilities for surface shipping. To the north were The Heads, the relatively narrow entrance to the harbor. And on the north coast were the high cliffs, with bays and more sandy beaches.

Grimes studied the aerial view of the city and its environs that was being transmitted to him. He could foresee no difficulties in making a landing. He would keep well to the west on his way down, so that if, in the event of a breakdown of his inertial drive, he were obliged to use the auxiliary reaction drive he would do no damage to the city.

He had wanted to adhere to the standard practice of the Survey Service and bring the ship down at dawn, but the mayor would not agree to this. "Come off it, Skip!" she remonstrated. "I don't like gettin' up at Matilda-less hours, even if you do! Wot's wrong wif ten hundred? The streets'll be aired by then, an' everybody'll be up an' dressed. We want ter *see* yer comin' down. We don't want ter be starin' up inter the gloom ter watch somethin' droppin' down outa the sky that could be no more than a solid-lookin' cloud wif a few lights hung on it!"

Grimes was obliged to agree. As a Survey Service captain he was supposed to make friends as well as to influence people. Meanwhile, as a preliminary measure, he had certain of the ship's clocks adjusted to synchronize with Paddington Local Time. Ten hundred hours Mavis had said, and he was determined that the pads of his tripedal landing gear would touch the turf of the Oval at precisely that time.

It was a fine, clear morning when *Discovery* dropped down through the atmosphere. Her inertial drive was working sweetly, but inevitably noisily, and Grimes wondered what the colonists would be thinking of the irregular beat of his engines, the loud, mechanical clangor driving down from above. Their own machines—with the exception of the few jet planes—were so silent. In the periscope screen the large island, the continent that had been named New Australia, showed in its entirety. Its outline was not dissimilar to that of the original Australia, although there was no Tasmania, and Port Jackson was on the north and not the east coast. The coastal fringe was green, but inland there were large desert areas, the sites of the solar power stations.

Grimes glanced at the control room clock, which was now keeping local time. There was time to spare; he could afford to take things easily.

"Target," announced Tangye. "Bearing 020, range fifty. Closing."

"Altitude?" asked Grimes.

"It's matching altitude with us, sir."

"It can't be one of the airships this high," said Grimes. He added nastily, "And, anyhow, we don't have Major Swinton at fire control this time."

He turned away from his console to look out of the viewports on the bearing indicated. Yes, there the thing was, a silvery speck, but expanding, closing fast.

"What if they *are* hostile, Captain?" asked Brabham. "We're a sitting duck."

"*If* they are hostile," Grimes told him, "we'll give them the privilege of firing the first shot."

"It's one of their jets," said Tangye.

"So it is," agreed Grimes. "So it is. They're doing the right thing; laying on an escort."

The aircraft closed them rapidly, circled them in a slowly descending spiral. It was, obviously, a passenger plane, with swept-back wings. Grimes could see men in the forward control cabin. They waved. He waved back, then returned his attention to handling the ship. He hoped that the jet pilot would not attempt to approach too close.

He could see Port Jackson plainly enough in the screen now, a great irregular bite out of the northern coastline. He could see the golden beaches with a cream of surf outlining them and—very small, a mere, crawling insect—one of the big schooners standing in toward The Heads. And there were two more targets announced by the radar-watching Tangye—airships this time, huge brutes with the sunlight reflected dazzlingly from their metal skins.

A familiar voice came from the speaker of the control room transceiver. "That's a noisy bitch yer've got there, Skip. Sounds like umpteen tons of old tin cans fallin' downstairs. Just as well yer didn't come in at sparrer fart."

"Do you have sparrows here?" asked Grimes interestedly.

"Nah. Not *reel* sparrers. But it's what we call one o' the native birds. Don't know how it got by before it had human bein's ter bludge on."

"Mphm. Excuse me, Mavis, but I'd like to concentrate on my pilotage now."

"That's what me late husband useter say. He was skipper o' one o' the coastal schooners. Oh, well, I can take a hint."

Grimes could see the city now—red roofs and gray, a few towers of pseudo-Gothic appearance. He could see the airport, with one big dirigible at its mooring mast like an oversized wind sock. And there, just beyond it, was the Bradman Oval, a darkly green recreation area with spectators' stands around it and, he was pleased to note, a triangle of red flashing lights, bright even in the general brightness of the morning. The radio beacon had been set up as requested by Grimes, but he preferred to use visual aids whenever possible.

The Oval expanded to fill the screen. The stands, Grimes saw, were crowded. He thought sourly, *These bastards have more faith in my innies than I do.* If the inertial drive were to break down, necessitating the use of the emergency reaction drive, there would be a shocking tragedy. But the beat of the engines still sounded healthy enough. He applied a touch of lateral thrust, brought the three beacons into the center of the screen. He looked at the clock: 0953. He was coming down just a little too fast. A slight, very slight increase of vertical thrust. The figures on the face of the radar altimeter flickered down in slightly slower succession.

That should do it, thought Grimes smugly.

Eleven . . . ten . . . nine . . .

And, on the clock, 0955.

Seven . . . six . . . five . . . four . . . three . . . two . . . one . . . 0959.

Gently, gently, thought Grimes.

Zero!

And, on the clock, the sweep second hand jumped to the same numeral.

The ship groaned and shuddered as her weight came onto the shock absorbers, and silence fell like a blow when the inertial drive was shut down. But there was another noise, a tumult that Grimes at first could not identify. Then he realized that it was cheering, noisy cheering, loud enough to be heard even inside the buttoned-up ship. And, faintly, there was the noise of a band. "Waltzing Matilda" (of course).

He looked out of the port at the waving crowds, at the blue flags, with their Union Jacks and Southern Crosses, flying from every mast around the Oval.

"So yer made it, Skip," the mayor's voice issued from the speaker. "Bang on time, too! Welcome to Botany Bay! Welcome to Paddo!"

"I'm glad to be here, Your Ladyship," replied Grimes formally.

"It's a pleasure ter have yer. But is it safe ter come near yer ship? You ain't radioactive or anythin', are yer?"

"Quite safe," said Grimes. "I'll meet you at the after airlock."

CHAPTER 26

Grimes, after issuing instructions, went down to his quarters to change. He had decided that this was an occasion for some show of formality, no matter how free and easy the people of this Lost Colony seemed to be. Or—he had his contrary moments—it was this very freeness and easiness that had induced in him the desire to be stiff and starchy. He got out of his comfortable shorts and open-necked shirt, replacing the latter with a stiff, snowy-white one. He knotted a black necktie about his throat, then thrust his legs into sharply creased black trousers. The bemedaled frock coat came next, then the sword belt and the quite useless ceremonial sword. Highly polished black shoes on his feet, the fore-and-aft hat with its trimmings of gold braid on his head. He inspected his reflection in the full-length mirror inside his wardrobe door, holding himself stiffly at attention. He'd do, he decided.

He took the elevator down to the after airlock. The others were waiting for him—the Mad Major, temporarily forgiven, with a half dozen of his men. The Marines, too, were in their dress finery, blue and scarlet and gleaming brass. Swinton was wearing a sword, his men carried archaic (but nonetheless lethal) rifles. Tangye, one of the few officers to possess a presentable full dress uniform, was there, as was Vinegar Nell, in the odd rig prescribed by the Survey Service for its female officers on state occasions, best described as a long-skirted, long-sleeved black evening frock, trimmed with gold braid and brass buttons and worn over a white shirt and black tie, topped with a hat like the one Grimes was wearing. But she carried it well.

The outer airlock door slowly opened, and as it did so the ramp was extruded, its end sinking to the close-cropped grass. Grimes stepped out into the warm, fresh air, the

139

bright sunlight. He was thankful that his uniform had been tailored from the lightest possible material. As he appeared there was a great welcoming roar from the crowds in the stands. He paused, saluted smartly, then continued down the ramp. After him came Tangye and the paymaster, and after them, their boots crashing rhythmically on the metal gangway, marched the Marines.

There was a stir among the crowd on the stand immediately facing the airlock. In the broad aisle between it and its neighbor a coach appeared, a vehicle drawn by four gleaming black horses, the first of what looked like a procession of such vehicles. Grimes, standing at the foot of the ramp, the others drawn up behind him, watched with interest. Yes, that was the mayor in the first coach, and other women and men with her. From this distance he could not be sure, but it did not look as though anybody had made any attempt to dress up. The driver was in some sort of khaki uniform with a broad-brimmed hat. But what was Brabham waiting for?

Suddenly, from overhead, there came a deafening *boom*, the first round of the twenty-one-gun salute, fired from one of the forty-millimeter cannon, using special blank cartridges.

Boom!

The coachmen were having trouble controlling their horses.

Boom!

The horses of the second and third coaches had bolted, had begun to gallop around the Oval like the start of a chariot race.

Grimes lifted his wrist transceiver to his mouth. "Brabham, hold . . ."

Boom!

"Brabham, hold your fire!"

"But that's only four rounds, sir," came the tinny whisper in reply.

"Never mind. Hold your fire."

The driver of the mayor's coach had his animals under control at last. He came on steadily, then reined in about ten meters from the foot of the ramp. From one of his pockets he produced a cigarette, lit it with a flaring lighter, then sat there stolidly with the little crumpled cylinder dangling from the corner of his mouth. He stared at Grimes and his entourage with a certain hostility.

Another khaki-uniformed man was first out. He assisted the mayor to the ground. She emerged from the vehicle with a lavish display of firm, brown thigh. She was wearing a short tunic, with sandals on her feet, only the mayoral chain of office adding a touch of formality. Her blue eyes were angry, her mouth drawn down in a scowl.

Grimes saluted with drawn sword. The Marines presented arms with a slap and rattle.

She demanded, "Wodyer playin' at, you stupid drongo? You said there'd be no bleedin' fireworks."

Grimes sheathed his sword. He said stiffly. "It is customary, Your Ladyship, to accord heads of state the courtesy of a twenty-one-gun salute."

"That may be where you come from, Skip, but it certainly ain't here. You scared shit outa the horses."

"Too flamin' right," commented the coachman. "Wodyer think me wheels was skiddin' on?"

"I'm sorry," Grimes began lamely.

The mayor smiled, broadly and dazzlingly. "So'm I. But this ain't a way for me to be welcomin' long-lost relatives from the old world." Suddenly she threw her plump arms about Grimes and drew him to her resilient breast, kissed him warmly full on the mouth. He felt himself responding— and was somehow aware of the disapproving glare that Vinegar Nell was directing at the back of his head.

"That's better," murmured the mayor, pulling reluctantly away. "A *lot* better. Kiss an' make up, that's what I always say. An' now, Skip, wot about introducin' me to the lady and these other gentlemen?"

"Your Ladyship," Grimes began.

"*Mavis,* you drongo. Even if you're all dressed up like a Christmas tree, I ain't."

"Mavis, may I introduce my paymaster."

"Pay*master?* Paymistress, if I'm any good at guessin'."

"Lieutenant Russell."

Vinegar Nell saluted and contrived to convey by her expression that she didn't want to be mauled.

"Major Swinton, my Marine officer."

Swinton's salute did not save him from a motherly kiss on the cheek.

"And Lieutenant Tangye, my navigator."

Tangye's face was scarlet when he was released.

"An' what about these other blokes?" demanded Mavis.

"Er . . ." began Grimes, embarrassed.

"Private Briggs," snapped Swinton, stepping smartly into the breach. "Private Townley. Private Gale. Private Roskov. Private O'Neill. Private Mackay."

"Well?" demanded the big woman. "Well?"

Now it was Swinton's turn to feel embarrassment. The six men stood stiffly like wooden soldiers.

"Well?"

"Stack your rifles," ordered Swinton.

The men did so.

"Advance to be greeted by Her Ladyship."

The order was obeyed with some enthusiasm.

When the introductions were over the mayor said, "Natterin' to you on the radio, Skip, I never dreamed that you were such a stuffed shirt. All o' yer are stuffed shirts. Looks like Earth ain't changed since our ancestors had the sense ter get the hell out."

"And this, I suppose," said Grimes, "is one of those worlds like Liberty Hall, where you can spit on the mat and call the cat a bastard."

"You said it, Skip, you said it!" exclaimed Mavis, bursting into delighted laughter. Grimes laughed too. He had thought that expression very funny the first time that he had heard it—how many years ago?—and he was delighted to be able to use it on somebody to whom it was new and brilliantly witty.

CHAPTER 27

Grimes had liked Mavis since his first sight of her in the monitor screen. He liked her still more now that he had actually met her. He kept on recalling a phrase that he had once heard—*A heart as big as all outdoors*. It applied to her. She was big in all ways, although in her dress that concealed little it was obvious that her body was all firm flesh, with no hint of flabbiness.

He was entertaining her and other officials in his day-cabin, with some of his own officers also present—Dr. Brandt, Brabham, and Vinegar Nell, who was kept busy refilling glasses and passing around dishes of savories. She, alone of all those present, seemed not to approve of the informality, the use of given names rather than titles and surnames. There was Jock, the man in the khaki shorts-and-shirt uniform who had assisted the mayor from the coach and who was City Constable. There was Pete, with a floral shirt over the inevitable shorts and sandals, who was president of the Air Pilots' Guild. There was Jimmy, similarly attired, who was master of the Seamen's Guild. There was Doug and Bert, mayors of Ballina and Esperance respectively, who had flown by fast jet from their cities to be present at *Discovery*'s landing.

Mavis, watching Vinegar Nell, said, "Why don't yer scarper, dearie, an' change inter somethin' more comfy? Any o' our barmaids havin' to wear wot you've got on 'd go on stroke, an' quite right, too!"

"What do your barmaids wear?" asked Grimes interestedly.

"At the beach eateries, nuffin'."

"So you have a culture similar to that of Arcadia?" asked Brandt.

"Arcadia? Where in hell's that?"

143

"It's a planet," explained Grimes, "with an ideal climate, where the people are all naturists."

"Naturists, Skip? Wot's that?"

"Nudists."

"You mean they run around in the nudie all the time?"

"Yes."

"No matter *wot* they're doin'?"

"Yes."

"Sounds screwy ter me—as screwy as wearin' anything when yer goin' inter the sea for a dip. Oh, well, takes all sorts ter make a universe, don't it?"

"Have I your permission to change into undress uniform, Commander Grimes?" asked Vinegar Nell coldly.

"Of course, Miss Russell." Grimes wondered what the effect would be if Vinegar Nell returned to the daycabin in the undress uniform in which he had often seen her.

"And ain't it time that you got outer yer admiral's suit?" Mavis asked Grimes.

"I think it is," he admitted.

He went into his bedroom, changed back into shirt and shorts. "Now yer look more human, Skip," said Mavis. She held out her empty glass to him. "Wot about some more Scotch? We do make whiskey here, but t'ain't a patch on this. But you should try our beer. Best in the universe. And our plonk ain't bad. Nor's our rum."

"You'll be tryin' it at ternight's party, Skipper," said Jimmy.

"An official reception?" Grimes asked the master of the Seamen's Guild.

"Not on yer nelly. If yer thinkin' o' gettin' all dressed up again, forget it. A beach barbecue. Come as yer please, preferably in civvies. Jock's makin' the arrangements."

"Twenty guests. Yerself an' nineteen others," said the City Constable. "There'll be other parties for the rest o' yer crowd. Transport'll be at yer gangway at 1900 hours."

"I'll pick up the skipper meself," said Mavis.

Vinegar Nell returned, wearing her shortest skirted uniform. The mayor looked at her and added, "When I drive meself, I use me little run-about. Only room for one passenger."

The paymaster said, "As you know, Commander Grimes, we have many guests aboard the ship. I have arranged for two sittings at lunch in the wardroom. I imagine that you will prefer second sitting."

"Don't bother about us, dearie," Mavis told her. "Just send up some more o' this Scotch, an' some more blottin' paper to soak it up afore it rots the belly linin'." She nibbled appreciatively. "This sorta sausage stuff is very moreish."

The other two mayors agreed with her enthusiastically.

"I'll see if there's any more of that Rimini salami left in the storeroom," said Vinegar Nell, conveying the impression that she hoped there wouldn't be. "It comes from Rimini, a world settled mainly by people of Italian ancestry. They make the salami out of a sort of fat worm."

"It still tastes good," said Mavis stoutly.

Grimes treated himself to an afternoon sleep after his guests had left. He felt guilty about it; he knew that as a conscientious Survey Service captain he should be making a start on the accumulation of data regarding this new world. It must be the climate, he thought, that was making him drowsy. It was a little too much to drink, he admitted.

He was awakened by somebody shaking him gently. He ungummed his eyes, found that he was looking up into the face of the mayor. She grinned down at him and said, "I had to pull me rank on that sodger you've got on yer gangway, but he let me come up after a bit of an argy-bargy."

"I . . . I must have dosed off, Mavis. What time is it?"

"Eighteen-thirty hours. All the others've gone, even that snooty popsy o' yours. They left a bit early for a bit of a run-around first."

"My steward should have called me at 1700," muttered Grimes.

"He did, Skip. There's the tray wif a pot o' very cold tea on yer bedside table."

Grimes raised himself on one elbow, poured himself a cup. It tasted vile, but it helped to wake him. He hesitated before throwing back the coverlet—he was naked under it— but Mavis showed no intention of leaving the bedroom. And he wanted a brief shower, and then he had to dress. He said over his shoulder, as he tried to walk to the bathroom with dignity, "What do I wear?"

"Come as you like if yer want to, Skip. It's a hot night, an' the weather bastards say it'll stay that way. But you've civvy shorts, ain't yer? An' a shirt an' sandals."

Grimes had his shower and was relieved, when he had finished drying himself, to find that Mavis had retired to the dayroom. It was not that he was prudish, but she was a large woman and the bedroom was small. He found a gaily patterned shirt with matching shorts, a pair of sandals. She said, when he joined her, "Now you *do* look human. Come on; the car's waitin' by the gangway."

"A drink first?"

"Ta, but no. There'll be plenty at the beach."

The Marine on gangway duty, smart in sharply pressed khaki, saluted. He said, "Have a nice night, sir."

"Thank you," replied Grimes. "I'll try."

"You'd better," the mayor told him.

Grimes took her arm as they walked down the ramp. Her skin was warm and smooth. He looked up at the clear sky. The sun was not yet set, but there was one very bright planet already shining low in the west. The light breeze was hotter than it had been in the morning. He was glad that he was not attending a full-dress function.

The mayor's car, a runabout, was little more than a box on relatively huge wheels, an open box. Grimes opened the door for her on the driver's side and she clambered in. She was wearing the shortest skirt in which he had yet seen her, and obviously nothing under it. *And yet,* thought Grimes, *she says that the Arcadians are odd.*

He got in on the other side. As he shut the door the car started with a soft hum of its electric motor. As it rolled smoothly over the grass toward the entrance to the Oval the mayor waved to groups of people who had come to stare up at the ship from the stars. They waved back. When she nudged him painfully, muttering something about stuck-up Pommy bastards, Grimes waved as well. They were worth waving to, he thought, the girls especially. Botany Bay might not be another Arcadia—but a bright shirt worn open over bare, suntanned breasts can be more attractive than complete nudity. He supposed that he would have to throw his ship open to the public soon, but by the time he did all hands would have enjoyed ample opportunity to blow off excess steam.

"We'll detour through the city," said Mavis. "This is the

time I fair love the dump, wif the sun just down an' the street lights comin' on."

Yes, the sun was just dipping below the rolling range to the west, and other stars were appearing to accompany the first bright planet. They drove slowly through the narrow, winding streets, where the elaborate cast-metal balconies of the houses were beginning to gleam, as though luminous, in the odd, soft greenish-yellow glow of the street lights.

"Gas lamps!" exclaimed Grimes.

"An' why not? Natural gas. There's plenty of it—an' we may's well use what's left after the helium's been extracted. An' it's a much *better* light."

Grimes agreed that it was.

"This is Jersey Road we're comin' inter. The city planners tried to make it as much like the old one as they could. I s'pose it's all been pulled down long since."

"It's still there," said Grimes, "although the old bricks are held together with preservative."

"An' how does it compare?" she asked. "Ours, I mean."

"Yours is better. It's much longer, and the gas lighting improves it."

"Good-oh. An' now we turn off on ter the West Head Road. That's Macquarie Head lighthouse we're just passin'. One lighthouse ter do the work o' two. The main guide beacon for the airport as well as for the harbor." Something big fluttered across their path, just ahead of them, briefly illumined in the glare of the headlights. Grimes had a brief impression of sharp, shining teeth and leathery wings. "Just a goanna," Mavis told him. "Flyin' goannas they useter be called, but as we've none o' the other kind here the 'flyin' part o' the name got dropped. They're good eatin'."

They sped through the deepening darkness, bushland to their left, the sea to their right. Out on the water the starboard sidelight, with a row of white accommodation lights below it, of a big schooner gleamed brightly.

"*Taroona*," said Mavis. "She's due in tonight. Ah, here's the turn-off. Hold on, Skip!"

The descent of the steep road—little more than a path—down to the beach was more hazardous, thought Grimes, than any that he had ever made through an atmosphere. But they got to the bottom without mishap. Away to their right a fire was blazing, its light reflected from the other vehicles parked in its vacinity. Dark figures moved in silhouette to the flames. There was the music of guitars, and singing.

"*Tie me kangaroo down, sport . . .*" Grimes heard.

"I got yer here, Skip," said Mavis.

"And in one piece," agreed Grimes.

"Come orf it!" she told him.

CHAPTER 28

As well as voices and music a savory smell of roasting meat drifted down the light breeze from the fire. Grimes realized that he was hungry. Unconsciously he quickened his step.

"Wot's the hurry?" asked Mavis.

He grinned—but at least she hadn't called him Gutsy Grimes. He said, "I want to join the party."

"Ain't I enough party for yer, Skip? I didn't think you'd be one fer chasin' the sheilas."

Grimes paused to kick his sandals off. The warm, dry sand felt good under his bare soles. He said, gesturing toward the parked cars, "I thought you people used horses for short journeys."

"Yair, we do—but not when we've a crowd o' spacemen along who, like as not, have never ridden a nag in their bleedin' lives."

"I have ridden a horse," said Grimes.

"An' what happened?"

"I fell off."

They both laughed, companionably, and then Grimes stopped laughing. He was able to distinguish faces in the firelight. This, obviously, was not an officers-only party. There was Langer, the burly bos'n, and with him Sergeant Washington. And there was Sally, the little slut of a stewardess who had ministered to the needs of his predecessor in the ship, Commander Tallis. Obviously their hosts were determined to maintain their egalitarian principles. Well, that was their right, he supposed.

"What's eatin' you, Skip?" asked Mavis.

"I'm thinking that it was time that I was eating something."

"Spacemen are the same as sailors, I suppose. Always

149

thinkin' o' their bellies." She raised her voice. "Hey, you drongoes! One o' yer bring the skipper a mug an' a sangwidge!"

Surprisingly it was the girl, Sally, who obliged, presenting him with a slab of steak between two halves of a thick roll. She seemed in an unusually happy mood as she walked toward him, her breasts—she had discarded her shirt—jouncing saucily. She said, "You see, Captain, I *can* make a sandwich when I want to." And it was Langer who came with a mug of beer in each hand, one of which he presented to Grimes. As he raised his own to his lips he said, "Your very good health, Captain."

"And yours, Bos'n. (He thought, *This may not be the finest beer in the universe, but it'll do till something better comes along.*)

"Here's to your luck, Captain. I knew *our* luck would change as soon as we got *you* in command."

"I hope it stays that way," said Grimes. (Damn it all, the man seemed positively to *love* him.)

He took a bite from his sandwich. It was excellent steak, with a flavor altogether lacking from the beef in the ship's tissue culture vats.

Dr. Rath drifted up. His informal civilian clothing was dark gray—but, amazingly, even he looked happy. He was smoking a long, thin cigar. "Ah, so you've joined us, Captain. Miss Russell was wondering when you were going to turn up."

"Oh. Where is she now?"

"Haven't a clue, my dear fellow. She sort of drifted off among the dunes with one of the local lads. Going for a swim, I think. At least, they'd taken off all their clothes."

"Mphm." What Vinegar Nell did, and with whom, was her own affair—but Grimes felt jealous. He accepted another mug of beer, then fumbled for his pipe.

"Have one of these, Captain," said Rath, offering him a cigar. "Not exactly Havanas, but not at all bad."

"Better than Havanas," said Langer.

And you'd know, thought Grimes uncharitably. *With your flogging of ship's stores you could always afford the best.* He accepted the slim, brown cylinder from the doctor, nonetheless, and a light from the attentive Sally.

Not bad, he thought, inhaling deeply. *Not bad. Must be a local tobacco.*

He turned to Mavis and said, "You certainly do your-
selves well on this world, darling." She seemed to have
changed, to have become much younger—and no less attractive. It must, he thought, be the effect of the firelight.
And how had he ever thought of her abundant hair as
silver? It was platinum-blonde.

She said, "We get by. We always have got by. We had no
bloody option, did we?" She took the cigar from his hand,
put it to her own lips, drew in. She went on, "Still an' all,
it's good to have you bastards with us at last, after all
these bleedin' years."

How had he ever thought her accent ugly?

She handed the cigar back, and again he inhaled. Another
mug of beer had somehow materialized in his free hand.
He drowned the smoke with a cool, tangy draft. He thought,
This is the life. Too bloody right it is.

By the fire the singing had started again, back by thrum-
ming guitars.

> *Farewell to Australia forever,*
> *Good-bye to old Sydney, good-bye,*
> *Farewell to the Bridge an' the Harbor,*
> *With the Opera House standin' on high.*

> *Singin' tooral-i-ooral-i-addy,*
> *Singin' tooral-i-ooral-i-aye,*
> *Singin' tooral-i-ooral-i-addy,*
> *We're bound out fer Botany Bay!*

"The opera house isn't all that high," complained Grimes.

"Never mind, dearie. It's only a song." She added almost
fiercely, "But it's *ours*."

> *Farewell to the Rocks an' to Paddo,*
> *An' good-bye to Woolloomooloo,*
> *Farewell to the Cross an' the Domain,*
> *Why were we such mugs as ter go?*

"You're better off here," said Grimes. "You've a good
world. Keep it that way."

"That's what I thought, after talkin' to some o' yer
people this arvo. But will you bastards let us?"

"You can play both ends against the middle," suggested

Grimes. He was not conscious of having been guilty of a grave indiscretion.

"Wodyer mean, Skip?"

"Your world is almost in the territorial space of the Empire of Waverley, and the emperor believes in extending his dominions as and when possible."

"So . . . the thot plickens." She laughed. "But this is a *party*, Skip. We're here to enjoy ourselves, not talk politics." Her hands went to a fastener at the back of her dress. It fell from her. She stood there briefly, luminous in the firelight. She was ample, but nowhere was there any sag. Her triangle of silvery pubic hair gleamed brightly in contrast to the golden tan of her body. Then she turned, ran, with surprising lightness, into the low surf. Grimes threw off his own clothing, followed her. The water was warm—*pee-warm,* he thought—but refreshing. Beyond the line of lazy breakers the water was gently undulant. He swam toward a flurry of foam that marked her position. She slowed as he approached her, switched from a crawl to an energy-conserving breaststroke.

He followed her as she swam, parallel to the beach. After a few moments of exertion he caught up with her. She kept on steadily until the fire and the music were well astern, then turned inshore. A low breaker caught them, swept them in, deposited them gently on the soft sand like stranded, four-limbed starfish. He got to his feet, then helped her up. Their bodies came into contact—and fused. Her mouth was hot on his, her strong arms were around him as she pulled him to her—and, after they had fallen again to the sand, above the tidemark, her legs embraced him in an unbreakable grip. Not that he wished to break it. She engulfed him warmly.

When they were finished he, at last, rolled off her, falling on his back onto the sand. He realized that he and Mavis had performed before an audience. Somehow he was not at all embarrassed—until he recognized, in the dim starlight, the naked woman who, with a young man beside her, was looking down at him.

"I hope you had a good time, Commander Grimes," said Vinegar Nell acidly.

"I did," he told her. "And you?" he asked politely.

"*No!*" she snapped.

"Fuck orf, why don't yer?" asked the mayor, who had raised herself on her elbows.

The young man turned at once, began to trudge toward the distant fire. Vinegar Nell made a short snarling noise, then followed him.

"That Col," remarked Mavis, "never was any good. "That sheila o' yours couldn't've picked a feebler bastard. All blow, no go, that's him."

"The trouble," said Grimes, "is that she is, as you put it, my sheila. Or thinks she is."

"Then wot the hell was she doin' out with Col?" she asked practically. "Oh, well, now we *are* alone, we may as well make the most of it."

CHAPTER 29

The next morning—not too early—Grimes held an inquest on the previous night's goings-on. He, himself, had no hangover, although he had forgotten to take an anti-alc capsule on his return to the ship, before retiring. He felt a little tired, but not unpleasantly so.

He opened by asking Brabham how he had spent the evening.

"I went to a party at Pete's place, sir."

"*Pete?*"

"The president of the Air Pilots' Guild."

"And what happened?"

"Well, we had a few drinks, and there was some sort of help-yourself casserole, and then we had a flight over the city and the countryside in one of the airships."

"Anything else?"

The first lieutenant oozed injured innocence. "What else would there be, Captain?"

"Any relaxation of what we regard as normal standards? Any . . . promiscuity?"

Brabham looked injured.

"Come on, Number One. Out with it. As long as you do your job your sex life is no concern of mine. But I have a good reason for wanting to know what happened." He grinned. "Some odd things happened to me. Normally I'm a very slow starter."

Brabham managed to raise a rather sour smile. "So *that's* what Vinegar Nell was dropping such broad hints about! Well, sir, I had it off with one of our tabbies—I'll not tell you which one—during the flight over the city. Have you ever done it on the transparent deck of a cabin in an airship, with the street lights drifting by below you?" The first lieutenant was beginning to show signs of enthusiasm.

"And then, after we got back to the airport, there was a local wench . . . I can't remember her name. I don't think that we were introduced."

"Mphm. And how do you feel?"

"What do you mean, sir?"

"Presumably you had plenty to drink, as we all did. Any hangover?"

"No, sir."

"Mphm. Commander MacMorris?"

"The Seamen's Guild laid it on for us, Captain. Plenty o' drinks. A smorgasbord. Plenty o' seawomen as well as seamen. There were a couple—engineers in the big schooners." He grinned. "Well, you can sort o' say it was all in the family."

"Mphm. Commander—or Doctor, if you prefer—Brandt?"

The scientist colored, his flush looking odd over his pointed beard. "I don't see that it is any concern of yours, Commander Grimes, but I was the guest of honor at a banquet at the university."

"And were you—er—suitably honored, Dr. Brandt?"

The flush deepened. "I suppose so."

"Try to forget your dignity, Doctor, and answer me as a scientist. What happened?"

"I've always been a reserved man, Commander Grimes. I was expecting an evening spent in intelligent conversation, not an—" He had trouble getting the word out. "Not an orgy. This morning I am shocked by the memory of what those outwardly respectable academics did. Last night I just joined in the party. Happily."

"As did we all," murmured Grimes. "Dr. Rath?"

The medical officer had reverted to his normal morose self. "You should know, Captain. You were there."

"What I'm getting at is this. What is your opinion of it all as a physician?"

"I'd say, Captain, that we were all under the influence of a combined relaxant and aphrodisiac."

"The beer?" suggested Grimes.

"I didn't touch it. There was some quite fair local red wine."

"And I was on what they call Scotch," contributed MacMorris. "It ain't Scotch, but you can force it down."

"And I," said Brandt, "do not drink."

"But all of us smoked, presumably."

"I do not smoke," said Brandt.

"But you were in a room where other people were doing just that," Grimes went on. "You were inhaling the fumes whether you wanted to or not."

"I think you've the answer, Captain," said Rath. "I wish I'd thought to bring a cigar stub aboard so I could analyze it."

"And we all feel fine this morning," said Grimes. "Even so, I want none of those cigars aboard the ship."

"Not even for analysis?" demanded the two doctors simultaneously.

"Oh, all right. Analyze if you must—although no doubt a complete analysis of the weed will be made available to you if you ask in the right quarters. Our hosts were just being hospitable, that's all."

"And how," murmured Brabham happily. "And how!"

The mayor came on board late in the forenoon. Grimes asked her about the cigars.

"Oh, we don't smoke 'em all day an' every day," she told him, "though there are some as'd like to. We regard 'em as hair-let-downers, as leg-openers. An' no party'd be a party without 'em."

You can say that again, thought Grimes. In the broad light of day, with nothing, not even alcohol, to blunt his sensibilities, Mavis no longer seemed quite so attractive. Her accent again jarred on his ear, and he didn't really like *big* women; Vinegar Nell was far more to his taste. Nonetheless, he did not regret what had happened the previous night and hoped that it would happen again. He was sorry about the paymaster, though; it must have been galling for her to witness a man whom she regarded as her own property making love to somebody else. But whose fault was that? If she had waited for him instead of wandering off with the highly unsatisfactory Col—

He said, "You've a good export there. Are they made from a native plant?"

"No, Skip. They first comers brought terbaccer wif 'em. Musta mutated like a bastard, or somethin'. An' now, I've a full day for yer. To begin wif, an official lunch wif all the mayors o' the planet, followed by a Mayors' Council. An' you'll be sayin' yer piece at the meetin'. About wot

you were tellin' me last night about the Empire o' Waverley
an' the Federation an' all the rest of it."

What did *I* say? Grimes asked himself. But he remembered
all too well. He had been hoping that she would have forgotten.

CHAPTER 30

Botany Bay was a good world, but speedily Grimes came to the conclusion that the sooner *Discovery* lifted from its surface and headed for Lindisfarne Base the better. She had never been and never would be a taut ship—and, in any case, Grimes hated that expression—but now standards of efficiency and discipline were falling to a deplorably low level. Rank meant nothing to the people of Botany Bay. In their own ships—air and surface—the captain was, of course, still the captain, but every crew member was entitled to officer status, an inevitable consequence of automation. Their attitude was rubbing off on to the ratings, petty officers, and junior officers of the spaceship.

Grimes set a date for departure. In the four weeks that this gave him he was able to make quite a good survey of the planet, using *Discovery*'s pinnace instead of one of the local aircraft. The mayors of the city-states cooperated fully, as did the universities of the state capitals. Loaded aboard the survey ship were microfilmed copies of the history of the colony from its first beginnings, from several viewpoints, as well as samples of its various arts from the first beginnings to the present time. There were the standard works on zoology, botany, and geology, as well as such specimens as could safely be carried. (The box of local cigars Grimes locked in his safe, of which only he knew the combination.) There were manuals of airmanship and seamanship. There was all the literature covering local industry. Mavis—who was no fool—insisted on taking out Galactic Patents on their contents after discovering, by shrewd questioning, that the captain of a survey vessel can function as a patents office director in exceptional circumstances.

It was, however, by no means a case of all-work-and-no-play. Grimes went to his share of parties. At most of them

158

he partook of what Mavis referred to as hair-let-downers, the cigars made from the leaves of the mutated tobacco. He had been assured by Dr. Rath that they were not habit-forming and no ill results would ensue from his smoking them. Usually his partner at such affairs was the mayor of Paddington, but there were others. On one occasion he found himself strongly attracted to Vinegar Nell—but she, even though she was smoking herself, rejected him and wandered away with the City Constable. Grimes shrugged it off. After all, as he had discovered, she wasn't the only fish in the sea, and on his return to Lindisfarne Base he would, he hoped, be able to resume where he had left off with Maggie Lazenby.

Brandt wanted to stay on Botany Bay, but expressed misgivings about the amount of time he would have to wait until contact with the Federation was established. Grimes told the scientist of the simple code that he had agreed upon with Captain Davinas. He said, "With any luck at all, *Sundowner* should drop in almost as soon as I've shoved off. As the sole representative of the Federation on this planet you'll be empowered to make your own deal with Davinas. And Davinas, of course, will be making *his* own deals with the Council of Mayors. I've told Mavis to expect him."

"It all *seems* foolproof enough, Commander Grimes," admitted Brandt.

"You can make anything foolproof, but it's hard to make it bloody foolproof," Grimes told him cheerfully. "All the same, neither Davinas nor myself come in that category."

"So you say," grumbled Brandt. Yet it was obvious that he was pleased to be able to get off the ship for an indefinite period. Grimes suspected that a romance had blossomed between him and a not very young, rather plain professor of physics at Paddington University. Quite possibly he would decide to resign his commission in the Survey Service and live on Botany Bay. There were quite a few others, Grimes knew, who had the same idea. That was why he wanted to get spaceborne before the rot set in properly.

Then there was the farewell party—the last, in fact, of a series of farewell parties. It was a beach barbecue. (The colonists *loved* beach barbecues.) It was a huge affair, with no fewer than a dozen fires going, held on the beach of Manly Cove, one of the bigger bays on the north coast but still within easy reach of the city. All hands were there, with the exception of the unlucky watchkeepers. The beer and the wine flowed freely and everybody was smoking the mutated tobacco. Grimes stayed with Mavis. He might see her again; he most probably would not. He wanted to make the most of this last evening. They found a lonely spot, a small floor of smooth sand among the rocks.

She said, "I shall miss yer, Skip."

"And I you."

"But when yer gotter go, yer gotter go. That's the way of it, ain't it?"

"Too right it is. Unluckily."

"Yer boys don't wanter go. Nor yer sheilas."

"There is such a thing as duty, you know."

"Duty be buggered. Ships have vanished without trace, as yer know bloody well. No one knows yer here."

"They'd soon guess. If there were any sort of flap about *Discovery*'s going missing, then Captain Davinas—the master of *Sundowner* I was telling you about—would soon spill his beans. And the Survey Service can be very vicious regarding the penalty of mutiny and similar crimes. I've no desire to be pushed out of the airlock, in Deep Space without a spacesuit."

"You mean they'd do *that* to yer?"

"Too bloody right, they would."

"An' I'm not worth takin' the risk for. But you sort of *explode* in a vacuum, don't yer? All right. I see yer point."

"I didn't think that there was enough light," said Grimes, looking down at her dimly visible nudity.

She laughed. "I didn't mean *that*. But seein' as how the subject has risen. For the third time, ain't it?"

"Third time lucky," murmured Grimes.

Liftoff had been set for 1200 hours the following day. As on the day of landing the stands were crowded, and the brave, blue flags were flying from every pole. Two of the big dirigibles cruised slowly in a circle above the Oval. Their captains would extend the radius before *Discovery* began to lift.

There were no absentees from the ship at departure time, although it was certain that many of her complement would have liked to have missed their passage. Grimes was the last man up the ramp. At the foot of the gangway he shook hands with Brandt, with the mayors of the city-states.

He had intended that his farewell to Mavis would be no more than a formal handshake, but her intentions were otherwise. He felt her mouth on his for the last time. When he pulled away he saw a tear glistening in the corner of her eye.

He marched stiffly up the ramp, which retracted as soon as he was in the airlock. He rode the elevator up to control. In the control room he went to his chair, strapped himself in. He looked at the telltale lights on his console. Everything was ready. His hand went out to the inertial drive start button.

Discovery growled, shook herself. (*Growl you may, but go you must!*) She shuddered, and from below came the unrhythmic rattle of loose fittings. She heaved herself off the grass. In the periscope screen Grimes could see a great circular patch of dead growth to mark where she had stood, with three deep indentations where the vanes had dug into the sod. He wondered, briefly when it would be possible to play a cricket match in the Oval again.

"Port Paddington to *Discovery*," came a voice from the speaker of the NST transceiver, "you know where we live now. Come back as soon as yer·like. Over."

"Thank you," said Grimes. "I hope I shall be back."

"Look after yourself, Skip!" It was Mavis' voice.

"I'll try," he told her. "And you look after *your*self."

She had the sense to realize that Grimes would be, from now on, fully occupied with his pilotage. But is was an easy ascent. There was little wind at any level, no turbulence. The old ship, once she had torn herself clear from the surface, seemed glad to be heading back into her natural element. After not very long, with trajectory set for Lindisfarne Base, Grimes was free to go below.

In his cabin he got out a message pad. He wrote: *Davinas, d/s/s Sundowner. Happy Anniversary. John.* He took it down to the radio officer on duty. He said, "I'd like this away as soon as possible. It might just catch him in time. On Botany Bay I rather lost track of the Standard Date."

"Didn't we all, sir?" The young man yawned. No doubt he had a good excuse for being tired, but his manner was little short of insolent. "Through the Carlotti station on Elsinore, sir?"

"Yes. A single transmission. I don't want the emperor's monitors getting a fix on us. Elsinore will relay it."

"As you say, sir."

The tiny Carlotti antenna, the rotating Moebius strip, synchronized with the main antenna now extruded from the hull, began to turn and hunt. Elsinore would receive the signal, over the light-years, almost instantaneously. How long would it be before Davinas got it, and where would he be? How long would it be before *Sundowner* made her landing on Botany Bay? How long would Brandt have to wait? Grimes found that he was envying the scientist.

He debated with himself whether or not to drop in on Flannery, but decided against it. The PCO had found no fellow telepaths, but he had found quite a few boozing pals. No doubt the man would be suffering from a monumental hangover.

He went up to his quarters. He started to think about writing his report. Then he thought about his first report, the one in which he had damned Swinton. Should he rewrite it? The Mad Major had been very well behaved on Botany Bay. People like him should smoke those cigars all the time. *Make love, not war*

Grimes decided to sleep on it. After all, it would be some days before the ship would be in a sector of space from which it would be safe to inform Lindisfarne Base of her whereabouts, and even then a long and detailed report of her activities would almost certainly be picked up and decoded by the Waverley monitors. It could wait until *Discovery* was back at Lindisfarne.

By the Standard Time kept by the ship it was late at night. And Grimes was tired. He turned in, and slept soundly.

CHAPTER 31

Discovery was not a happy ship.

All hands went about their duties sullenly, with a complete lack of enthusiasm. Grimes could understand why. They had been made too much of on Botany Bay. It had been the sort of planet that spacemen dream about, but rarely visit. It had been a world that made the truth of Dr. Johnson's famous dictum all too true. How did it go? *A ship is like a prison where you stand a good chance of getting drowned. . . .* Something like that, Grimes told himself. And though the chances of getting drowned while serving in a spaceship were rather remote there were much worse ways of making one's exit if things went badly wrong.

He went down to the farm deck to have a yarn with Flannery. The PCO had recovered slightly from his excesses but, as usual, was in the process of taking several hairs of the dog that had bitten him. The bottle, Grimes noted, contained rum, distilled on Botany Bay.

"Oh, t'is you, Skipper. Could I persuade ye? No? I was hopin' ye'd be takin' a drop with me. I have to finish this rotgut afore I can get back to me own tipple."

"So you enjoyed yourself on Botany Bay," remarked Grimes.

"An' didn't we all, each in his own way? But the good times are all gone, an' we have to travel on."

"That seems to be the general attitude, Mr. Flannery."

"Yours included, Skipper. Howiver did ye manage to make yer own flight from the mayor's nest?"

"Mphm."

"Iverybody had the time of his life but poor ould Ned." Flannery gestured toward the canine brain suspended in its sphere of murky nutrient fluid. "He'd've loved to have been

163

out, in a body, runnin' over the green grass of a world so
like his own native land."

"I didn't think the dingo ever did much running over
green grass," remarked Grimes sourly. "Through the bush,
over the desert, yes. But green grass, no."

"Ye know what I'm meanin'." Flannery suddenly became
serious. "What are ye wantin' from me, Skipper?" *It always
used to be "Captain,"* thought Grimes. *Flannery's been tainted
by Botany Bay as much as anybody else.* "Don't tell me. I
know. Ye're wonderin' how things are in this rustbucket. I
don't snoop on me shipmates, as well ye know. But I can
give ye some advice, if ye'll only listen. Ride with a loose
rein. Don't go puttin' yer foot down with a firm hand. An' it
might help if ye let it be known that ye're not bringin'
charges against the Mad Major when we're back on
Lindisfarne. Oh—an' ye could try bein' nice to Vinegar
Nell."

"Is that all?" asked Grimes coldly.

"That's all, Skipper. If it's any consolation to ye, Ned
still likes ye. He's hopin' that ye don't go makin' the same
mistake as Grimes was always afther makin'."

"*Grimes?*" asked Grimes bewilderedly.

"T'was Bligh I was meanin'."

"Damn Bligh!" swore Grimes. "This ship isn't HMS
Bounty. This, in case you haven't noticed, is FSS *Discovery*,
with communications equipment that can reach out across
the galaxy. *Bounty* only had signal flags."

"Ye asked me, Skipper, an' I told ye." Flannery's manner was deliberately offhand. "Would there be anythin'
else?"

"No!" snapped Grimes.

He went up to the main radio office, had a few words
with the operator on duty. He was told there was very little
traffic, and all of it signals from extremely distant stations
and none of it concerning *Discovery*. He carried on to the
control room, stared out through the viewports at the
weirdly distorted universe observed from a ship running
under Mannschenn Drive, tactfully turning his back while
the officer of the watch hastily erased the three-dimensional
ticktacktoe lattice from the plotting tank. *Ride with a loose
rein,* Flannery had warned. He would do so. He looked at
the arrays of telltale lights. All seemed to be in order.

He went down to the paymaster's office. Vinegar Nell

was there, diligently filling in forms in quintuplicate. He tried to be nice to her, but she had no time for him. "Can't you see that I'm busy, Commander Grimes?" she asked coldly. "All this work was neglected while we were on Botany Bay." She contrived to imply that this was Grimes's fault.

Then Grimes, as he sometimes did, called in to the wardroom to have morning coffee with his officers. Their manner toward him was reserved, chilly. *We were having a good time,* their attitude implied, *and this old bastard had to drag us away from it.*

So went the day. There was something going on—of that he was sure. He was, once again, the outsider, the intruder into this micro-society, resented by all. And there was nothing he could do about it. (And if there were, should he do it?)

He was a man of regular habits. In space he required that he be called, by his steward, with a pot of morning coffee at precisely 0700 hours. This gave him an hour to make his leisurely toilet and to get dressed before breakfast. During this time he would listen to a program of music, selected the previous night, from his little playmaster. It was the steward's duty to switch this on as soon as he entered the daycabin.

He awakened, this morning (as he always did) to the strains of music. *Odd,* he thought. He could not recall having put that particular tape into the machine. It was a sentimental song which, nonetheless, he had always liked—but it was not, somehow, the sort of melody to start the day with.

> *Spaceman, the stars are calling,*
> *Spaceman, you have to roam,*
> *Spaceman, through light-years falling,*
> *Remember I wait at home. . . .*

He heard Mullins come into the bedroom, the faint rattle of the coffee things on the tray. He smelled something. *Was the man smoking?* He jerked into wakefulness, his eyes wide open. It was not Mullins. It was the girl, Sally, who had been his predecessor's servant. She was not in uniform. She was wearing something diaphanous that concealed nothing and accentuated plenty. One of the thin cigars dangled from a corner of her full mouth. She took it out. "Here you are, Skipper. Have a drag. It'll put you in the mood."

Grimes slapped the smoldering cylinder away from his face. "In the mood for what?" he snapped.

"You mean to say that you don't know? Not after your carryings-on with the fat cow on Botany Bay, to say nothing of that scrawny bitch of a paymaster . . . ?" She let her robe drop open. "Look at me, Skipper. I'm better than both of 'em, aren't I?"

"Get out of here!" ordered Grimes. "I'll see you later."

"You can see me now, Skipper." Her robe had fallen from her. "Take a good look—an' then try to tell me that you don't like what you see!"

Grimes did like it; that was the trouble. The girl had an excellent figure, although a little on the plump side. He thought of getting on to his telephone to demand the immediate presence of both Vinegar Nell and Brabham, then decided against it. Both of them would be quite capable of putting the worst possible construction on the situation. On the other hand, he had no intention of letting things go too far.

Decisively he threw aside the covers, jumped out of the bed. The girl opened her arms, smiling suggestively. He said, "Not yet, Sally. I always like a shower first."

She said, "I'll wash your back, Skipper."

"Good."

He pushed her into the shower cubicle before she could change her mind. And would it work? he wondered. On Botany Bay a swim in the warm sea had led to no diminishment of the effects of the smoke of the mutated tobacco— but the sea had always been warm. The shower would not be. When Grimes turned on the water he made sure that she did not see the setting. She screamed when the icy torrent hit her warm skin. Grimes felt like screaming too. He was not and never had been a cold shower addict. She struggled in his arms, even tried to bring her knee up into his crotch. He thought, as he blocked the attack, *You'd have a job finding anything!*

She squeaked, "Turn on the hot, you stupid bastard!"

He muttered, through chattering teeth, "This is hurting me at least as much as it's hurting you. Now, tell me. What's all this about?"

Her struggles were weaker now. The cold water was draining her of strength. She whispered, "If you turn on the hot, I'll tell you."

"You'll tell me first."

"It—it was just a bet . . . with the other tabbies. An' the hunks. That—that I'd get in with you, same as I was in with Commander Tallis."

"Where did you get the cigar? Out of my safe?"

"I'm not a thief, Skipper. The—the ship's lousy with the things. They'll be worth a helluva lot back on Lindisfarne. You know how people'll pay."

Grimes shook her. "Anything else?"

"No, no. Please, Skipper, please. I'll never be warm again."

Gratefully, Grimes adjusted the shower control. He felt at first as though he were being boiled alive. When he was sufficiently thawed he left the cubicle, with the naked girl still luxuriating in the gloriously hot water. He dressed hastily. He phoned up to the control room, got the officer of the watch. "Mr. Farrell, ring the alarm for boat stations."

"Boat stations, sir? But—"

"There's nothing like a drill at an unexpected time to make sure that all hands are on the ball. Make it boat stations. Now."

There was a delay of about three seconds, then the clangor of alarm bells echoed through the ship, drowning out the irregular beat of the inertial drive, the thin, high whine of the Mannschenn Drive. A taped voice repeated loudly, "All hands to boat stations! All hands to boat stations!"

Sally emerged from the shower cubicle, dripping, her hair plastered to her head. She looked frightened. She snatched up her robe, threw it over her wet body. "Captain, what's wrong?" she cried.

"It's an emergency," Grimes told her. "Get to your station."

In the doorway to the dayroom she almost collided with Brabham on his way in.

"What's going on, sir?" demanded the first lieutenant harshly.

"Sit down," ordered Grimes. He waited until he was sure that Sally was out of earshot. Then he said, "I gave orders, Commander Brabham, that none of that mutated tobacco, in any form, was to be brought aboard the ship."

"You were smoking enough of it yourself on Botany Bay, Captain."

"I was. In those circumstances it was quite harmless."

"It will be quite harmless at parties back at Lindisfarne Base, Captain."

"So you're in it, too."

"I didn't say so, sir."

Grimes snarled. "Did you consider the effects of smoking the muck aboard this ship, with the sexes in such gross disproportion?"

"Nobody would be so stupid—"

"You passed that stewardess on her way out when you came in. She's one of the stupid ones. And now, with all hands at their stations, you and I are going to make a search of the accommodation."

"If that's the way you want it. Sir."

They started in the officers' flat, in Brabham's cabin. The first drawer that Grimes pulled out was full of neatly packed boxes. And the second.

"You're pretty blatant about this, Number One," remarked Grimes.

"I hardly expected that the captain would be pawing through my personal possessions with his own fair hands. Sir."

"Not only me."

"Lindisfarne Base is not a commercial spaceport. Sir. There are no customs."

"But the dockyard police exercise the same function," snapped Grimes. But he knew, as well as Brabham did, that those same dockyard police would turn a blind eye to anything as long as they, personally, profited.

All the officers, Grimes discovered, had disobeyed his orders, working on the good old principle of *What he doesn't know won't bother him.* Now he did know. Using his master key he went down through compartment after airtight compartment. Stewards and stewardesses . . . petty officers . . . Marines . . . general purpose ratings . . . it was even worse than he had thought. In the catering staff's general room he found butts in the ashtrays. They must, he thought, have enjoyed quite a nice little orgy last night—and he had been pulled in at the tail end of it.

He and a sullen Brabham rode the elevator up to the

control room. Grimes went at once to the intercom microphone. He said harshly, "Attention, all hands. This is the captain speaking. It has come to my attention that large quantities of Botany Bay tobacco are being carried aboard this ship. All—I repeat *all*—stocks of this drug are to be taken to the after airlock, from which they will be dumped."

"You can't do that, Captain!" expostulated Brabham.

"I am doing it, mister."

"But it's private property."

"And this ship is the property of the Federation Survey Service. We are all the property of the Service, and are bound to abide by its regulations. See that my orders are carried out, Commander Brabham."

"But—"

"Jump to it!"

"You'll do the jumping, Commander Grimes!" It was Swinton who spoke. He had entered the control room unnoticed. He was carrying a twenty-millimeter projectile pistol, a nasty weapon designed for use inside a ship, its slug heavy and relatively slow moving, incapable of penetrating the shell plating or bulkheads of a ship. But it would make a very nasty mess of a human body.

"Swinton! Put that thing down!"

"Are you going to try to make me, Commander Grimes?"

Grimes looked at Brabham and the watch officer. Brabham said, "We're all in this, Captain. Almost all of us, that is. This business of the cigars pushed us past the point of no return."

"Mutiny?" asked Grimes quietly.

"Yes. Mutiny. We owe the Survey Service nothing. From now on we're looking after ourselves."

"You must be mad," Grimes told him. "The moment Lindisfarne gets word of this there'll be a fleet out after you."

"The Sparkses are with us," said Swinton. "There'll be no word sent out on Carlotti radio. As for that drunken bum Flannery—the first thing I did was to smash that dog's brain in aspic of his. Without his amplifier he's powerless."

"He'll never forgive you," said Grimes.

"The least of my worries," sneered Swinton.

"And just what do you intend to do?" Grimes asked quietly. If he could keep them talking there was a chance, a faint chance, that he might be able to grab that weapon.

"Return to Botany Bay of course," said Brabham.

"You bloody fool!" snarled Swinton.

"Why?" asked the first lieutenant calmly. "Dead men tell no tales."

"And even Botany Bay has laws and policemen," remarked Grimes.

"Do you think we haven't thought of that?" Brabham demanded. "We intend to loaf around a bit, and make our return to Botany Bay after an interval that should correspond roughly to the time taken by a voyage to Lindisfarne and back. Our story will be that you were relieved of your command on return to Base and that I was promoted."

"You'll have to do better than that," said Grimes. "You'll have Brandt to convince as well as the colonists."

"Oh, we'll polish our story until it gleams while we're cruising. We'll make it all as watertight as a duck's down."

"Down to the airlock!" ordered Swinton, gesturing with his pistol.

"Better do as the major says," came a deep voice from behind Grimes.

He turned. Sergeant Washington had come into the control room, and two other Marines with him. They were all armed.

So, he thought, this was it. This was the end of the penny section. His famous luck had at last deserted him. In any ship but this one there would be a fair number of loyalists—but whom could he count on in *Discovery*? Poor, drunken, useless Flannery, his one weapon, his ability to throw his thoughts across the light-years, destroyed with the killing to his psionic amplifier? Perhaps he was dead himself. He had never been popular with his shipmates. Dr. Rath, perhaps —but what could he do? Plenty, maybe—but nothing in time to save Grimes. And who else?

He tensed himself to spring at Swinton, to wrest the pistol from his grasp before it could be fired. Perhaps. It would be suicidal—but quicker and less painful than a spacewalk without a suit. Or would it be? He realized the truth, the bitter truth, of the old adage, *While there's life, there's hope.* Perhaps he hadn't run out of luck. Perhaps something, anything, might happen between this moment and the final moment when, locked in the cell of the airlock chamber, he realized that the air was being evacuated prior to the opening of the outer door.

"All right," he said. "I'm coming."

"You'll soon be going," Brabham quipped grimly.

CHAPTER **32**

There was a crowd by the airlock—Langer, the bos'n; Mullins, who had been Grimes's steward; the little slut Sally; MacMorris and several of his juniors; the radio officers. They made way for Grimes and his escorts, raised an ironic cheer. There were two men already in the chamber, facing the leveled pistols of Swinton's Marines with pitiful defiance. One, surprisingly, was Dr. Rath; the other was Flannery. The PCO was bleeding about the face and one of his eyes was closed. No doubt he had made a vain attempt to save his macabre pet from destruction. The doctor looked, as always, as though he were on his way to a funeral. *And so he is,* thought Grimes with gallows humor. *His own.*

Swinton painfully jabbed Grimes in the small of the back with his pistol. "Inside, you!" he snarled. Grimes tried hard to think of some fitting, cutting retort, but could not. Probably he would when it was too late, when there was no air left in his lungs to speak with.

"Inside, bastard!"

That pistol muzzle hurt. With what little dignity he could muster Grimes joined the two loyalists, then turned to face his tormentors. He said, reasonably, "I don't know why you hate me so much."

"Because you've achieved everything that we haven't," growled Brabham. "*Lucky* Grimes. But throughout your service career you've committed all the crimes that *we* have, and got away with them, while our promotions have been blocked. You're no better than us. Just luckier, that's all. I've always prayed that I'd be around when your luck finally ran out. It seems that the Odd Gods of the Galaxy have seen fit to answer my prayers." He turned to MacMorris. "Chief, what about shutting down the time-twister? We can't make any changes in the mass of the ship with the Mannschenn Drive running."

So you thought of that, commented Grimes to himself. *A pity.*

Suddenly there was a commotion at the rear of the crowd. Vinegar Nell, followed by Tangye, was forcing her way through, using her sharp elbows vigorously. *So she wants to be in at the kill,* thought Grimes bitterly.

She demanded, "What do you think you're doing?"

"What does it look like?" asked Brabham.

She snapped, "I'll not stand for murder!"

"Now, isn't that just too bad?" drawled Swinton. "Perhaps you'd like to take a little spacewalk yourself. Just as a personal favor we'll let you do it in your birthday suit."

One of the Marines put an eager hand out to the neck of her shirt. She slapped it away, glared at the man. "Keep your filthy paws off me, you ape!" Then, to Swinton and Brabham, "You can't touch *me!*"

"Why not?" demanded the major.

"Try to use your brains—if you have any. How many people aboard this ship are trained as ecologists?" She pointed at Dr. Rath. "You're about to dispose of one of them. And that leaves me. Without me to take care of the environment you'd all be poisoned or asphyxiated long before you got back to Botany Bay." She added nastily, "And *with* me you could still meet the same fate if I had good reason not to feel happy."

Swinton laughed. "I think, Miss Russell, that I could persuade you to cooperate. After all, such persuasion is part of *my* training."

"Hold on," put in Brabham. After all he, with all his faults, was a competent spaceman, was keenly aware that the blunder, intentional or otherwise, of one key technician can destroy a ship. He asked the paymaster, "What proposals do you have regarding the disposition of the . . . er . . . prisoners? You realize that we can't take them back to Botany Bay. Not when Grimes and that fat cow of a mayor are eating out of each other's hands."

"Mr. Tangye will tell you," she said.

"We'll set them adrift in a boat," stated the navigating officer.

"Are you quite mad, Tangye?" demanded Brabham.

"No, I'm not. We're in no great hurry, are we? We have

time on our hands, time to waste. It'll be less than an hour's work to remove the Carlotti transceiver and the mini-Mann-schenn from whichever boat we're letting them have."

"*And* the inertial drive," added Brabham thoughtfully.

"Hardly necessary. How far will they get, even at maximum acceleration, even with a long lifetime to do it in, on inertial drive only?"

"You've forgotten about Flannery," objected Swinton.

"We haven't," Vinegar Nell assured him. "Without his horrid amplifier he couldn't think his way out of a paper bag."

"Murder," admitted Brabham suddenly, "has never been my cup of tea."

"Or mutiny?" asked Grimes hopefully, but everybody ignored him.

"It has mine," asserted Swinton, far too cheerfully.

"I say, give the skipper an' his pals a chance!" shouted Sally.

"I second that," grunted Langer.

And what sort of chance will it be? wondered Grimes. *A life sentence, instead of a death sentence. A life sentence, locked for years in a cell, with absolutely no chance of escape. And in company certainly not of my choosing.* He had, not so long ago, made a long boat voyage with an attractive girl as his only companion. It had started well, but had finished with himself and the wench hating each other's guts.

He said, "Thank you, Miss Russell. And Mr. Tangye. I appreciate your efforts on my behalf. But I think I'd prefer the spacewalk."

Swinton laughed, although it sounded more like a snarl. "So there is such a thing as a fate worse than death, after all. All right, Brabham, you'd better start getting one of the boats ready for the long passage. The long, long passage. Meanwhile, this airlock will do for a holding cell."

The inner door sighed shut, sealing off the prisoners from the mutineers.

"You might have warned me!" Grimes said bitterly to Flannery.

The telepath looked at him mournfully from his one good eye. "I did so, Captain. Ride with a loose rein, I told ye. Don't go puttin' yer foot down with a firm hand. An' don't go makin' the same mistakes as Bligh did. With him it was a squabble over coconuts or some such the first time, an' rum the last time. With you it was cigars. I did so warn ye. I was a-goin' to warn ye again, but it all flared up sudden like. An' I had me poor hands full tryin' to save Ned."

"I hope," said Grimes, "that you now appreciate the folly of trying to run with the fox and hunt with the hounds." He turned to Rath. "And what brings you into this galley, Doctor?"

"I have my standards, Captain," replied the medical officer stiffly.

"Mphm. Then don't you think you'd better do something about Mr. Flannery? He seems in rather bad shape."

"It's only superficial damage," said Rath briskly. "It can wait until we're in the boat. The medicine chests in all the lifecraft are well stocked. I saw to that myself."

"That's a comfort," said Grimes. "I suppose that you'll do your damnedest to keep us all alive for the maximum time."

"Of course. And when the boat *is* picked up—I presume that it will be eventually—my notes and journal will be of great value to the medical authorities of that future time. My journal may well become one of the standard works on space medicine."

"What a pity," sneered Grimes, "that you won't be around to collect the royalties."

The doctor assumed a dignity that made Grimes ashamed of his sarcasm, but said nothing further. And Flannery, who had long since lost any interest in the conversation of his companions, was huddled up on the deck and muttering, "Ned—Ned . . . what did they have to do that to ye for? The only livin' bein' in this accursed ship who never hurt anybody."

CHAPTER 33

In little more than an hour's time the inner airlock door opened. During this period Grimes and Rath had talked things over, had decided that there was nothing at all that they could do. Flannery refused to be stirred from his grief-ridden apathy, muttering only, "Too much hate runnin' loose in this ship . . . too much hate . . . an' it's all come to the top, all at once, like some filthy bubble."

The inner airlock door opened, and Swinton stood there, backed by Sergeant Washington and six of his men. All were armed, and all were trained in the use of arms. They said nothing, merely gestured with their pistols. Grimes and his companions said nothing either; what was there to say? They walked slowly out of the chamber, and were hustled onto the spiral staircase running up and around the axial shaft. In the cramped confines of the elevator cage, Grimes realized, it would have been possible—although not probable—for weapons to be seized and turned upon their owners.

Grimes slowly climbed the staircase, with Rath behind him, and Flannery bringing up the dejected rear. Behind them were the Marines. They came at last to one of the after boat bays. The boat was ready for them. The mini-Mannschenn unit and the Carlotti transceiver, each removed in its entirety, were standing on the deck well clear of the airlock hatch.

Brabham was there, and Tangye, and Vinegar Nell, with other officers and ratings. Grimes tried to read the expressions on their faces. There were flickers of doubt, perhaps, and a growing realization of the enormity of their crime—but also an unwavering resolution. After all, it would be many, many years (if ever) before the Admiralty learned that there had been a mutiny. Or would it be? Grimes suddenly remembered what he should have remembered before—that

Captain Davinas, in his *Sundowner*, would, provided that his owners were agreeable, soon be dropping down on Botany Bay. But what could Davinas do? He commanded an unarmed ship with a small crew. The mutineers would see to it that Davinas and his people did not survive long enough to tell any sort of tale. But if he told Swinton and Brabham about his coded message to the tramp captain, then *Sundowner*'s fate would surely be sealed. If he kept his knowledge to himself there was just a chance, a faint chance, that Davinas would be able to punch out some sort of distress message before being silenced.

"The carriage waits, my lord," announced Swinton sardonically.

"So I see," replied Grimes mildly.

"Then get in the bloody thing!" snarled the Mad Major.

Flannery was first through the little airlock. Then Rath. Grimes was about to follow, when Vinegar Nell put out a hand to stop him. With the other she thrust at him what she had been carrying—his favorite pipe, a large tin of tobacco. Grimes accepted the gift. "Thank you," he said simply. "Think nothing of it," she replied. Her face was expressionless.

"Very touching," sneered Swinton. Then, to one of his men, "Take that stinking rubbish away from him!"

"Let him keep it," said Vinegar Nell. "Don't forget, Major, that you have to keep me happy."

"She's right," concurred Brabham, adding, in a whisper, *"The bitch!"*

"All right. Inside, Grimes, and take your baby's comforter with you. You can button up the boat if you feel like it. But it's all one to me if you don't."

Grimes obeyed, clambering into and through the little airlock. He thought briefly of starting the inertial drive at once and slamming out through the hull before the door could be opened. It would be suicide—but all those in the boat bay would die with him. But—of course—the small hydrogen fusion power unit had not yet been actuated, and there would be no power for any of the boat's machinery until it was. The fuel cells supplied current—but that was sufficient only for closing the airlock doors and then, eventually, for starting the fusion process. So he went to the forward cabin, sat in the pilot's seat, strapped himself in. He told the others to secure themselves. He sealed the airlock.

The needle of the external pressure gauge flickered, then turned rapidly anti-clockwise to zero. So the boat bay was now clear of people and its atmosphere pumped back into the ship. Yet the noise of *Discovery*'s propulsive machinery was still audible, transmitted into the boat through the metal of the cradle on which it was resting. The high, thin note of the Mannschenn Drive faded, however, dying, dying—and with the shutting down of the temporal precession field came the uncanny disorientation in time and space. Grimes, looking at his reflection in the polished transparency of the forward viewscreen, saw briefly an image of himself, much older and wearing a uniform with strange insignia.

The boat bay doors opened. Beyond them was the interstellar night, bright with a myriad stars and hazy drifts of cosmic dust. *Any moment now*, thought Grimes—but the shock of the firing of the catapult took him unawares, pressing him deep into the padding of his seat. When he had recovered, the first thing to be done was the starting of the fusion power unit, without which the life-support systems would not function. And those same life-support systems, cycling and recycling all wastes, using sewage as nutriment for the specialized algae, would go on working long beyond the normal lifetimes of the three men in the boat.

But Grimes, somehow and suddenly, was not worried by this dismal prospect.

He said, "All right, now let's get ourselves organized. I intend to proceed at a low quarter gravity, just enough for comfort. You, Doctor, can patch Flannery up."

"In his condition, Captain, I'd better keep him under heavy sedation for a while."

"You will not. As for you, Mr. Flannery, I want you to listen as you've never listened before in your misspent life."

"But there's no traffic at all, at all, in this sector o' space, Skipper."

"For a start, you can keep me informed as to how things are aboard *Discovery*, while you can still pick up her psionic broadcasts. It won't surprise me a bit if there are one or two mutinies yet to come. But, mainly, you keep your psionic ears skinned for *Sundowner*."

"*Sundowner*?" demanded Rath. "What would she be doing out here?"

"You'll be surprised," said Grimes. He thought, *I hope you will.*

CHAPTER 34

A ship's boat is not the ideal craft in which to make a long voyage. Even when it is not loaded to capacity with survivors there is an inevitable lack of privacy. Its life-support systems are not designed for the production of gourmet food, although there is a continuous flow of scientifically balanced nutriment. Grimes—who, after a couple of disastrous experiments by Dr. Rath, had appointed himself cook—did his best to make the processed algae palatable, using sparingly (he did not know how long he would have to make them last) the synthetic flavorings he found in a locker in the tiny galley. But always at the back of his mind—and at the backs of the minds of his two companions—was the off-putting knowledge that the vegetable matter from the tanks had been nourished directly by human wastes.

The main trouble, however, was not the food, but the company. Rath had no conversation. Flannery, at the slightest excuse, would wax maudlin over the death of Ned, his hapless psionic amplifier. Lacking this aid to telepathic communication, and with nobody aboard *Discovery* a strong natural transmitter, he was not able for long to keep Grimes informed as to what was going on aboard the ship. It was learned, however, that Brabham and Swinton were not on the best of terms, each thinking that he should be captain. And Sally had been the victim of a gang rape—which, said Flannery, grinning lubriciously, she had enjoyed at the beginning but not at all toward the finish. And Vinegar Nell had taken up with Brabham. Grimes, puffing at his vile pipe, felt some sympathy for her. The only way that she stood a chance of escaping Sally's fate was by becoming the woman of one of the leaders of the mutiny.

And then *Discovery*, as the distance between her and the boat rapidly increased, faded from Flannery's ken. It was at

179

this time that the three men became acutely conscious of their utter loneliness, the frightening awareness that they were in a frail metal and plastic bubble crawling, at a pitiful one quarter G acceleration, across the empty immensities between the uncaring stars. They were on a voyage from nowhere to nowhere—and unless Davinas happened along it would take a lifetime.

The days passed. The weeks passed—and Grimes was beginning to face the sickening realization that his famous luck had indeed run out. And yet, he knew, he had to hang on. As long as Rath and Flannery wanted to go on living (what for?) he was responsible for them. He was captain here, just as he had been captain of *Discovery*. He was in charge, and he would stay in charge. He hoped.

One evening—according to the boat's chronometer—he and Rath were playing a desultory game of chess. Flannery was watching without much interest. Suddenly the telepath stiffened. He whispered, vocalizing what he was hearing in his mind, "Two no trumps."

"We are playing chess, not bridge!" snapped Rath irritably.

"Quiet!" warned Grimes.

"I wish I could tell Jim what I have in my hand," murmured Flannery, almost inaudibly. "But I have to observe the code. But surely he knows he can afford to bid three over Bill's two hearts."

"Farley?" asked Grimes in a low, intent voice.

"Farley," agreed Flannery.

"*Farley?*" demanded Rath.

"He *was* PCO of *Sundowner*," Grimes told him. "When *Sundowner*'s owners had her fitted with Carlotti equipment he became redundant. But he qualified as a Carlotti operator, and stayed in the ship."

"He was a traitor to our cloth, so he was," muttered Flannery. "An' he knows it. When I met him, on New Maine, he told me that he was bitter ashamed o' goin' over to the enemy. He said that he envied me, he did, an' that he'd sell his blessed soul to be in my place, with a sweet amplifier like Ned as a true companion. But we didn't know then what was goin' to happen to Ned, lyin' all broken on the cruel hard deck, wi' the murtherin' bastard Swinton's boot a-crashin' into his soft, naked tissues."

"*Damn Ned!*" swore Grimes, shocking the telepath out of his self-induced misery. "Forget about that bloody dingo and get on with the job! Concentrate on getting a message through to Farley. *Sundowner* can't be far off if you can pick up his random thoughts."

"I am so concentratin'," said Flannery, with injured dignity. "But ye'll have to help."

"How? I'm no telepath."

"But ye have to be me amplifier. The blessed God an' all His saints know that ye're no Ned, nor ever will be, but ye have to do. Give me a . . . a carrier wave. Ye saw the ship. Ye were aboard her. You got the *feel* of her. Now, concentrate. Hard. Visualize the ould bitch, how she was lookin' when she was sittin' on her pad, how she was, inside, when ye were suppin' yer drinks with the man Davinas."

Grimes concentrated, making almost a physical effort of it. He formed in his mind a picture of the shabby star tramp as he had first seen her, at her loading berth in the New Maine commercial spaceport. He recalled his conversation with Captain Davinas in the master's comfortable dayroom. And then he could not help recalling the later events of that night, back aboard his own ship, when Vinegar Nell had offered herself to him on a silver tray, trimmed with parsley.

"Forget that bitch!" growled Flannery. "Bad cess to her, wherever she is, whatever she's a-doin'." And then, "Farley, come in, damn ye. Farley, t'is yer boozin' pal Flannery here, an' t'is in desperate straits I am. Oh, the man's all wrapped up in his silly game o' cards. He's just gone down, doubled an' redoubled. I'm touchin' him, but not hard enough."

"Drink this," interrupted Rath, thrusting a full tumbler into the telepath's hand. It was, Grimes realized, brandy from the small stock kept in the medicine chest. Flannery took it, downed it in one gulp. The doctor whispered to Grimes, "I should have thought of that before. He's not used to operating in a state of stone-cold sobriety."

"An' t'is right ye are, me good doctor," murmured the telepath. "T'was fuel that the engine o' me brain was needin'. Farley, come in, or be damned to ye. Come in, man, come in. Yes, t'is Flannery here. Ye met me on New Maine. Yes, this is an SOS." He turned to Grimes. "Have ye a position, Captain? No? An' ye're supposed to be a navigator." Then, resuming his intent whisper, "We don't know where we are. There's three of us in a boat—the Old Man, the Quack, an' meself? No mini-Mannschenn, no Carlotti. Ye can home on us, can't ye? Yes, yes, I know ye have no psionic amplifier, but nor have I, now. An' what was that? Oh. Captain Davinas sends his regards to Commander Grimes. I'll pass that on. An' you can tell Captain Davinas that Commander Grimes sends *his* regards. An' tell Captain Davinas, urgently, on no account to break radio silence on his Carlotti. There's a shipload o' mutineers, armed to the teeth, scullin' around in this sector o' space." Then, to the doctor, "Me fuel's runnin' low." Rath got him another glass of brandy. "I'll keep on transmittin', Farley. Just be tellin' your Old Man which way to point his ship, an' ye'll be on to us in two shakes o' the lamb's tail. Good . . . good."

Grimes looked at Rath, and Rath looked at Grimes. A slow smile spread over the doctor's normally glum face. He said, "I really don't think that I could have stood your company much longer, Captain."

"Or I yours, Doctor." He laughed. "And this means goodbye to your prospects of posthumous fame."

"There may be another opportunity," said Rath, still smiling, "but, frankly, I hope not!"

CHAPTER 35

It took longer for Davinas to effect the rescue than had at first been anticipated. Like many merchant ships at that period *Sundowner* was not equipped with a Mass Proximity Indicator, the only form of radar capable of operating in a ship running under Mannschenn Drive. The merchant captain feared that if he were not extremely careful he might break through into the normal continuum in the position occupied by the boat. It is axiomatic that two solid bodies cannot occupy the same space at the same time. Any attempt to make them do so is bound to have catastrophic consequences.

So Davinas, running on Mannschenn Drive, steering as instructed by Farley, kept the boat right ahead—and then, as soon as the ex-PCO reported that the relative bearing was now right astern, shut down his time-twister and his inertial drive, turned the ship, restarted inertial drive and ran back on the reciprocal trajectory, scanning the space ahead with his long-range radar. At last he picked up the tiny spark in his screen, and, after that, it was a matter of a few hours only.

Sundowner's holds were empty; Captain Davinas had persuaded his owners to let him make a special voyage to Botany Bay to make such advantageous arrangements as he could both with the local authorities and whatever scientific staff had been left on the Lost Colony by *Discovery*. It was decided to bring the boat into the ship through one of the cargo ports. This was achieved without any difficulty, Grimes jockeying the little craft in through the circular aperture with ease, and onto the cradle that had been prepared for her. Then, when the atmosphere had been reintroduced into the compartment, he opened his airlock doors. The air of *Sundowner* was better, he decided, than that inside the boat. It carried the taints inevitable in the atmosphere of all space-

183

ships—hot machinery, the smell of cooking, the odor of living humanity—but not in concentrated form.

Gratefully Grimes jumped down from the airlock door to the deck; Davinas had restarted his inertial drive and the ship had resumed acceleration. He was greeted by *Sundowner's* chief officer, still spacesuited but with his helmet visor open. "Good to have you aboard, Commander Grimes."

"And it's good to be aboard."

"The master is waiting for you in the control room, sir. I'll lead the way."

"Thank you."

Grimes and his companions followed the officer to the doorway into the axial shaft. They rode up to control in the elevator. Davinas was waiting in the control room. After the handshakings and the introductions he said, "Now, Commander, I'd like some information from you. With all due respect to your Mr. Flannery and my Mr. Farley, I got a rather confused picture. I *was* proceeding to Botany Bay, as I learn that the Lost Colony is called. At the moment I'm heading nowhere in particular; the inertial drive's on only to give us gravity. Do you want me to set course for the Lost Colony again?"

"No," said Grimes at last. *Discovery,* he knew, would be deliberately wasting time before her return to Botany Bay, and there was quite a good chance that *Sundowner* would get there first. But what could she do? She was not armed, and on the world itself there was a paucity of weaponry. There was no army, only a minimal constabulary. There was no navy, no air force. He had no doubt that the colonists would have no trouble manufacturing weapons, and very effective ones, if given time—but time was what they would not have. And if they tried to arrest the mutineers, knowing them to be criminals, immediately after their landing a massacre would be the result. (Swinton tended to specialize in massacres.)

"I could pile on the lumes," said Davinas.

"No, Captain. This is not a warship, and Botany Bay has nothing in the way of arms beyond a few sporting rifles. I think you'd better take us straight to Lindisfarne Base." He added, seeing the disappointment on the other's face, "You'll not lose by it. Your owners will be in pocket. The cost of your deviation, freight on the boat, passages for myself and Dr. Rath and Mr. Flannery. And I'll do my damnedest to see that you get your charter as a liaison ship as soon as this mess is cleared up."

"I see your point," admitted Davinas at last. "And do you want me to get off a Carlottigram to your bosses on Lindisfarne, reporting the mutiny and all the rest of it?"

"No. I don't have my code books with me, and I've no desire to broadcast to the whole bloody galaxy that the Survey Service has a mutiny on its hands. And I don't want *Discovery* to know that I've been picked up. It's strict radio silence, I'm afraid, until we start talking on NST before we land on Lindisfarne. That's the only safe way."

Davinas agreed, then gave orders to his navigator. That young man, Grimes noted, was far more efficient than Tangye. (But Tangye was one of those to whom he owed his continued existence.) The change of trajectory was carried out with no fuss and bother, and in a very short time *Sundowner* was lined up on the target star. Davinas went down then, asking Grimes to accompany him.

Over drinks Grimes filled Davinas in on all (well, not quite all) that had happened since their last meeting. The tramp captain asked, "And what will happen to your mutineers, John?"

"Plenty," replied Grimes grimly. "There are two crimes of which the Survey Service takes a very dim view—piracy is one, and mutiny is the other. The penalty for both is the same—a spacewalk without a spacesuit."

"Even when there was nobody killed during the mutiny?"

"Even then." Grimes stared thoughtfully at the trickle of smoke issuing from the bowl of his pipe. "Somehow, I wish it weren't so. There's only one man among 'em who's really bad, all the way through. That's Swinton, of course. The others . . . I can sympathize with them. They'd reached the stage, all of them, when they felt that they owed the Service no loyalty."

"Poor, stupid bastards," murmured Davinas. Then, "I thought your paymaster was a very attractive woman. I'd never have thought that she'd have been among the mutineers."

"She stopped me from being pushed out from the airlock," said Grimes.

"And yet she'll still have to pay the same penalty as the others," stated Davinas.

"I suppose so," said Grimes. "I suppose so." He did not like the vision that flickered across his mind, of that slim body bursting in hard vacuum, its erupting fluids immediately frozen.

"There are times," Davinas said, "when I'm glad I'm a merchant spaceman. Being a galactic policeman is no job for the squeamish."

CHAPTER 36

"You will have to face a court-martial, of course," said the admiral coldly.

"Of course, sir," agreed Grimes glumly.

"Not only did you lose your ship, but there was that unfortunate affair on the first world you visited. Yes, yes, I know that fire was opened against your orders—but you, at the time, were captain of *Discovery*."

"I suppose so, sir."

"You suppose! There's no supposition about it. And then"—the old man was warming up nicely—"there's the odd private deal you made with that tramp skipper, Davinas."

"I acted as I thought fit, sir."

"In other words—it seemed a good idea at the time. Hrrmph. All in all, young man, you've made a right royal balls of things. I warned you, before you lifted off in *Discovery*, not to put a foot wrong. I told you, too, that you were expected to lick the ship into shape. You should have known that a crew of misfits, such as those you had under you, would be demoralized by an extended sojourn on a world such as Botany Bay."

"Yes, sir."

"The court-martial will not be convened until your return, however."

"My return, sir?"

"From Botany Bay, of course. You will be proceeding there in the frigate *Vega*, as adviser to Commander Delamere, whose instructions are to apprehend the mutineers and bring them to Lindisfarne for trial."

Delamere, of all people! thought Grimes. He had always hated the man, and Delamere had always hated him. Of

187

Delamere it had been said that he would stand on his mother's grave to get a foot nearer to his objective.

"That is all, Commander," snapped the admiral. "You will remain on Base until sent for."

"Very good, sir."

"Try to reply in a more spacemanlike manner, young man. You're a naval officer—still a naval officer, that is—not a shopwalker."

"Aye, aye, sir."

Grimes saluted with what smartness he could muster, turned and strode out of the admiral's office.

CHAPTER 37

"You're in a mess, John," said Commander Maggie Lazenby soberly. Her fine-featured face, under the glossy auburn hair, was serious.

"A blinding glimpse of the obvious," said Grimes.

"This is no laughing matter, you oaf. I've been keeping my ears flapping all day for gossip. And there's plenty. Not everybody in this Base regards you as a little friend to all the universe, my dear. You've enemies—bad ones. You've friends, too—but I doubt if they're numerous or powerful enough. And Frankie Delamere hates you."

"That's no news."

"When you're aboard his ship, don't put a foot wrong."

"I've heard that advice before."

"But it's *good* advice. I tell you, John, that you'll be lucky to keep your rank after the court-martial. Or your commission, even."

"Bligh kept his," said Grimes. "And then he rose to admiral's rank."

"Bligh? Who was he? I can't remember any Admiral Bligh in the Survey Service."

"Never mind," said Grimes. He filled and lit his pipe. "You know, Maggie . . . I've been thinking. Why should I stay in the Service? No matter how the court-martial goes—and I don't see how they can crucify me for Brabham's and Swinton's sins—it looks as though I shall never, now, make the jump from commander to a four-ring captain."

"But you just said that Bligh, whoever he was—"

"All right. Bligh did, and he'd lost his ship because of a mutiny, the same as I've done. I might be as lucky as Bligh— if Bligh ever was lucky, which I doubt. But let's forget him, shall we? The question before the meeting is this: do I resign my commission, and go out to the Rim Worlds?"

189

"The Rim Worlds, John? Are you quite mad?"

"No. I'm not. They've a new state shipping line, Rim Runners, which is expanding. There's a demand for officers."

"As long as you don't mind making a fresh start as third mate of a star tramp."

"With prospects. Now we come to the second question before the meeting. If I resign my commission, will you resign yours, and come out to the Rim with me? They're frontier worlds, as you know, and there's bound to be a demand for scientists, like yourself."

She got to her feet, stood over him as he sprawled in his easy chair. "I'm sorry, John, but you're asking too much. I wasn't cut out to be a frontierswoman. When *I* leave the Service I shall retire to Arcadia, my home world, where the climate, at least, is decent. From what I've heard of the Rim Worlds the climate on all of them is quite vile. My advice to you, for what it's worth, is to stick it out. As I said, you have got friends, and your sins might be forgotten."

"And I'd still have you," he said.

"Yes. You'd still have me."

"But to ship out under Delamere—"

"Not under. With. You hold the same rank. Forget your blasted pride, John. And who's more important in your life? Me, or Handsome Frankie?"

"You," he told her.

"All right," she said practically. "We don't have many nights before you push off. Let's go to bed."

CHAPTER 38

Commander Frank Delamere could have posed for a Survey Service recruiting poster. He was tall, blond, blue-eyed, with a straight nose, a jutting chin, a firm mouth. He was an indefatigable skirt-chaser, although not always a successful one. (Women have rather more sense than is generally assumed.) More than once the definitely unhandsome Grimes had succeeded where he had failed. Nonetheless, his womanizing had contributed to his professional success; he was engaged to the ugly daughter of the Base commanding officer. He prided himself on running a taut ship. As he had always been fortunate enough to have under his command easily cowed personnel he had got away with it.

Commander John Grimes walked up the ramp to *Vega*'s after airlock slowly, without enthusiasm. Apart from the mutual dislike existing between himself and the frigate's captain he just did not like traveling in somebody else's ship. For many years now he had sailed only in command—in Serpent Class couriers (with the rank of lieutenant), in the Census Ship *Seeker*, and, finally, in the ill-fated *Discovery*. He had no doubt that Delamere would extract the ultimate in sadistic enjoyment from his present lack of status.

The Marine at the head of the ramp saluted him smartly. *And was that a flicker of sympathy in the man's eyes?* "Commander Grimes, sir, the captain would like to see you in his quarters. I'll organize a guide."

"Thank you," said Grimes. "But it's not necessary. I'll find my own way up."

He went to the axial shaft, pressed the button for the elevator. He had to wait only seconds. The cage bore him swiftly up past level after level, stopped when the words CAPTAIN'S FLAT flashed on the indicator. He stepped out,

191

found himself facing a door with the tally CAPTAIN'S DAYROOM. It slid open as he approached it.

"Come in!" called Delamere irritably. "I've been waiting long enough for you!" He did not get up from his chair, did not extend his hand in greeting.

"It is," said Grimes, looking at his wristwatch, "one hour and forty-three minutes prior to liftoff."

"You know that I require all hands to be aboard two full hours before departure."

"I am not one of your hands, Commander Delamere," said Grimes mildly.

"As long as you're aboard my ship you're under my command, Grimes."

"Am I? My orders are to accompany you as an adviser."

"When I need *your* advice that'll be the sunny Friday!"

Grimes sighed. Once again he was getting off on the wrong foot. He said mildly, "Perhaps I should go down to my quarters to get myself organized before liftoff. I take it that my gear has already been sent aboard."

"It has. And your dogbox is on the deck abaft this. I'll see you again as soon as we're on trajectory."

So he was not to be a guest in the control room during liftoff, thought Grimes. He was not to be the recipient of the courtesies normally extended to one captain by another. It was just as well, perhaps. Delamere was notorious rather than famous for the quality of his spacemanship, and Grimes would have found it hard to refrain from back-seat driving.

He left Delamere in his solitary majesty, went out into the circular alleyway. He did not bother to call the elevator, descended the one level by the spiral staircase. The compartment immediately below the captain's flat was that occupied by the senior officers. There was nobody around to tell him which cabin was his, but between CHIEF ENGINEER and FIRST LIEUTENANT he found a door labeled SPARE. Presumably this was where he was to live. Going inside he found his gear, two new suitcases, officers, for the use of, large, and one new suitcase, officers, for the use of, small. He looked around the room. It was not large—but he had lived, for weeks at a time, in smaller ones when serving in the couriers. It was clean, and promised to be comfortable. It had its own tiny adjoining toilet room. It would do.

Grimes began to unpack, stowing the things from the collapsible cases into drawers and lockers. Everything was new.

He had been obliged completely to reequip himself after his return to Base. He wondered gloomily how much wear he would get out of the uniforms.

The intercom speaker came to life. "Attention, attention! Secure all! Secure all! This is the first warning."

A little spacewoman poked her head inside the door, a very pale blonde, a tiny white mouse of a girl. "Oh, you're here, sir. Do you want any help? The captain's very fussy."

"Thank you," said Grimes, "but I think I've everything stowed now." He looked at his watch. "It's still over forty minutes before liftoff."

"Yes, sir, but he wants to be *sure.*"

"Better to be safe than sorry, I suppose," said Grimes. "But since you're here you can fill me in on a few things. Mealtimes, for a start."

"In space, breakfast at 0800 hours. Lunch at 1230 hours. Dinner at 1900 hours. Commander Delamere expects all officers to dress for dinner."

He would, thought Grimes. Luckily, mess dress had been included in the uniform issue that he had drawn.

"And then there're the drills. The captain is very fond of his drills. Action Stations, Boat Stations, Collision Stations."

"At fixed times?"

"Oh, no, sir. He says that the real thing is liable to happen at unexpected times, and so the drills have to happen likewise. If he wakes up in the middle of the night with indigestion he's liable to push one of the panic buttons."

And then, thought Grimes, *he'll be standing there in his control room, his uniform carefully casual, imagining that he's fighting a single ship action against the Grand Flight of the Hallichek Hegemony.*

"You seem to have fun in this ship," he said. "Everything, in fact, but a mutiny."

The girl blushed in embarrassment, the sudden rush of color to her pale cheeks startling. "I didn't think you'd be able to joke about *that*, sir."

"It's a poor funeral without at least one good laugh," said Grimes.

"Attention, attention!" barked the bulkhead speaker. "Secure all! Secure all! This is the second warning!"

"I have to be going, sir," said the girl. "I have to check the other cabins."

Grimes picked up a novel that he had brought with him,

lay down on the bunk, strapped himself in. There was no hurry, but he might as well wait in comfort. He was well into the first chapter when the third warning was given. He had almost finished it when an amplified voice announced, "This is the final countdown. Ten . . . nine . . . eight . . ."

And about bloody time, after all that yapping, thought Grimes.

". . . Three . . . two . . . one . . . *lift!*"

It was at least another three seconds before the inertial drive rumbled and clattered into life. And to Grimes, traveling as a mere passenger, away from the control room, where he could have seen what was going on, the climb through Lindisfarne's atmosphere seemed painfully slow. At last, at long last, *Vega* was up and clear, swinging about her axes on her directional gyroscopes. She seemed to be taking an unconscionable time finding the target star. And was Delamere never going to start the Mannschenn Drive, restart the inertial drive?

"Attention, attention! The Mannschenn Drive is about to be started. Temporal disorientation is to be expected."

You amaze me, thought Grimes.

He heard the thin, high whine of the Drive building up, stared at the geometry of his cabin that had suddenly become alien, at the colors that flared and faded, sagging down the spectrum. There was the feeling of *déjà vu,* and the other feeling that he, by making a small effort only, could peer into the future, his own future. And he was frightened to.

Sounds, colors, and angles returned to normal. The temporal precession field had built up.

"Attention, attention! Normal acceleration is about to be resumed."

The ship shuddered to the arhythmic beat of the inertial drive.

"Attention, attention! Will Commander Grimes please report to the captain's daycabin?"

I suppose I'd better do as the man says, thought Grimes, unsnapping the safety straps.

CHAPTER 39

"Come in," grunted Delamere. "Sit down," he said reluctantly.

Grimes took what looked like the most comfortable chair.

"To begin with, Commander Grimes," said the captain, "you were appointed to my ship against my wishes."

"And against mine, Commander Delamere," said Grimes. "That makes us even, doesn't it?"

"No. It does not. I'm the captain of *Vega*, and you'd better not forget it. Furthermore, I consider myself quite capable of mopping up your mess without any assistance from you. I have *carte blanche* from our lords and masters. I am empowered to treat with the government of Botany Bay as I see fit. When we get to that planet I do not expect to have you working against me, behind my back." He picked up a thick folder from his desk. "This is the transcript of all evidence so far taken. Yours, of course. And Dr. Rath's. And Mr. Flannery's. From the stories of those two officers it would appear that you entered into a liaison with one of the local dignitaries, the Lady Mayor of Paddington."

"What if I did, Delamere? Who are you to presume to judge my morals?"

"At least I have too much sense to mix business with pleasure, Grimes."

"You can't be getting much pleasure out of your affair with the admiral's daughter," agreed Grimes pleasantly. "A strictly business relationship, from your viewpoint."

"Watch your tongue, Grimes!"

"Oh, all right, all right. That must be rather a sore point with you. Now, what do you want me for?"

"I suppose I have to put you in the picture. You're the alleged expert on Botany Bay. I'm proceeding directly there, with no stopovers. I arrest the mutineers, using whatever force is necessary. I put a prize crew aboard *Discovery*—of which *you* will not be in command—and then the two vessels will return, in company, to Lindisfarne." He smiled nastily. "Then there will be the courts-martial, yours included."

"A busy voyage," commented Grimes.

"Yes. And during the voyage you, as a member of this ship's company, will be expected to attend all drills and musters. You are to regard yourself as one of my officers—without, however, any executive powers."

"You'd better read the regulations, Frankie," said Grimes. He quoted, having memorized this passage, " 'A senior officer, traveling in a Survey Service vessel commanded by an officer of no higher rank than himself, shall be subject to that officer's orders only during periods of actual emergency such as enemy action, shipwreck etc.' "

"You bloody space lawyer!" snarled Delamere.

"I have to be, in your company," said Grimes. "Get this straight. I'm here to advise, nothing else. Anything you want to know about Botany Bay, ask me. I'll tell you. And I'll turn up for your drills and musters; even a civilian passenger in a commercial space liner has to do that. I might even brush up on my navigation if you'll let me into your sacred control room."

"Get out!" snapped Delamere. "I'll send for you when I want you again."

"Temper, temper," chided Grimes. In other circumstances he would have rebuked himself for having been so unwise as to make a dangerous enemy—but he and Delamere had always been enemies, and always would be, and nothing that he could do or say would have any effect upon the situation.

CHAPTER 40

There were times during the voyage to Botany Bay when Grimes toyed with the idea of becoming the ringleader of a mutiny himself. Delamere was insufferable. The only members of his crew who took him seriously, however, were among that too sizable minority who have a slavish respect for rank, no matter how earned. The others—officers and ratings alike—paid lip service to their captain's oft iterated determination to run a taut ship, then did pretty well as they pleased. None of them, however, was foolish enough not to attend the drills that Delamere delighted in springing at odd times, although at every one of these there was much yawning and shuffling of feet.

Grimes did not succeed in making friends with any of *Vega*'s people. They were, he decided, afraid of him. His run of good luck had been followed by one spectacularly bad piece of luck—and the fear was there that his bad luck would rub off on them. After a subjective week or so he no longer bothered to try to be sociable. He spoke when he was spoken to, he took his place at table at mealtimes, he had an occasional drink with the frigate's senior officers. Delamere never invited him to have a drink, and plainly resented the fact that Service protocol required him to have Grimes seated at his right hand at table.

At last he was obliged to make use of Grimes's advisory services. It was when the voyage was almost over, when *Vega*, her Mannschenn Drive shut down, proceeding under inertial drive only, was approaching Botany Bay. He called Grimes up to the control room. "You're the expert," he sneered. "What am I supposed to do now, Commander?"

"To begin with, Commander, you can make a start by monitoring the local radio stations. They have newscasts every hour, on the hour."

"On what frequencies?"

"I don't know. I left all such sordid details to my radio officers." There was an unsuccessfully suppressed snigger from the Senior Sparks, who was in the control room. Grimes went on. "It will be advisable, too, to make a check to see if there's anything in orbit about the planet. There weren't any artificial satellites when I was here—but it's possible that Brabham may have put up an armed pinnace as a guard ship."

"I'd already thought of that, Commander," said Delamere. (It was obvious that he hadn't.) He turned to his navigator. "Mr. Prokieff, will you make the necessary observations? We should be close enough to the planet by now."

Grimes looked at the gleaming instrumentation in the control room, all far more up to date than what he had been obliged to make do with in *Discovery*. *With* that *gear,* he thought, *the satellite search could have been initiated days ago, as soon as we reemerged into normal space-time.*

A voice came through the intercom speaker. "Radio office here, control room. We are monitoring a news broadcast. Shall we put it through to your NST transceiver?"

Delamere turned to his senior radio officer. "That was quick work, Mr. Tamworthy."

"We've been trying for some time, sir. Commander Grimes suggested it."

"Commander Grimes—" Delamere made it sound like a particularly foul oath. Nonetheless, he walked to the NST set, the screen of which was now alive with a picture. Grimes followed him. It seemed to be the coverage of a wedding. There was the bride, tall and slim in white, on the arm of a man in the uniform of an airship captain, smiling directly at the camera. In the background were faces that Grimes recognized—Mavis, and Brabham, and Tangye, and the Paddington City Constable, and the president of the Air Pilots' Guild, and Brandt. But he knew none of them as well as he did the bride.

". . . the wedding of Miss Ellen Russell," the news reader was saying, in that accent that Grimes, now, had no trouble in understanding, "to Skipper Benny Jones, of the air liner *Flying Cloud.* As you all know, Miss Russell—sorry, Mrs. Jones! —was paymaster o' the Terry spaceship *Discovery,* but Commander Brabham has accepted her resignation so that she may become a citizen of our planet. Our first immigrant, folks, in one helluva of a long time."

Local girl makes good, thought Grimes—and then his wry amusement abruptly faded. Vinegar Nell, no less than the other mutineers, was a criminal, and would be arrested, and tried, and would pay the penalty for her crime.

"Talkin' of *Discovery*," the news reader went on, "Commander Brabham has informed us that it would be unwise for him to attempt to send a message to his Base on Lindisfarne. Such a signal, he says, would be picked up and decoded by the monitors of the Empire of Waverley. He says that his instructions are to stay here until relieved. Unless he's relieved soon his ship'll be growing roots, an' more of his crew will be followin' the good example o' the fair Miss Russell."

There followed a shot of *Discovery*. This time she was not berthed in the middle of the Oval. Grimes recognized the site, however. It was in a field to the west of the airport. The people of Paddington could hardly be expected to cancel their cricket fixtures a second time.

"There's your precious ship, Commander," sneered Delamere. "What a rustbucket!"

"Meanwhile—I hate ter have ter say it, but it's true—not all of *Discovery*'s people are endearin' themselves to us. Her Marines—who should have provided a guard of honor at the weddin'—are all in jail, even their commandin' officer, Major Swinton. It seems they went on a bender last night. As luck would have it we had a camera crew at the Red Kangaroo, to get some shots o' the new floor show there. There was a floor show all right—o' the wrong kind."

A picture of a large, garishly decorated room filled the screen. Seated around a big oval table were the Marines, including Swinton and Washington. The tabletop was covered with bottles and glasses. Swinton got unsteadily to his feet. "Where's the music?" he bawled. "Where's the dancing girls? We were told there'd be both in this dump!"

"We'll provide our own, Major!" yelled one of his men. "Come on, now! All of yer!"

> *"We're the hellhounds o' the galaxy,*
> *We're the toughest ever seen!*
> *Ain't no one fit ter wipe the arse*
> *Of an FSS Marine!"*

"Gentlemen, please!" It was the manager, a thin, worried-looking man. "The floor show's about ter start."

"Stuff yer floor show, an' you with it!" The man who had started the singing swung viciously with his right, and the manager crumpled to the floor. Then half a dozen tough-looking waiters were converging on the scene. The Marines picked up bottles by their necks, smashed them on the edge of the table, held them like vicious, jagged daggers. The waiters hesitated, then snatched up chairs, not caring whom they spilled in the process. People were throwing things. A missile of some kind struck Swinton on the forehead, felling him. Someone yelled, "Get the Terry bastards!" Women screamed. The waiters, reinforced by customers, holding their chairs before them as a protection from the broken bottles, advanced in a rush.

It was then that the scene became chaotic—and blanked out abruptly. "That," said the news reader, "was when some bastard put his boot through our camera. Over twenty of our people finished up in the hospital. The condition of the manager o' the Red Roo is critical. An' the Marines, bein' behind bars, missed out on their charmin' shipmate's weddin'.

"An' that, folks, is all the news to date."

"Disgusting," said Delamere, somehow implying that it was all Grimes's fault.

"Marines will be Marines," said Grimes.

"Not *my* Marines," Delamere stated smugly.

"What are they, then?" Grimes asked interestedly.

Delamere ignored this. He said, "I anticipate no difficulties in rounding up this rabble of yours. And now, Mr. Adviser, what do you advise? Don't bother to answer. I've already decided what I am going to do. I shall drop in, unannounced, just after dawn, local time. I shall land close to *Discovery*, covering her with my guns."

"*Discovery* has guns too, you know," remarked Grimes.

"I shall have the advantage of surprise," said Delamere. "I'll blow her off the ground before my vanes kiss the dirt."

"I thought," said Grimes, "that your instructions were to put a prize crew aboard her and bring her back to Base. You'll not be at all popular if you destroy such a large and expensive hunk of Federation property."

Delamere considered this. He asked, reluctantly, at last, "Then what do you suggest, Commander?"

"Put *Vega* in orbit, one that keeps her always over the daylight hemisphere. That way she won't be spotted visually. Get your artificers working on sonic insulation for the boats you'll be using for the landing. Send your force down for a dawn landing, and then go and call on the mayor. She won't like being called at such a godless time, but I think I'll be able to smooth things over."

"Too complicated," said Delamere.

"Then what are your ideas on the subject?"

"One Falcon missile, with a Somnopon warhead. That should be ample for a city the size of Paddington. And then, while all the Paddingtonians *and* your mutineers are snoring their heads off, we land and take over."

"You can't do that!" exclaimed Grimes. "It will be an act of war."

"Rubbish. Somnopon's nonlethal."

"Even at night," said Grimes, "there are people up and about, doing various jobs. If they fall asleep, suddenly, there are bound to be casualties. Civilian casualties."

"I think that Commander Grimes is right," said *Vega*'s first lieutenant.

"You're not paid to think, Lieutenant Commander Bissett."

"I beg your pardon, sir," Bissett said firmly, "but that is one of the things that I am paid for. High-handed action on our part will, inevitably, drive Botany Bay into the arms of Waverley."

"Those colonists have never heard of the Empire of Waverley," said Delamere stubbornly.

"You heard that news broadcast, sir. The Empire of Waverley was specifically mentioned. If you like, I'll get Sparks to play the tape back."

Delamere glared at his executive officer, and then at Grimes. He snarled, "All right, all right. Then please tell me, somebody, why I shouldn't bring *Vega* down in broad daylight, with flags flying and brass bands playing? Or why I shouldn't do the same as Grimes did before *his* first landing— announce it on the normal broadcast channels?"

"Because," Grimes pointed out, "either course of action would give the mutineers ample warning. And if we have to fight a battle right over a major city we shall not endear ourselves to the inhabitants."

"Commander Grimes is right," said Bissett.

"I'm always right," Grimes could not resist saying.

CHAPTER 41

After a long discussion, during which Delamere's officers made useful suggestions—which is more than could be said for their captain—it was decided to send only one boat down for the initial landing. This was to be piloted by Grimes himself, accompanied by Major Briggs, *Vega*'s Marine officer, and six of his men. All of the Marines came either from Australia or from Australian colonies and, with a little practice, were able to speak with a fair approximation to the Botany Bay accent. All of the landing party wore civilian clothing—gaily patterned shirts, shorts, and sandals.

Vega's artificers had made a good job of soundproofing the inertial drive of the boat. When the engine was run in neutral gear, in the confined space of the boat bay, the noise, which normally would have been deafening, was little more than an irritable mutter. And, as Grimes well knew, the Lost Colonists liked their sleep and it took a lot to rouse them from it, especially after a heavy night.

He felt almost happy as he maneuvered the little craft down through the atmosphere. It was good to have a command again, even if it was only a ship's boat, especially after a passage in a vessel captained by Delamere. Once clear of the ship he had steered to a position over the night hemisphere, a little to the west of the terminator. Conditions were cloudless, and he could see, without any difficulty, the diffuse patch of soft light that was Paddington and, as he steadily lost altitude, the hard, bright, coded flash of the Macquarie Light. As he dropped toward it the picture formed on the radar screen, a chart drawn in pale-green luminescence—the northern coastline and the great, irregular bite out of it that was Port Jackson. Lower yet, and lower, and he could see the outlines of the finger jetties. He had decided to land in the southeastern corner of the harbor where several old hulks were moored, a marine junkyard.

Dawn was pale in the east when, at last, the boat dropped to the surface of the calm water with hardly a ripple. Grimes steered her toward the shadowy forms of the obsolete shipping, threading a cautious way between the looming dark hulls. There was, he remembered, a rickety little jetty just about here, used by work boats and the like. He came alongside it cautiously, opened the airlock doors. The Marines scrambled out onto the warped and weatherworn planking. Grimes followed. And then, working as quietly as possible, they succeeded in pushing and pulling the boat under the jetty, squeezing her in, somehow, between the marine-growth-encrusted piles. She would not be found unless somebody were making a deliberate search for her.

Grimes led the way inland. There was just enough light—although it was growing stronger—for them to pick their way through the rusty tangle of obstacles: anchors, lengths of chain cable, a big, four-bladed propeller. One of the Marines swore as he stubbed his bare toe on some unseen obstruction. Then they came to a road leading down to the water's edge, and the first, sleeping houses. The light of the gas street lamps was paling as the dawn brightened. Ahead of them, quite suddenly, the sun came up and, simultaneously, the lamps went out. Somewhere a dog was barking, and there was a brief and startling clamor overhead as a flock of birdlike things emerged from the trees, circled and assembled, then flew steadily toward the north on some unknown mission.

"It—it's like time travel, sir," whispered the Marine officer.

"What do you mean, Major?"

"This—this city. It's like something out of Earth's past. So . . . quiet. The way a morning should be, but hardly ever is. And these houses . . . nothing over three stories. And all the trees."

"This is the way they wanted it," said Grimes, "and this is the way they got it."

It was not far to the mayor's palace—a big, low structure, built in the long-dead (on Earth) colonial style. Grimes marched up to the front door, the gravel of the driveway grating under his sandals. The others followed him into the portico, the major looking with admiration at the graceful, cast-aluminum pillars with their ornate floral designs. He tapped one. He said, "Should be cast-iron, really, but aluminum's more practical."

"This isn't a sight-seeing tour, Major Briggs," Grimes told him. He added, "But I wish it were."

He pressed the bell firmly. He heard a distant, muffled shrilling inside the house. He pressed it again, and again.

The door suddenly opened. A girl stood there, glaring at them. Grimes recognized her. She was one of Mavis' staff. She demanded, "Wot the hell do yer want at this Jesus-less hour?"

"A word with Her Ladyship," said Grimes.

"Then yer can come back later. Noonish. Mavis left word that she wants her breakfast in bed at 1000 hours an' not a bleedin' second before."

"This is important," Grimes told her.

"Here, let me look at yer!" She put out a shapely arm and pulled him close to her. "Commander Grimes, ain't it? Cor stone the bleedin' crows, wot are you doin' back here, Skip? Wait till I tell Mavis. She won't half be beside her bleedin' self!"

"Not a word to anybody else, Shirley. Nobody must know I'm here."

"A secret mission, is it? I knew there was somethin' wrong, somewhere. Come on in, all o' yer. I'll put yer in her study while I drag her out. An' I'll rustle up some tea an' scones while yer waitin'."

She led them through a long corridor into a large, book-lined room, told them to be seated, then hurried out. The Marines, after Briggs had nodded his permission, disposed themselves on a long settee. Grimes went to the big window, accompanied by the major, and looked out. The city was, at last, showing some slight signs of life. A large coach drove by, obviously bound to the airport to meet an incoming passenger-carrying dirigible. There were a few, a very few, pedestrians.

"Skip, you old bastard!" It was Mavis, her abundant charms barely concealed by a thin wrapper. She grabbed Grimes as he turned to face her, almost smothered him in a tight embrace. "Gawd! It's good to see yer back!" Then her face clouded. "But I don't suppose yer came back just to see me. An' where's yer ship? Don't try ter tell me that yer walked all the way!"

"The ship's in orbit," began Grimes.

"An' who're yer pals? Don't think I know 'em."

Grimes made introductions, and while he was in the middle of them Shirley came in with a big tray, with tea things and a great dish of hot, buttered, lavishly jammed scones.

"An' now," asked Mavis, speaking through a mouthful, "wot *is* all this about, Skip? You come droppin' in unannounced, wif a goon squad, an' I don't think the bulges under their shirts are male tits!"

"Nothing more lethal than stunguns," Grimes assured her. "Now, I'll be frank with you. I'm here on a police mission."

"We have our own police force, Skip, an' we ain't members of your Federation."

"That's so, Mavis. But you're harboring criminals."

"An' what concern is that o' yours, Skip?"

"Plenty. The criminals are the entire crew of *Discovery*."

"Garn!"

"It's true, Mavis. There was a mutiny."

"You can't tell *me* that Commander Brabham'd do a thing like that. As nice a bloke as you'd ever meet. Not as nice as you, perhaps"—she smiled—"but nice enough."

"Brabham did do it, Mavis. He and Swinton were the ringleaders."

"Oh, Swinton. *Him.* And his bloody pongoes. That doesn't surprise me."

"They were going to push Dr. Rath and Mr. Flannery and myself out through the airlock. Without spacesuits."

"What!"

"Yes. I'm not kidding, Mavis. And then Vinegar Nell and Tangye persuaded the others to set us adrift in a small boat, with no Deep Space radio and no Deep Space drive. Where we were, we'd have died of old age long before we got anywhere."

"Is this *true*, Skip?"

"Of course it's true. We picked up a few news broadcasts before I came down in the boat, including the one about Vinegar Nell's wedding. Your news reader made the point that there has been absolutely no communication between *Discovery* and Lindisfarne Base. Brabham has his story to account for that, but it doesn't hold water, does it?"

"I . . . I s'pose not. But how did yer get yer boat back here?" She laughed at the stupidity of her own question. "But, o' course, you didn't. You were picked up, weren't yer?"

"Yes. By a ship called *Sundowner*, commanded by a friend

of mine. He took us back to Lindisfarne. And the admira
commanding the base has sent a frigate to arrest the muti
neers and take them back for trial."

"Wot'll happen to 'em?"

"The same as was going to happen to me. An unsuite
spacewalk."

"It's a bastard of a universe you live in, Skip. I'm not sur
that I'd like Botany Bay dragged inter it. Swinton an' hi
drongoes *we* can deal with. The others? They're integratin
nicely."

"We must take them, Mavis. All of them."

"An' what if we refuse to give 'em up?"

"Then we have to use force. Under Federation Law, we'r
entitled to."

"But we ain't members o' your bleedin' Federation."

"You're still subject to Interstellar Law, which is subscribe
to by all spacefaring races."

"We aren't."

"I'm sorry, Mavis, but you are. You have been sinc
Discovery's first landing."

"You might've told me. A right bastard I clasped to m
bosom when I made yer free of the body beautiful."

"Look, Mavis. I've a job to do. Send for the City Con
stable, but don't tell him what for until he gets here."

"I'll call him—an' tell him to warn all yer so-called muti
neers to go bush. They've too many friends on this bleedin
world for you ever ter find 'em. If they'd killed yer, I'
be thinkin' differently. But you're alive, ain't yer? Wot's ye
beef?"

"You won't cooperate, Mavis?"

"No. Skip, an' that's definite." She turned to the girl. "Ge
on the blower, will yer, Shirl? Warn 'em aboard *Discovery*."

Major Briggs said, "I'm sorry, Commander Grimes, bu
your way of doing things doesn't seem to be working." He
raised his wrist transceiver, a special long-range model, to hi
mouth. "Briggs to *Vega*. Do you read me? Over."

"*Vega* to Briggs. Captain here, Major. How are thing
going?" Delamere's voice was faint and distant, but all in the
room could hear the words.

"Operation Sweet Sleep, sir," said Briggs.

"And about bloody time. We've given Commander Grime
his chance to look up his old flames. Over."

"What's goin' on, Skip?" demanded Mavis.

Grimes did not answer her, turned on Briggs. "I thought this landing party was under *my* orders, Major."

"I had my own orders, sir, directly from the captain."

"He's a bloody fool," snarled Grimes, "and so are you! I know what you're doing can be argued, by the right lawyers in the right court, to be legally correct—but you've lost Botany Bay to the Federation."

The first dull thud sounded from overhead. Delamere's trigger finger must have been itchy. Grimes visualized the exploding missile, the heavy, odorless, invisible gas drifting slowly downward. He heard a second thud, and a third. Frankie was making sure.

The last thing he saw as he drifted into unconsciousness was Mavis' hurt, accusing face.

CHAPTER 42

When Grimes slowly awakened he was conscious, first of all, of the dull ache in his upper arm, where he had been injected with an antidote to the gas, and then of the too handsome, too cheerful face of Delamere grinning down at him. "Rise and shine, Grimesy boy! You can wake up now. We've done all your work for you!"

Grimes, unassisted, got groggily to his feet. He looked around the mayor's study. The Marines were gone, of course. They would have been given *their* shots before leaving the ship. Mavis and Shirley were still unconscious. *Vega*'s surgeon was bending over the lady mayor, a hypodermic spraygun in his hand. He used it, on the fleshy part of a generously exposed thigh, then turned to the younger woman.

"What—what time is it?" asked Grimes.

"Fifteen hundred hours, local. We have full control of the city. Such officials as we have awakened are cooperating with us. Most of the mutineers—with their popsies—were aboard *Discovery*. We carted 'em off to the dressing rooms in the stadium—the mutineers, that is, not the popsies—and they're there under guard. Safer there than in that apology for a jail." Delamere paused. "Oh, your girlfriend, or ex-girlfriend—" Grimes looked toward Mavis, who was listening intently. "No. Not *her*. Your paymaster. We had to persuade some of her friends to talk. We found out that she and her new husband were spending their honeymoon on" —he made a grimace of distaste—"Daydream Island. Only half an hour's flying time in one of my pinnaces."

"So you've got her too," said Grimes.

"What the hell else did you expect?" demanded Delamere.

Mavis was on her feet now, glaring at the spacemen, clutching her thin wrap around her. She was about to say something when the ringing of a telephone bell broke the

208

silence. It came, thought Grimes, from her office. She asked coldly, "I s'pose I can answer me own phone, in me own palace?"

"Of course, madam," replied Delamere airily. "If it's for me, let me know, will you?"

"Bastard!" she snarled, making her exit.

"I suppose you brought the ship down," said Grimes.

"Yes. I'm parked in that big oval sports arena. One of the first natives we woke up was quite hostile. He screamed about a big match due today, and accused me of buggering the pitch. He actually ordered me off. We had to use a stungun on him."

"You mightn't make many friends, Delamere," said Grimes, "but you sure influence people."

"Not to worry. We've got what we came for."

Mavis, her face pale under the dark tan, returned to the study. She said, in a low, venomous voice, "You bloody murderers!"

"The gas we used, madam," Delamere told her, "is no more than an instant anesthetic. Those whom we have not already revived will wake, quite naturally, in about one hour, feeling no ill effects whatsoever."

"An' wot about those who won't wake? Wot about the young couple who were killed in bed when a dirty great hunk o' rocket casin' crashed through their roof? Wot about that power station engineer who fell against somethin' an' got fried? An' wot about *Flyin' Scud*? She was comin' in ter the moorin' mast when the skipper passed out, an' she kept on goin', an' gutted herself. An' that's just the start of it."

"I am sure, madam," said Delamere stiffly, "that the Federation will pay generous compensation."

"In Federation money, I s'pose," she sneered. "Wot bloody use will that be? Specially since we won't join your bloody Federation now, not for all the gold in the galaxy." She turned on Grimes. "An' as for you, you . . . you dingo! I thought you were a man. Wot a bloody hope! Not only do yer help this bastard ter murder *my* people, you're goin' ter stand back an' let yer own crew be dragged off ter be butchered."

"But, Mavis—"

"Gah! Yer make me sick!"

"Delamere," demanded Grimes, "have you done anything about the crash at the airport, and the other accidents?"

"When we got around to it, Grimes. Our first job was to round up the mutineers." He added smugly, "You can't make an omelet without breaking eggs, you know."

"There was no need to run amuck in the kitchen," said Grimes.

"Out!" yelled Mavis suddenly. "Out o' me palace, you Terry bastards! I've work to do!"

"So have we, madam," said Delamere. "A very good afternoon to you. Come, Doctor. And you, Grimes."

"But, Mavis," Grimes began.

"Out! All o' yer. That includes you, lover boy!"

"You do have the oddest girlfriends," remarked Delamere as the three of them passed out through the front door.

Grimes did not reply. He was full of bitter self-reproach. He should have guessed that Delamere would have his own secret plans. He could have stopped Major Briggs from making that call . . . or could he? His name, he admitted wryly, was not Superman.

He followed the other two into the commandeered electric car that was waiting for them.

CHAPTER 43

They drove to the Oval, in the middle of which, an alien, menacing tower, stood *Vega*. They did not go straight to the ship but dismounted at the entrance to the sports ground. At the doors to the dressing rooms under the stands stood armed Marines and spacemen.

Delamere led the way to one of the doors, which was opened by a sentry. He sneered as he pointed to the scene inside, and said disgustedly, "What a rabble! I can't see how anybody could have ever sailed in the same ship with them!"

Yes, they were a rabble—as the crew of any ship would be if dragged naked and unconscious from their beds, to awake in captivity. The only ones clothed, in dirty, torn uniforms, were Swinton and his Marines. Swinton, followed by the huge Washington, pushed through the mob of his hapless shipmates. He stood there defiantly, glaring at Grimes and his companions. He demanded, "Have you come to gloat? Go on, damn you! Gloat to your heart's bloody content!"

"I haven't come to gloat," said Grimes.

"Then what the hell have you come for? But it's my fault. I should never have listened to Vinegar Nell and that puppy Tangye. We should have made sure of you while we had you."

"But you didn't," said Grimes. "Unluckily for you. Luckily for me."

"Grimes's famous luck!" sneered the Mad Major.

Vinegar Nell came slowly to stand beside the Marine. She had been conscious when she had been captured, and obviously had put up a fight. She looked steadily at Grimes. She said, "So you made it, John. Am I glad, or sorry? I'm glad for you. Genuinely. As for me—" She shrugged. "Whatever I say will make no difference."

"*Very* touching," commented Delamere.

"Shut up!" snapped Grimes. He turned to face Brabham—who, like the majority of the prisoners, was without clothing. His ex-first lieutenant looked fit, far fitter than he had ever looked aboard *Discovery*. Life on Botany Bay had agreed with him.

"You win, Captain," he said glumly. Then he actually smiled. "But it was good while it lasted!"

"I'm sorry," said Grimes inadequately.

"Hearts and flowers," murmured Delamere.

"Captain," went on Brabham, "I know I've no right to ask favors of you. But do you think you could persuade Commander Delamere to let us have some clothing? And I think, too, that the women should have separate quarters."

"Mutineers have no rights," stated Delamere.

"Human beings have!" retorted Grimes. "And don't forget that we, on this world, are ambassadors of the Federation. We've made a bad enough impression already. Don't let's make it worse."

"Who cares?" asked Delamere.

"Every do-gooder and bleeding heart in the galaxy, that's who. I've often hated that breed myself—but I'll have no hesitation in making use of them."

The two commanders glared at each other, and then Delamere turned to one of his officers. "You might see that the prisoners have some rags to cover their disgusting nakedness, Mr. Fleming. And you can sort out the cows from the goats and have them penned separately."

"Thank you," said Brabham—to Grimes. Then, "How long are they keeping us here, Captain?"

"Until we've converted *Discovery*'s holds into palatial quarters for you bastards!" snarled Delamere.

Grimes turned away.

He could not help feeling sorry for those who had abandoned him in a hopeless situation. They were guilty of a crime for which there could be no forgiveness, let alone pardon, and yet . . . on this planet they had been given the second chance to make something of their hitherto wasted lives. They could have become useful citizens. Botany Bay would have benefited from their knowledge of different technologies.

"I'm going aboard now," said Delamere.

"I'm not," said Grimes.

"We have things to discuss."

"They can wait."

He walked slowly into the tree-lined street—which, at last, was becoming alive with dazed-looking citizens. He hoped that nobody would recognize him. But somebody did. His way was blocked by a man in a light blue shorts-and-shirt uniform.

"Commander Grimes?"

"Yes?"

"Don't you remember me? I'm Benny Jones, skipper o' *Flyin' Cloud.*"

Grimes remembered the airship captain, had taken a flight in the big dirigible. And he knew, too, that the man was Vinegar Nell's husband. No wonder he looked almost out of his mind with worry.

"Nell's a fine person, Commander. She came straight with me. She told me all sorts of things that she had no need to. I—I know about you an' her. An' so what? But are you goin' to stand back an' let her be dragged away to be—to be—"

"I—I don't have much choice in the matter, Skipper."

"I know yer don't. You have ter take yer orders from the bastards above yer. But— Look, Commander. You know the sort o' routine they have aboard that bastard ship that's ruinin' the turf in the Oval. I'm told that you're in her just as an adviser. Can't yer be an adviser to— All right. To me?"

I owe Nell something, thought Grimes, pulling his pipe out from his pocket, and looking at it. *I owe her a lot. And there was nothing that* she *could have done to stop the mutiny— but that won't save her from the spacewalk along with the others. She saved* me *from a spacewalk.*

"I take it that you want to rescue Nell, Skipper."

"Wot the bloody hell else? But how? But how?"

But how? Grimes asked himself. He began to see the glimmerings of an answer. He thought that the chemists on Botany Bay might already, after the salutary lesson of that morning, be working on it. And Brandt, after his long residence at the university, would be on intimate terms with the local scientists. Brandt, too, had always made it plain that he had no time for Survey Service regulations.

But he, Grimes . . . ? When it came to the crunch where did his loyalties lie? To his Service, or to an ex-mistress?

Certainly not, he decided, to the obnoxious Delamere.

He said, as he slowly filled his pipe, "We may be able to do something, Skipper. But only for Nell. Only for Nell. Shall we take a stroll to the university?"

CHAPTER 44

They found Brandt without any trouble. The scientist was unchanged, as irascible as ever. He demanded, "What *is* going on here, Commander Grimes? A dawn attack on our world by a Federation warship—"

"*Our* world, Doctor?"

"Yes. I'm married now, and I resigned my commission, and applied for citizenship."

"You resigned your commission?"

"Must you parrot every word, Commander Grimes? Commander Brabham was the senior officer of the Survey Service on Botany Bay, so I handed my resignation in to him. He accepted it. I got tired of waiting for that chum of yours, Captain Davinas."

"Did you tell Brabham about Davinas?" asked Grimes.

"Of course not. I knew that it was some private deal between you and him, so I kept my mouth shut."

"Just as well," said Grimes. "If Brabham and his crowd had been expecting *Sundowner* they'd have been more alert."

"What do you mean, just as well? If they'd been alert, they'd have stood a fighting chance."

"But they're mutineers, Doctor."

"Mutineers, shmutineers . . . a mutiny's only a strike, but with the strikers wearing uniform."

"Mphm," grunted Grimes. "That's one way of looking at it, I suppose. But I'm lucky to be alive, Doctor."

"You're always lucky. Well, what can I do for you?"

"Are there any supplies of Somnopon gas on this world, Doctor? Or anything like it?"

"Not as far as I know. We're a peaceful planet. We could make some, I suppose. Do you know the formula?"

"I've seen it, in gunnery manuals, but I didn't memorize it."

"You wouldn't. You're a typical spaceman, always bludging

215

on the scientists and technologists. But what do you want it for?"

"Can we trust this bastard?" asked Jones.

"Why not?" countered Grimes. "He's one of yours, now." He turned to Brandt. "This gentleman is Miss Russell's husband."

"He has my sympathy," said Brandt.

Grimes looked at him sharply. That remark could be taken two ways. He said, "Naturally, he does not wish to see his wife taken away to be tried and executed, as she will be. The trial will be a mere formality. On every occasion that the Survey Service has had a mutiny the entire crew has been made an example of. That, I suppose, is why mutiny is such a rare crime. But Miss Russell—or Mrs. Jones, as she is now —saved my life. I want to reciprocate."

"Uncommonly decent of you, Commander Grimes. Beneath that rugged exterior there beats a heart of gold."

"Let me finish, damn you. What I want is enough Somnopon, or something like it, so that Skipper Jones and his friends can put the entire Oval, including *Vega*, to sleep. Then Jones rescues Nell—and surely, with the population of an entire planet shielding her, she'll never be found." He added, "There's always plastic surgery."

"I like her the way she is!" growled Jones.

"All very ingenious, Grimes, and it keeps *your* yardarm clear, as you would put it. But you don't remember the formula. I've no doubt that we could work it out for ourselves, but that would take time. Too much time." He picked up a telephone on his desk. "Rene, could you get hold of Doc Travis? Tell her it's urgent. Yes, in my office."

"Is Dr. Travis a chemist?" asked Grimes.

"No. A psychologist. You've no idea what dirt she can drag out of people's minds by hypnosis."

"A brain drain?" demanded Grimes, alarmed.

"Nothing like as drastic," Brandt assured him. "It'll just be a sleep from which you'll awake with your mind, such as it is, quite intact."

Grimes looked at Jones. The airship captain's strong face was drawn with worry and his eyes held a deep misery.

"All right," he said.

The hypnosis session bore little relationship to the brain drain techniques used by the Intelligence Branch of the Survey Service. There was no complicated electronic apparatus, no screens with the wavering, luminescent traces of brain waves. There was only a soft-voiced, attractive blonde, whose soothing contralto suggested that Grimes, sitting on his shoulder blades in a deep, comfortable chair, relax, relax, relax. He relaxed. He must have dozed off. He was awakened by the snapping of the hypnotist's fingers. He was as refreshed as he would have been by a full night's sleep. He felt exceptionally alert.

"We got it," said Brandt.

"Nothing else?" asked Grimes suspiciously.

"No," replied the scientist virtuously.

"No posthypnotic suggestions?"

"Wot d'yer take us for?" demanded Dr. Travis indignantly. "You do the right thing by us, we do the right thing by you." She looked thoughtful. "As you know, we ain't got any telepaths on this planet. There'll be at least one aboard that frigate. Wot're the chances o' him snoopin'?"

"That's a chance we have to take, Doctor. But you can't snoop all of the people all of the time. Anyhow, there're quite a few people aboard *Vega* who'd like to see their gallant captain come a gutser, and he's one of them."

"Some time, Dolly," said Brandt, "you must make a study of the micro-societies of ships. I assure you that it would be fascinating. And now, while we're waiting for Dr. Ronson and his team to let us know what they can do with the formula, we'll have a drink. Skipper Jones, at least, looks as though he could use one."

Ronson phoned through to say that he would have a supply of the gas ready within forty-eight hours. It would take more than that time to bring *Discovery* back to full spaceworthiness as well as to modify her for her new role as a prison ship.

CHAPTER 45

Delamere, after a stormy session with Mavis—who was backed by Grimes—reluctantly agreed to allow the prisoners some small privileges before their removal from Botany Bay. "You must remember," Grimes told him, "that these Lost Colonists are descended from other colonists, and that those other colonists have always distrusted brassbound authority, and often with good reason. Who else would make a folk hero out of a bushranger like Ned Kelly?"

"You've Australian blood yourself, Grimes, haven't you? That accounts for your own attitude toward authority. My authority, specifically."

"I'm speaking as a man, Delamere, not as an Australian, nor as an officer of the Survey Service, nor as any other bloody thing. Those mutineers—and I admit that most of 'em are as guilty as all hell—have made friends on this planet, have formed very close relationships. You're hurting those people, who'll never see their friends or lovers again, as much as you're hurting the criminals. Don't forget what I said about the bleeding hearts, the sob sisters, and the do-gooders."

"Good on yer, Skip!" murmured Mavis.

"I haven't forgotten, Grimes," admitted Delamere coldly. "And I haven't forgotten the rather dubious part you've played in affairs ever since we lifted ship for this blasted planet." Then, to Mavis, "All right, madam. I'll allow your people to visit their boyfriends and girlfriends, at times to be arranged by myself, under strict supervision. And I give you fair warning—if there's any attempt to smuggle in weapons or escape tools, then may the Odd Gods of the Galaxy help you! You'll need their help."

"Thank you, sir, Commander, sir," simpered Mavis infuriatingly.

There were visitors. The visitors brought gifts—mainly cakes. The cakes were, of course, X-rayed. There was nothing of a metallic nature inside them. They were sliced, and samples chemically analyzed. There was not a trace of plastic explosive. Delamere's PCO was on hand during each visiting period to scan the minds of the visitors, and reported that although, naturally, there was considerable hostility to Delamere—and to Grimes himself—there was no knowledge of any planned jailbreak. Oddly enough, Skipper Jones did not visit his wife, and it was obvious that she was deeply hurt. Grimes knew the reason. He dare not tell Vinegar Nell. He dare not visit her himself. Jones, of course, knew of the clandestine manufacture of Somnopon. There was another slight oddity of which Grimes thought nothing—at the time. Many of the cakes and other edible goodies came from the kitchens of the mayor's palace. But that was just another example of Mavis' essential goodheartedness.

When the big night came—it was early evening, actually —Grimes was standing with Brandt and Jones on the flat roof of one of the towers of the university. From it they could see the airport, and just beyond it the huge, floodlit shape of *Discovery*. They could see the Oval, and the even larger, brightly illumined tower that was *Vega*. They returned their attention to the airport. One of the dirigibles was about to cast off—*Duchess of Paddington,* a cargo carrier, commanded by a friend of Jones's. Grimes watched through borrowed binoculars. He could make out the mooring mast, with its flashing red light on top, quite well, and the long cigar shape that trailed from it like a wind sock. He saw the airship's red and green navigation lights come on. So she had let go. *Duchess of Paddington* drifted away from the mast, gaining altitude. She was making way, and slowly circled *Discovery*. Grimes wondered vaguely why she was doing that; *Discovery* was not the target. A dry run, perhaps. Now she was steering toward the Oval, a dimly seen blob, foreshortened to the appearance of a sphere, in the darkling sky, two stars, one ruby and one emerald, brighter far than the other, distant stars that were appearing one by one in the firmament. The throbbing beat of her airscrews came faintly down the light breeze.

The airship passed slowly over the university.

"Conditions ideal," whispered Jones. "Smithy'll be openin' his valves about now. Let's go!"

The party descended to ground level by an express elevator, piled into a waiting car. Jones took something off the back seat, thrust it at Grimes. "Take this, Commander. You'll be needin' it."

Grimes turned the thing over in his hands. It was a respirator. He asked, "What about the rest of you?"

"We're all full o' the antidote. I hope it works. Ronson assured us that it will."

"Wouldn't it be simpler if I had a shot?"

"We took it orally. But we're protectin' you, Commander. When the fun's over you take off yer mask an' just pass out, same as all the other bastards. If there ain't enough Somnopon still lyin' around, we've a spare bottle."

"You've thought of everything," admitted Grimes. He put on the respirator, looked out at the tree-lined, gaslit streets sliding past the car. A few pedestrians, he saw, had succumbed to stray eddies of the anesthetic. Gas is always a chancy weapon.

They were approaching the entrance to the Oval. They could already hear, over the hum of their engine, loud voices, the crashing of the main gate as it was forced. Grimes expected a rattle of fire from *Vega*—but her people had been taken unawares, even as the mutineers had been.

The car stopped. Jones jumped out. "Good-bye, Commander. An' thanks. I wish I could've known you better." He extended his hand for a brief, but firm, handshake.

"I'll see you again," said Grimes.

"You won't. I sincerely hope you won't. Nothin' against *you*, mind you." He ran off, toward the stands.

Grimes got out of the car, realized that many vehicles were already on the scene, that more were arriving. He was almost knocked over by a mob rushing the transport. There was Jones, towing a bewildered Vinegar Nell by the hand. There were Brabham, MacMorris, Tangye, Sally. . . .

"To the ship!" Jones was shouting. "To *Discovery*!"

"To *Discovery*!" the cry was going up. "To *Discovery*!" Not only were there mutineers in the mob, but many local women.

Enough was enough, thought Grimes. He stepped forward to try to stem the rush. He saw Swinton leveling a weapon taken from one of the guards—and saw Vinegar Nell knock it to one side just as it exploded. Nell clawed the respirator from his face, crying, "Keep out of this, John! The less you know the better!" She swung the gas mask to hit him in the belly, and he gasped.

That was all he knew.

CHAPTER 46

He awoke suddenly. Once again there was the dull ache
in his arm where a hypodermic spray had been used. He
opened his eyes, saw a khaki-uniformed man bending over
him. One of Delamere's Marines . . . ?

"You're under arrest," said the man. "All you Terry
bastards're under arrest."

What the hell was going on? The man, Grimes saw, was
wearing a wide-brimmed hat, with the brim turned up on
one side. The beam of a light shone on a badge of polished
brass, a rising-sun design. Not a Marine . . . a policeman.

"Don't be so bloody silly, Vince." It was Mavis' voice.
"The skipper's a pal o' mine."

"But the orders were—"

"Who gives the orders round here? Get inside, to the
Oval. There's plenty o' Terries in there to arrest, an' quite a
few wantin' first aid!" She added admiringly, "That bloody
Brabham! He's made a clean getaway, an' there'll be no
chase!" She put out a hand and helped Grimes to his feet.
"Thinkin' it over, Skip, I'd better have yer arrested with the
others. But we'll walk an' talk a while, first."

They went in through the main entrance, picking their
way carefully through the wreckage of the gate. Grimes
cried out in dismay. *Vega* was there still, but no longer
illumined by the glare of her own floodlights, no longer
proudly erect. She was on her side, the great length of her
picked out by the headlights of at least two dozen heavy-
duty vehicles. Externally she seemed undamaged. Internal-
ly? She would be a mess, Grimes knew.

"The cricket season's well an' truly buggered," said Mavis
cheerfully. "Never could see anythin' in the game meself."

"What happened?" demanded Grimes.

"That bloody Brabham . . . or it could've been Jonesy's idea. It was as much airmanship as spacemanship."

"Jones? He's with the mutineers?"

"An' quite a few more. I couldn't stop 'em. Not that I wanted to."

"But what happened?"

"Oh, they all made a rush for your *Discovery* after the breakout. *Your* crew, an' Jones, an' . . . oh, we'll have ter sort it out later, how many darlin' daughters an' even wives are missin'. Where was I? Oh, yes. *Discovery* lifted off. But she didn't go straight up. She sorta drifted across the city, her engines goin' like the hammers o' Hell, just scrapin' the rooftops. Then she lifted, but only a little, just so's her backside was nuzzlin' *Vega*'s nose. Like two dogs, it was. An' she sorta *wriggled,* an' *Vega* wriggled too, more an' more, until . . . *Crash!* An' then Brabham went upstairs as though the sheriff an' his posse were after him."

"Delamere was lucky," said Grimes.

"Bloody *un*lucky, if you ask me."

"No. Lucky. Brabham could have used his weaponry. Or he could have sat on top of *Vega* and cooked her with the auxiliary rocket drive." He managed a grin. "I guess you people must have had a civilizing influence on him. Oh, one more thing. How was it that the mutineers weren't affected by the gas?"

"They were all immune, that's why. Ain't many people can resist the goodies that come out o' *my* kitchen! But we made sure that none o' the popsies deliverin' the pies an' cakes knew the secret ingredient. Not with a nasty, pryin' telepath pickin' up every thought. But that'll have ter do. Here come the mug coppers wi' yer pal Frankie. He's under arrest, same as you are."

Delamere, battered and bruised, held up by the two men of his police escort, staggered toward the mayor. He saw Grimes, stiffened.

"I might have known that you'd be at the bottom of this, you bastard!"

"How the hell could he be?" asked Mavis. "My police found him sprawled, unconscious, by the main entrance."

"You're in this too, you bitch! You'll laugh on the other side of your face when this world is under Federation military occupation!"

"An' is your precious Federation willin' ter fight a war

over Botany Bay, specially at the end o' long supply lines
Dr. Brandt showed us how ter build a Carlotti set. We use
it, ternight. We got through ter Waverley without an'
trouble at all. The emperor's willin' to put us under hi
protection."

"Grimes, you'll pay for this. This is a big black mark o'
your Service record that'll never be erased!"

This was so, Grimes knew. It would be extremely unwis
for him to return to Lindisfarne to face court-martial. H
would resign, here and now, by Carlottigram. After that
The Imperial Navy, if they'd have him? With his record
probably not.

The Rim Worlds? Rim Runners would take anybody, a
long as he had some qualifications and rigor mortis hadn'
set in.

The implications of it all he would work out later. Th
full appreciation of the desperate situation into which he ha
been maneuvered—by Mavis as much as by anybody—
would sink in slowly.

He looked up at the night sky, at the distant stars.

Would *Discovery* find her Pitcairn Island?

Would the fate of her people be happier than that o
those other, long ago and faraway, mutineers?

In spite of all that had been done to him by them, i
spite of all that had happened because of them, he rathe
hoped so.